SARAH NEGOVETICH

RITE of REJECTION

SarahNegovetich@Gmail.com

www.SarahNegovetich.com

ISBN-13: 978-1500675653
ISBN-10: 1500675652

The text was set in Garamond 12pt.

Cover design by Deranged Doctor Design.

To my mom, for teaching me to read.
It's a gift that has impacted my life in more positive ways than I can count.
This book is for you.

One

Before You Stands the Future. The dark-red banner strung across the storefront awning matches the dozens of others lining the streets of the shopping district. Each one with the same clock counting down to Acceptance. Tomorrow morning can't get here soon enough.

I push the glowing blue button and the door slides open with a staccato puff of air. Overhead, an electric bell dings as I shuffle into the upscale boutique packed with other Candidates. Cheryl is right behind me, bouncing on her toes with each step. My mother would die of embarrassment if I showed the same lack of decorum as my best friend, but I'm bouncing on the inside. Our mothers walk in behind us and the door slides shut with another whoosh of air.

We visited half the shops in Cardinal City this morning in our search for the perfect dresses and dyed-to-match shoes. I got a thrill buying my first pair of silk gloves,

Cheryl and I gushing over the tiny pearl buttons, but this is the purchase I'm looking forward to the most.

Shelves bursting with dance cards cover every square inch of wall space. Dozens of girls sigh and squeal over the small books we'll use to record the names of our dance partners for tomorrow's ball. I wipe damp palms against the cool material of my skirt and force myself to focus on the goal. One of these books is the perfect one for me. Hopefully, by the end of tomorrow night, it will hold the name of my future husband.

"Isn't anyone going to help us?" My mother stares through the crowd of sixteen-year-old girls fawning over the books covering the display cases.

"Now, Mavis, we can hardly expect too much out of the salesmen." Cheryl's mother's smile covers her face like a masquerade-ball mask. "Their pay is even less than a processor's." She lays a hand on her chest, appearing absolutely scandalized to the untrained eye.

"Dreadful," my mother responds, her gloved fingers gripping the top of her handbag. "Of course, we both know all the money in the world can't buy good manners."

I've been watching this back-and-forth all day. Cheryl's mother making little comments about how expensive Cardinal City must be for some people, knowing full well that my father's processor salary doesn't make a trip like this easy. My mother responding about the number of things money can't buy, being equally aware that Cheryl's occasional lack of refinement is a sore spot for her mother.

Maybe shopping together was a bad idea, but this is such a special weekend and I can't imagine not sharing it with Cheryl. We only get one Acceptance ceremony, one chance to make the right first impression on our entrance into society. Between the ceremony and the celebration ball later in the evening, tomorrow is the most important day of our lives. I grab Cheryl's elbow and lead her over to one of the less-crowded cases so our mothers can snip at each other without us.

Cheryl takes one look at the case and turns back toward the most crowded section of the room. "Rebecca, these books are so old-fashioned. I'm looking for a dance card that speaks volumes about the kind of woman a man can expect me to be."

Speaking volumes is one of the first things he'll notice about Cheryl.

I bite my lip for even thinking such an ugly thing. My mother must be rubbing off on me today. Cheryl may be chatty, but she's the sweetest person I know. Any young man would be lucky to sign her dance card. "I think the newer books are closer to the front of the store. You go ahead. I want to wait until it clears out a bit first."

Cheryl gives my arm a squeeze and practically skips over to the other cases. The books here are older, but there's something charming about them. The newer ones in the display window have a small screen on the front that flashes the owner's name. Gentlemen can type in their name to reserve dances for the ball or even scan their OneCard once we get them after the ceremony.

I'm sure plenty of girls think having everything so automated is the height of elegance. For me, there's something unromantic about asking a young lady to dance the same way you pay for lunch or clock in at work.

A light-blue book catches my eye and I lift it off the soft velvet stand, fingering the raised silver filigree along the edges. Inside, the paper is stiff and slightly yellowed. This dance card has to be at least twenty years old. A relic from the days when people still used ink pens instead of sending messages through a Noteboard.

The flowing script leaves a spot on each page for a single dance partner to sign his name, with plenty of pages for an entire evening of dancing. The girl who can fill this book will leave the ball tomorrow night with sore feet and several potential suitors.

"I must say." A white-haired salesman, moving too slow to still be working, but with an endearing smile, walks out from a room behind the display cases. "It's nice to see a young lady take an interest in a card that doesn't go flash, bam, whiz at the touch of a button."

I smile back at him because that's the polite thing to do, but also because he makes me feel smart for wanting something so old. "It's beautiful."

"That it is, and this dance card has something those modern imitations don't." He takes the book and flips back all the pages to show the inside of the thick cover. Hidden in the binding is a small clasp he flicks with the tip of his nail. The back cover bends open to reveal a hidden pad of paper tucked inside.

"A false binding," I say, keeping my voice down as if we're discussing national secrets. "What is it for?"

The salesman beams at me, any trace of tiredness eclipsed by his wide smile and the mischievous twinkle in his eye. "The front pages are for the young men to make their intentions known, but these pages are for you. A place for your memories." He folds the false cover back in on itself until a small click indicates it's secure before closing the book up and holding it out to me.

"Thank you so much." I clutch the book to my chest, its glorious potential pulsing in my hands like a living thing.

"For a beautiful young lady such as you," he says, winking, "it's my pleasure." He pushes back from the counter, and shuffles off to help the next Candidate looking for the perfect dance card.

I twirl a golden curl of hair around my finger and scan the room for Cheryl and our mothers. The salesman called me beautiful, but that might be stretching the truth a bit. I'm pretty, at best. It's a good face; not beautiful, but pretty.

Leaning back against the counter, I enjoy a rare moment of solitude. It doesn't last long.

"Rebecca, there you are." My mother strides as fast as she can across the plush carpet in her ridiculously high heels and pulls my hand down to my side. "If you insist on wearing your hair loose, the least you can do is leave it alone. You'll knot it to death and we still have lunch."

I hold my breath and wait for her 'importance of appearance' lecture, but lucky for me she's distracted by my book choice. She plucks the blue dance card from my hands and examines it from top to bottom. After picking out my entire outfit for tomorrow, I should have known she'd want to weigh in on this as well.

She may have an opinion on everything, but her choices for me are almost always spot-on. It makes life easier for both of us if I go along with whatever she suggests, but picking out a dance card is the one thing I really wanted to do on my own. Letting my mother select it takes some of the romance out of attending my first ball.

She glances over at the newer books, with their flashing screens, and I prepare to be disappointed. "It reminds me of my Acceptance ball dance card." She tucks it under her arm, the barest trace of a wispy smile on her bright-red lips. "It's a lovely choice. Now let's be sharp. I want to be at lunch when the most people will be there."

I follow her across the room to the sales desk in a state of shock. My mother approved of one of my choices. Maybe now that I'm about to become an official member of society she's seeing me in a different light. As a woman who'll start a family of her own in a few years.

Cheryl and her mother are already at the sales desk where a younger man in a cheap suit is helping them. He wraps a bright-emerald book with a crystal-embossed 'C' on the front cover in airy tissue paper before settling it into a lacy white bag. Cheryl's mother spins around, bag in hand, and raises an eyebrow at my selection. "I suppose the older books are a bit more affordable."

I strap on my best 'I am a lady' smile. I love Cheryl like a sister, but sometimes her mother drives me to the brink. "I rather fancy the idea of something a bit more traditional. Plus, a boy signing your book is so much more intimate an experience than scanning his OneCard."

Cheryl's jubilant smile comes crashing down and her shoulders sag. Of course, the book she selected would be fitted with the newest bits of technology. She probably doesn't even realize how hurtful her mother's comments are. I'd certainly never bring it up, but in my haste to put her mother in her place, I've put a damper on my best friend's excitement.

"Cheryl, please," I grab her hand and give it a quick squeeze, "With your beautiful smile the boys will be staring so much, you could ask them to sign your shoe."

The sheer force of will it takes my mother not to roll her eyes at me is astounding. Her facial muscles actually tense with the effort. She takes my dance card to the desk and Cheryl and I step outside to wait.

Spring is in full swing in Cardinal City and the events of the weekend make the warm air whirl with life. Down the street, the setup is going on in the central square. The gathering space here in the capital is at least three times as big as the one back home. A huge screen covers the entire side of one of the buildings flanking the grassy area where the Acceptance ceremony will take place. A projector flashes the official Acceptance slogan "Before You Stands the Future" in bright-red letters against the white backdrop.

"Can you believe it?" I say, fighting to keep the squeal out of my words. "Tomorrow everything changes. We'll go through Acceptance, attend our first ball."

"And meet our future husbands." Cheryl does squeal out the words, but I can't blame her. This is our one and only chance to meet young men from the other Territories.

Thanks to my mother, I've already met every eligible boy back home and none of them are right for me.

I want a husband who can walk in the room and command attention. A man who deserves my respect and admiration. I need a husband who I know will always be there to take care of me and our children. If I want to meet the man of my dreams, and avoid a Compulsory marriage to a complete stranger, tomorrow is the night.

In the square, a team of red-uniformed workers rolls a lacquered black podium onto the stage. That's where the Cardinal will give the traditional opening speech before the ceremony starts. For as long as I can remember, I've sat on the green floral couch in our living room and listened to his speech on the radio. His stern voice pumped through the speaker as if he was talking directly to me. The thought of seeing him in person sends chills of excitement and fear up my arms. "Sometimes the Cardinal gives me the creeps."

"Rebecca!" Cheryl stares at me wide-eyed, newly manicured fingers covering her gaping mouth.

I shouldn't have said that out loud. The Cardinal's rules are the foundation that keeps us from sliding back into violent chaos. Acceptance weeds out the violent criminals, Assignment makes sure every man has a productive role to benefit society, and Compulsories keep families intact.

But just because I understand why the rules are in place doesn't mean I have to like them all. How can Assignment be such a great idea if my father's job makes him miserable? He would never say a word about it, but it's hard not to see how bored he is with the menial work or hear my parents' regular arguments over money.

It's a good thing negative thoughts about the Cardinal won't jeopardize my Acceptance. Only criminals and deviants are Rejected. Still, it's bad form to speak ill of the man who brought the United Territories out of a spiral to destruction. Without him, there wouldn't be any jobs to complain about or an Acceptance to attend.

"Sorry." I roll the thin, knotted pendant of my necklace between my fingers. "I'm just nervous about tomorrow night."

Cheryl pats my hand, always willing to overlook my random outburst. "Don't be. It's going to be magical." Cheryl's eyes glaze over and the goofy grin on her face is a sure sign she's lost in thoughts of charming suitors and romantic waltzes.

"What if it's not?" I drop my pendant and weave an arm through Cheryl's. "What if there isn't a boy out there perfect for me that also meets my mother's expectations?"

Cheryl presses her lips together and nods. My mother has made no secret about her desire for me to "marry up". But I've seen what happens when a girl marries for stability instead of love. A part of me thinks a Compulsory would be better.

"You can't think that way," Cheryl says, giving my arm a little squeeze. "Mr. Right is here. I can feel it."

"Lunchtime. Let's go, girls." My mother lets the door slide shut behind her and takes off down the street without a backward glance.

I dismiss my thoughts about Mr. Right and scurry after her, Cheryl right beside me. Tomorrow, everything changes and I have to believe Cheryl's right; it's going to be magical.

* * *

My stomach growls as we walk past a nearly empty restaurant. "Couldn't we just eat the sandwiches in the icebox back in the hotel room?"

My mother shakes her head without missing a step. "After all," she says as we pass yet another tempting deli door, "how can the boys get a good look at you if you spend the whole day hidden away in the hotel?"

We all stop in front of a bustling eatery, both our mothers nodding their acceptance. Inside, a smiling greeter shows us to a small, round table. All around the café, tables are packed with other teens and their families here for Acceptance. Once again, my mother is right.

A small man with a pleasant smile arrives at our table to take our order. Cheryl's stomach is unfazed by tomorrow's importance. She orders an expensive steak in a voice loud enough to be heard across the crowded restaurant, giggling when our server says, "Excellent choice." I stick with a salad. Despite my hunger, ordering a bigger meal would be pointless. The nerves flittering in my stomach about the ceremony happening in nineteen hours and twenty-seven minutes will probably keep me from doing much more than pick at my food.

The waiter gathers our menus and heads back to the kitchen, winding through the tightly packed tables like he's dancing one of the waltzes from tomorrow's ball. The back of his head bobs in time to silent music as he hurries away.

"What are you looking at?" My mother cranes her neck around to see what has captured my attention.

"The waiter. What did the Assignment see in him when it decided his optimal career would be food server? Does he have a naturally helpful disposition or strong arms for carrying heavy trays?" More importantly, is he happy?

My mother laughs, a short, terse noise making it clear I've said the wrong thing. "What does it matter why he's a server? That's his role; end of story."

I've stuck my foot in it, now. Still, with the ball tomorrow night, this is information I need to know. "It's just, if I can't tell why a man was Assigned as a waiter, how can I tell which boys will be Assigned good jobs like doctor, lawyer, or accountant?"

"Oh." My mother taps the tips of her fingers against the edge of the table.

Shortly after her own Acceptance Ceremony, my mother caught the eye of the bank manager's son. She started planning for a life on the high side of society. There was every reason to believe a young man from such a prominent family would do well in life. My parents got engaged only a few short months before his Assignment came down as paper processor. No one was more disappointed than the future Mrs. Stanley Collins.

Mother could have broken off the engagement, but by then they were both already eighteen. If she didn't marry my father she'd only have three years to find another husband before she'd be forced into a Compulsory marriage. In my opinion, nothing is more humiliating than being forced to marry a complete stranger because neither of you could find a partner on your own. My mother must have felt the same way.

"That's why I tell Cheryl, make sure a young man's family is present before he signs your dance card. Of course, we all know good lineage can only take a man so far."

"Mother, you are so old-fashioned," Cheryl says, laughing loud enough to draw the glances of several good-looking boys to our table. She's oblivious to the sharp jab her mother shot at mine. That, or she pretends to be so we can both stay outside of our mothers' squabbles.

Cheryl pulls out her new dance card and holds it up so all the boys glancing in our direction can get a good look. Apparently, she's decided to tempt fate. It's tradition for boys to wait until after the ceremony to ask for dances. It stems back to when the Acceptance was first put into place and a much higher percentage of teens were rejected.

That was what the people clamored for. An answer to the paralyzing crime rates that crippled the United Territories with fear. But that was a long time ago, back when the Territories were states and there was no way to tell if someone was a criminal until they committed a crime.

Things are better now, with the deviants removed from society and families able to raise their children without the constant threat of violence. When the Machine was invented, over eighty years ago, the Acceptance ceremony was tense with apprehension and fear. Now, it's almost all formality. Everyone knows that the kids brought in on buses, with parents who spend their money on contraband liquor and tobacco instead of Acceptance dresses and transport tickets, are the ones most likely to end up in the Permanent Isolation Territory.

Despite the tradition of waiting until after the ceremony, it's become a new tradition for the most eligible bachelors to ask for their first dance the day before. Clearly, Cheryl hopes to receive one of those coveted and rebellious invitations.

I look around the restaurant, watching the other families enjoying Acceptance weekend while I wait for my salad to arrive. Across the room, a young man sits with his parents, and I find myself drawn to their interactions.

He's certainly handsome with his blond, wavy hair and angular jaw, but that's not what catches my attention. It's the way he holds himself, with his back straight and arms demanding a place of importance at the table that makes me want to know more about him. He has a rare air of confidence.

He pivots in his seat and meets my stare with clear, blue eyes. I turn back to my own table, head down, but not before I catch his warm smile that raises the hair on the back of my neck. Busying myself by refolding the napkin in my lap, I lean in and try to pay attention to Cheryl, who's demonstrating the high-tech features of her flashy new dance card.

"Excuse me, ladies." A deep voice falls across the table from over my shoulder. "I apologize for interrupting your lunch. My name is Dr. Harold Dunstan. I'd like to introduce my son, Eric."

"No apologies needed," Cheryl's mom answers right away. "I'm Mrs. Thomas Pierce, and this is my daughter Cheryl."

Cheryl stands, the picture of perfection in her stylish dress and smooth ponytail. The boy with the straight back shakes her hand and polite hellos are spoken. Eric turns his attention to me and his warm smile brings a flaring heat to my empty stomach.

"I'm Mrs. Stanley Collins, and this is my daughter Rebecca."

Eric takes another step closer to me. I stand and lift my hand to shake his, but he takes my wrist and lifts it to his lips to kiss the back of my hand. "Rebecca, my name is Eric Dunstan. Very pleased to meet you."

All the air rushes out of my chest and there's nothing left in my lungs to say anything. It doesn't matter, really, since I have no idea what I'm supposed to say when a boy I've just met kisses my hand.

Eric laughs, a light chuckle that makes his blue eyes twinkle, but doesn't miss a beat. His eyes stay glued to mine. "I realize this is a little early, but I was hoping you'd allow me to sign your dance card for tomorrow."

I suck in a quick gasp of air. Behind Eric, the bottom half of Cheryl's face breaks into a huge grin. Clearly, she's thrilled, but it's my mother's opinion I need now. Her eyes are wide and bright, but her bleached-white teeth bite her lower lip. I wait while her brain works at warp speed to calculate the risk of an early dance invitation against the prestige of the asker. She nods her head, reaches into the lacy bag and pushes the soft-leather book into my hand.

“Of course,” I say, handing over my card with a smile I hope doesn’t show my nerves. This is the exact scene I pictured in my head when I chose the light-blue book with the swooping silver scrollwork along the edges.

“A pretty card, for a pretty lady.” Eric pulls an old-fashioned fountain pen from a pocket inside his jacket and signs his name in the spot designated for the first dance, the traditional opening waltz. “I look forward to our dance.”

Eric and his father walk back to their table, and I sink into my chair. My mother is beaming next to me. She runs the tips of her fingers under Eric’s name, careful not to smear the wet ink, and slides the priceless book back into the bag. Tomorrow can’t get here soon enough.

Two

Bright and early Saturday morning, Cardinal City is plastered with people along all the streets and sidewalks. As far as the eye can see, sixteen-year-olds in formal gowns and suits of every shade of the rainbow cloud the landscape. In front of the bright-red Cardinal building a large platform is raised with several chairs sitting in judgment behind the Machine. I've only ever seen pictures of the Machine in our history books. The black-and-white pictures of the mechanical brain that weeds out future criminals always looked sinister to me. In person, there really isn't much to it.

The round disc is only large enough for a single person to stand with their feet together. Two poles extend up from the base, topped with flat readers for our hands. That's where the Machine gets its information, though how it works is a mystery. A small horizontal bar in the front that links the readers will display the green and red lights that indicate each person's status. I've seen video games at the teen center that looked more sophisticated.

"Rebecca, Rebecca, over here!" Cheryl's voice rings out above the din from where she stands next to a small shop. "Isn't this exciting?" she asks when my parents and I finally wind our way through the crowd to join her. "Did you see the cameras?"

I stop moving and take in the square for the first time. I was so absorbed with the Machine I completely missed the video cameras positioned on high stands around the platform and throughout the crowd. Off to the side a raised booth towers over the crowd with more cameras. It reminds me of the booths used by the newsman when they show the Thanksgiving Day Parade every summer to commemorate the election of the Cardinal.

"Why are they there?" I ask.

"They're going to film the ceremony, of course. Do you think they'll show it to all the Territories?" Cheryl grabs my hands and pumps our arms up and down, nearly hitting several other people on the tightly packed sidewalk. "Just think, everyone back home will get to see us in our Acceptance gowns when it's our turn at the Machine."

Thanks to Cheryl's speculation, my mother is now fussing with every part of me within arm's reach. My dress is smoothed, my curls bounced and hairpins checked to make certain that no rogue strand of hair can mar my on-screen debut. "Stop twisting your necklace, Rebecca," she says, batting at my fingers. "It makes you look nervous." I am nervous.

I push my arms down to my sides, but it's hard to keep them still. It would be nice to have everyone from home see me in something other than the plain, collared dresses that make up my normal wardrobe. But this isn't a fashion show. Not everyone on that stage will make it to the ball tonight. Some among us will be Rejected and sent to the PIT. There isn't any tolerance for heathens who threaten our peace. The PIT keeps them away from us where they can only hurt each other.

I take a deep breath and release the fists knotted at my side. I can't go into the ceremony expecting the worst. It doesn't matter how horrible the PIT is. I won't be going there. A strong, deep voice calling out from the loudspeaker brings me back to the present.

"Ladies and Gentlemen, would all those participating in today's Acceptance ceremony please report to the right side of the stage. Our ceremony will begin momentarily."

Sure enough, the banners all around the square show less than thirty minutes on their countdown.

"Oh, Rebecca. My little girl all grown up." My mother gives me a quick peck on the cheek and a light hug, careful to avoid wrinkling my dress.

"We love you," my father says, pulling me into a deeper hug despite the clicks of disapproval from my mother. My father is a man of few words, so the ones he does say count extra. I lean in and hug him back, tighter than I have in years.

Cheryl and I head off arm in arm toward the stage that will mark our true entrance into society.

Despite the need to corral close to one thousand teens into order, the waiting area is well organized. An official-looking man is collecting names of everyone as they join the line and entering them on the flat, rectangular screen of his Noteboard.

"Hurry, Rebecca. I don't want to be at the end and have to wait all day to be called." We slide into line behind another girl in a butter-yellow dress. Somewhere by the stage a band is playing, its trumpets and drums adding to the holiday-like atmosphere.

"Good morning, ladies."

I turn around and stare straight into the pair of sky-blue eyes that held me captive yesterday at lunch.

"Becca, you are lovelier than I remember." Eric takes my hand in his again, raising goose bumps along the bare skin of my arm. "Perhaps I should ask for a second dance now, before the other boys get a chance to fill your dance card."

I want so badly to say something smart back to him, but my mouth is completely dry. My fingers twirl the knotted pendant of my grandmother's necklace. The best I can manage is a tight smile, but it feels weak compared to the wide one he's giving me.

"Your necklace is beautiful."

I smile wider because this time we are in complete agreement, though most people don't see the beauty in the chain's simplicity.

"It's a shame, but you won't be able to wear your gloves on the Machine. May I?" he asks, holding the tips of my fingers.

Eric is completely in his element while I can't manage to string together two words in a coherent sentence. I nod and hope he doesn't think I'm a complete moron.

Eric turns his attention to removing my gloves. While his piercing eyes are concentrated on undoing my tiny pearl buttons, I take the opportunity to study him up close. His suit is cut to fit him perfectly, the black material shimmering in the rays of the early morning sun. I don't know much about men's fashion, or any fashion really, but even I can tell his suit must have cost a fortune. No one back home wears anything this nice, even someone with wealth like Cheryl's father.

Eric removes one glove and hands it to me. Cheryl takes it for me and closes her eyes, the edges of her mouth lifted in a slight smile. No doubt she's already planning our engagement party.

He bends his head to work on my other glove and a few strands of hair fall down in front of his eyes. His blond locks are slightly longer than what my mother would consider appropriate, but I don't mind. I have a strong desire to sweep them back off his forehead, but manage to keep my hands to myself.

A booming voice from the speakers cuts over the chatter of a thousand excited teenagers. "Everyone in line, please."

Eric hands me my second glove and brushes his lips against the knuckles of my right hand. "Until this evening, then." Cheryl and I follow his movements toward the back of the line.

"Oh, Rebecca, he is absolutely divine. Promise to introduce me to his friends when he takes a break from wooing you."

I tuck the gloves into my pocketbook and fight to control the butterflies conducting aerial maneuvers in the pit of my stomach. "I'll introduce you to everyone he knows if you'll teach me how to not act like a bumbling fool every time he comes within five feet of me."

A hush settles over the crowd, silencing Cheryl's response. The Cardinal and his council advisors parade on to the stage, and the spectators break out into applause. The Cardinal looks nicer than I pictured; plenty of wide smiles and energetic nods to the crowd and his faithful citizens. His height and wide girth only add to his larger-than-life presence as he clomps across the platform. Stepping to the podium, he waves to the crowd, and they show appreciation for the man who has done so much to bring peace to the Territories.

This is the Cardinal I think about when good things happen back home. The Cardinal watching over us, guiding our futures to the path we're best suited, protecting us from those who would do us harm. He's never smiling in any of the photographs I've seen of him. In his weekly radio address he's all business, and his stern, clipped words leave me in awe of his power.

The Cardinal brings up his hands for silence. The last cheers disappear into the crowd and the band cuts off its peppy tune as every countdown on the square hits zero.

"Ladies and Gentlemen, welcome to this year's Acceptance ceremony. Cardinal City always comes alive when the citizens of the Territories come to visit for this special occasion. As you can see, we made a slight modification to this year's ceremony. The cameras here will broadcast back to the Territories so your friends and family at home can join in the celebration of welcoming new citizens into our fold."

The crowd bursts into another smattering of applause, though I can't tell if it's for those of us waiting for our Acceptance or for the Cardinal's decision to broadcast the ceremony. It doesn't really matter.

"Yes. We are all so proud of our young people and it's only right that we share our joy across the Territories." The Cardinal leans into the podium and his broad smile is replaced by a serious look, the one from his pictures that makes me nervous. "But, in addition to sharing in our celebration, all citizens of the Territories will be a witness. Everyone will be able to see that while our world is safer today, we can never falter in our diligence to protect our way of life.

"We don't have to look far into our past to see what happens when rule and order break down. But together we worked to a common goal of reshaping this great nation into a shining gem. We are the envy of the world and for good reason."

The Cardinal holds out his left arm and as one, every man and woman in the crowd turns their attention to us. "In just a few minutes we will welcome a new generation of citizens into our fold, granting them the honor of acceptance into the United Territories. These young men will be given a purpose and function in a few years at

Assignment. These young women will marry and bring new life into the world, carrying the great responsibility of raising the future. But not everyone deserves a place among us."

The crowd shifts with the fidgeting movements of thousands of people. "Among these young hopefuls are those who do not honor our rules and laws. Hidden among the bright and happy faces of these Candidates are those who desire to subvert our ways and bring harm to your families. While today is first and foremost a celebration, it is also a cautionary tale to anyone who does not respect our laws."

The Cardinal turns to face the line of us waiting to the side of the stage. His face is no longer just serious. It is alive with conviction. "You cannot hide. We will find you and you will be stopped." He raises his hands toward the awed crowd of parents. "My commitment to all of you, as your Cardinal, is that you can live your lives and raise your families in a world free from crime."

The roar is deafening as the streets of citizens erupt in cheers and applause. Cheryl and I clap right along. We respect the laws. We don't want to disrupt our society or hurt anyone's family. We have nothing to fear from the Machine.

"Thank you, thank you," the Cardinal says, bringing the crowd down from its fever pitch with the wave of his hand and the return of his disarming smile. "And now, let us begin the festivities. Ladies and Gentlemen of the Territories, before you stands the future."

In a whirl of activity and more deafening applause, the Cardinal takes his seat among the other diplomats, a team of red-uniformed Capital employees move the podium to the side, and another team places the Machine front and center on the stage. The crowd reaches a new fever pitch as the tower of steel and cables powers to life. What looked almost innocent with the crowd between us is now imposing, menacing. The flashing lights indicating different stages of readiness give the Machine an otherworldly appearance.

Up at the front of the line, the ceremony is starting, and the first girl steps up on the stage. The strong male voice booms over the speakers throughout the crowd. His prior announcements were all business, but now his voice has an air of excitement, like the commentators at the annual Inter-Territory Competition. "Ernestine Baker, WestCoast Territory."

A girl with perfect brown curls and a dress the color of spring grass walks toward the Machine like someone who's accustomed to being first. She holds her head high, meeting the eyes of everyone in the front row. Her steps are smooth and purposeful. Unlike my own quaking limbs, her arms don't betray even the slightest hint of nervousness.

Ernestine Baker of the WestCoast Territory steps onto the small, circular disk and places her feet on the two outlines of a shoe indicating where to stand. Before she makes contact with the readers, she takes a minute to look back at the Cardinal. Bold as day she flashes him a brilliant smile and nods her head as if to say, "Yes, I am the future." I want to be sick for her. No one should be that confident.

Ernestine turns back to the crowd and places her hands on the readers to her left and right. Immediately, the pads burst to life in flashes of color. A swirl of reds, blues, and greens pulse around her hands while she smiles out at the crowd. No one is watching Ernestine's smiling face or steady hands. All eyes and every video camera I can see are focused on the arch that runs in front of her and connects the readers. The lights stop after what feels like half an hour, but is probably less than ten seconds. The blues and reds have disappeared, and all that remains is a bright green strip of light running across the newly Accepted.

A polite round of applause breaks out through the crowd. It's a bit disappointing after the roars of celebration earlier. Ernestine steps down off the platform with the same proud smile on her face that she wore stepping on. She's off to find her family who will welcome her with hugs and smiles as an official member of society.

I envy that for her the waiting is over. She'll probably stay at the ceremony for a while longer, especially if she has any close friends still in line. Besides, as my mother would be only too happy to explain to Ernestine, an early exit doesn't allow enough time for potential dance partners to go through Acceptance and spot her in the crowd. For Ernestine, it's now a delicate balance of waiting long enough to secure at least a few names on her dance card and leaving early enough to prepare for the ball.

Cheryl nudges me out of my thoughts, and I realize I've completely missed several Candidates moving through the Machine. I look up in time to see the next Candidate, a boy with bright-red hair and a face full of freckles, moving across the stage at a snail's pace. His shuffling steps make it look like he's attempting a soft dance to music only he can hear. His eyes are glued to the floor directly in front of his feet, giving the crowd a prime view of the top of his head. Eventually he reaches the Machine and trudges on to the small, round disc. He places his hands on the readers the way someone might attempt to pet a stray dog, uncertain if the animal will snap back and bite off a few fingers at the first contact.

The lights flash the second his palms make contact with the readers. I wonder if they're a crucial part of the Machine's process or just there to add to the show. I could ask my father after the ceremony, but he probably won't know. The only people who really know how the Machine works are the experts who built it and the few assigned to keep it working. Important details about the Machine are a closely guarded secret in the government, although there are rumors of discussions with other countries interested in creating their own Machines.

The flashing lights stop and the bar across the front of the Machine flashes red. Without missing a beat, two large men in standard Cardinal uniforms step out of the shadows of the platform. I grab on to Cheryl's arm and fight against the desire to run onto the platform to protect him. The crowd is indifferent. They are already looking to the next person in line.

On the stage, the Rejected boy braces against the guards' approach, his wide eyes darting left and right, but there's nowhere for him to go. His shouts of protest die off as the guards drag him off the platform and out of sight.

The next name is called and the ceremony continues as if nothing happened.

Nothing to us, but not to the boy headed to the PIT, wherever that is. His life is over. Even if he's not slaughtered by the deranged criminals inside, he'll never go to Assignment or get married. He's not a citizen and that means he doesn't exist. I jerk my hand away from my pendant. My mother doesn't need to be standing next to me for me to hear her telling me not to fidget.

Cheryl places a hand over mine and mouths "Are you okay?" I nod my head and pull my hand away to twirl the knot of my necklace. That boy looked so scared, and harmless, but that's why we're here. Because you can't tell who's bad just by looking.

Those poor people who live in a place where your next-door neighbor could be a criminal. How can they trust anyone? Sometimes, when my parents watch the news, reports come in from other countries of murders and violent attacks, especially on women and children. The people in those news stories always look so frightened and sad. They must spend their days in a constant state of fear. The Cardinal needs to share the technology behind the Machine with every country.

The line of Candidates moves quickly. I stopped counting after the first dozen rejections. The shock of the red lights wearing off a bit more with each one. The sun hasn't yet reached the highest point in the sky when it's Cheryl's turn. She gives me a quick wink and squeezes my hand. "See you soon." Before I can be nervous, it's all over.

Cheryl is at the Machine and the bar shines a bright green at the crowd.

The announcer asks for my name and Territory and punches it into his Noteboard. In seconds he nods his head and holds the microphone to his mouth.

"Rebecca Collins, MidWest Territory."

I rush onto the platform, but remind myself to slow down after a few hurried steps. Tripping on stage would embarrass my mother to tears. Waiting in line, it was easy to forget about the cameras, but up on the platform, they are everywhere. I count out slow, waltz-like steps and pretend I'm dancing with Eric.

It doesn't take long before the Machine looms in front of me. It's so much bigger up close and the cold metal radiates judgment. I pause for only a second, a move I hope my mother doesn't notice, and lay my hands on the readers. Colors flash to life under my clammy palms, but I force my eyes up to scan the crowd for my parents. I want to find them now so I don't have to waste time later wandering through the thick crowd.

Cheryl will want to stay at the ceremony until she has at least a few names on her dance card. I hope I can convince her potential dance partners have to eat lunch, too. I'm only halfway through scanning the crowd when the flashing lights on the readers stop. Strong hands grab my wrists and upper arms just as I find my parents; their looks of horror are the last thing I see as I'm whisked off the stage.

Three

My escorts pull me to a dark corner at the back of the stage where the video cameras can't follow us. The unfamiliar faces on stage blur past us. I need to find my family. My feet fall out from under me and the red-suited guards carry me under my arms down a short set of stairs and through open metal doors. I crane my neck back toward the stage, but we're moving too fast for my eyes to focus. My stomach reels; I'm going to be sick. I plant my feet, but lurch forward when the guards keep marching.

"Where are we going? Where are my parents?" Nothing but silence answers my pleas. The guards move forward without so much as a sideways glance my way. I squeeze my eyes shut. Bad idea. Behind my eyelids, the bright, flashing red lights of the Machine burn into my eyes.

I pull back again, using my limited body weight to stop our progress. The guards pause and loosen their grip on me. Yes, let's go back. I shouldn't be here. A heavy, gloved hand flies from my right and slaps my cheek. The crack of leather meeting skin echoes down the dimly lit hallway. I gasp out a choked cry. No one has ever slapped me before. Who would? The Cardinal's guards would. The truth of it reverberates around my head like another slap. The full realization of the situation is like another slap. I failed Acceptance. Slap. I've been Rejected. Slap.

"Stop, please stop! There's been a mistake." My words tumble out between ragged, sobbing breaths, but there is no one except the guards to hear my cries. Hallways whiz by me, but I can't make out any details through my heavy tears. I could disappear here and no one would ever know. I don't exist.

The silent guards open a door and march me outside into a narrow alley. Most of the dingy space is taken up by a bright-orange Airbus, "PIT Transport" printed along the side in large, black, block lettering.

"Collins, Rebecca," one of the guards barks out to a tall, wiry man standing next to the bus.

He gives a sharp nod, not even glancing up from his Noteboard.

My guards push me forward. I want to plead with the man with the Noteboard, explain to him there's been a mistake, but I can't talk through the thick sobs racking from deep in my chest. A hard shove from behind forces me up the stairs of the Airbus. I turn around, but the door slides shut in my face leaving me alone on a bus full of society's Rejects.

Most of the seats are already filled. Dozens of bloodshot eyes stare back at me, only no one is actually looking at me. Some of the Rejected teens are crying. My own sobs silenced the minute I stepped on the bus, though wet drops still slide down my face. A paralyzing fear has replaced all the other emotions that were swirling through me. Who on this bus is a future murderer, thief, or rapist? I curl into a ball on an empty seat near the front and stare out the small, round window. I can't look at the others who now share my fate.

The wiry man with the Noteboard steps inside and whispers to the Airbus controller. The packed bus powers to life and a soft hum fills the tense silence.

Noteboard man steps toward the first row, pushes his thick glasses farther up his nose and clears his throat. His eyes roam around the bus, pausing to look at each of us for a moment. His eyes meet mine and tell me everything I need to know. It doesn't matter what kind of person I was before today. Nothing I've done matters. As of right now, I'm a criminal.

"You are departing now for the Permanent Isolation Territory. Anyone unable to control themselves for the short trip will spend their first week of the PIT in Quarantine. I don't care what kind of misguided, barbaric lives you lived until today. The full strength of the Cardinal has its eye on you now."

He pushes his glasses back up his nose, steps down the stairs, and off the bus. The Airbus slides forward and I sink down lower into the seat. Outside the window, scenes of the city and the plush residential district of the capital flash by. We cross over the Great Dividing River and the landscape turns to flat farms. The bus picks up speed and the farms disappear, leaving a great expanse of trees too deep to see through. I have no idea where the PIT is and it doesn't really matter. None of the places flying past the Airbus exist for me anymore.

I turn away from the window; looking outside hurts too much. I close my eyes and lay my head on my arm. I want to sleep, let dreams take me away from this bus, but my brain won't shut down.

I keep thinking about Constance Berger, even if the rest of the MidWest Territory erased her name from their memories. When Constance didn't come back from Acceptance six years ago, everyone assumed she found a husband and went to live with a foster family in his Territory until the wedding. After all, Constance was a model teen. She got good grades in school, participated in the annual civic parade and never stepped a toe out of line as far as anyone knew.

When months went by without a visit, people began to talk. When a year went by and no one received a wedding invitation people stopped talking. It was a scandal for a middle-class teen in the MidWest Territory to fail Acceptance, but any word of it was spoken only in private homes in soft, shocked whispers.

Did Constance know going in that she would be Rejected? Did she have a feeling about it? Did my parents know this would happen? My father so rarely shows his affection and yet he hugged me like he might never see me again before the ceremony. Did he know that would be our last hug?

What are they going to do? I don't have any siblings. My mother put all her hopes on me finding a good husband and pulling her up into social circles she felt she deserved to be in. With a daughter in the PIT she'll be excluded from every ladies lunch and social tea for the next twenty years. I've ruined everything for her.

And my father. Cardinal save him, alone in that house with her.

The Airbus slows down, and the empty feeling in my stomach is more than just a missed lunch. My mother used tales about the Permanent Isolation Territory to scare me into obedience since I was a child. The PIT is where the criminals are sent so they can't hurt anyone but themselves. Her stories revolved around evil, monster-like people who would kill you if they didn't like the look of you. In the PIT, no one is safe and every day is a fight for survival.

All my life, I listened to her tales and made sure I never behaved in any way that would put me in jeopardy of landing here. I never argued with my parents, always made it back to the house hours before curfew and never tried to get contraband items, like tobacco, the way some of my classmates did. I was good. A good student, a good daughter, a good person. But none of that matters. The Machine knew the truth even if I didn't.

The bus stops and I stare at the door, waiting for the skinny Noteboard man to come back to get us. I should know better. A man like that would never soil himself with an actual trip to the PIT. Instead a uniformed man with a chest as big around as a rain barrel enters the bus and barks out orders in a voice that cuts through the silence like a sharpened blade.

"Everyone up and on your feet, and I don't want to hear any lip about it. When you step off the bus, boys to the left, girls to the right. Do not dawdle, do not talk to anyone, do not attempt to leave the line. Move. NOW!"

I don't waste any time getting out of my seat. I hustle in line with the rest of the bus's passengers and step off into the PIT. Sixteen-year-old girls in varying degrees of finery move with unfocused speed toward an uncertain future.

Up ahead, a small, barn-shaped building stands with its door open, beckoning us inside. I walk through the door behind a red-haired girl and another huge man issues out a new string of commands.

"Remove all shoes, belts, stockings, jewelry, hair accessories, bags and gloves. You are not permitted to take these items into the PIT. Smuggling contraband into the PIT is a fast way to earn a trip to Quarantine. When you have removed these items, move forward into the dress room and wait for additional instructions."

Around the room, half a dozen girls methodically dismantle their carefully crafted Acceptance ensembles. Everyone keeps their head down, but lowered eyes can't hide the whimper of soft cries. A small girl next to me is shaking so bad she can't undo the buckle of her shiny white shoes. I should offer her some comforting words, but I don't have any. Back at home I might have offered assurances, like "it'll all be okay," but in here, that would be a lie.

I slip off my new satin shoes, dyed perfectly to match my dress, and lay them on the rough wood table next to my beaded handbag. My hands shake, but I manage to use the back of one of them to wipe tears off my cheek. Heels are probably the most impractical shoes imaginable in the PIT, but at the moment I don't care. I know exactly how many hours of stamping forms and sending them on to the next department those shoes cost my father.

I take a deep breath and prepare myself for what I need to do next. My grandmother gave me the delicate knotted pendant right before we left for the capital. It isn't valuable. The plain silver metal is common in any jewelry store and it doesn't have any precious gems in it. It was hers when she was my age and she'd held on to it all these years. I absolutely despise the idea of taking it off and leaving it here in this room. What will happen to it? Who will love it despite its lack of value?

I can't worry about that now. Not standing here in only my dress, my bare feet on the cold, concrete floor. Not while guards stand around in their bright-red Cardinal uniforms, watching my every move like I'm some kind of street rat. I can't mourn the pendant when I'm losing so much more. I take the necklace off and leave it with the rest of my worldly possessions. There's nothing left for me here.

"Do you think I'm stupid, scum?" A rough, callused hand grabs my arm while another tears through my carefully sculpted curls pulling out bobby pins and clumps of hair. "Think I won't notice you trying to sneak in weapons? Think because you're a girl, I'll forget the evil you carry inside?"

"Ow, I'm sorry, I'm sorry. I forgot, I promise. I wasn't trying to sneak anything. I'm sorry."

Another round of tears stings my cheeks, and I fight the urge to sink to the concrete floor and sob. My scalp burns from the patches of hair torn out by the bullish man directing our group. We've been in the PIT less than ten minutes and already I've had enough.

"I have my eye on you, girly. Now move it."

I sprint into the dress room, my bare feet slapping against the ground and echoing through the small room. I want as much distance as possible between me and that guard. In this room, the beefy guard is replaced by an older woman. Her grey hair tufts out of her head like weeds, drawing attention to the deep lines carved into her face. Her small frame isn't physically intimidating, but the snarl stretched across the bottom half of her sagging face makes me give her a wide berth.

All around us, tables are piled with some of the saddest dresses I've ever seen.

"Take off your dresses," the older woman croaks out, revealing a few yellowed teeth surrounded by black empty gaps. "You won't be attending any dinner parties where you're going." She cackles at her own joke and flecks of spit fly between her cracked lips. "Throw them in the corner here and find something to wear from the tables. And be quick about it. The next group won't be long, and they'll beat me blue if you fall behind schedule."

She isn't wearing the Cardinal's uniform like the other guards. I doubt they even make uniforms for women. Women stay home, raise the children, and prepare the meals. What is she doing? A wave of nausea sweeps through me, my head spinning. She isn't a guard. This bitter old woman is one of us, a fellow Reject sent to the girls dress room to keep an eye on us while we change. I bite my lip to keep from screaming. I look at her and see myself fifty years from now, a rail-thin shadow of who I used to be.

My fingers fumble with the buttons on the back of my dress. Only hours ago, my mother lovingly fastened each of these buttons, fussed with my hair, and cooed about her little girl being all grown up. That was a lifetime ago. I step out of the most expensive dress I've ever owned. I should be sad about losing it, but I'm actually glad to be rid of it. The sharp swish of satin with my every movement was a constant reminder of where I should be right now.

I'm not at the Acceptance ball, giggling behind gloved hands with Cheryl. Dancing with Eric. A stabbing pain pushes on my chest. Eric is back in Cardinal City sharing the first waltz with someone else. It should be me there, dancing in time to the music. Instead I'm here, sorting through threadbare cotton shifts to find something that doesn't have any holes and isn't missing a zipper.

All those hours wasted trying on dress after dress. Hours of freedom I didn't know were numbered. The hours here don't matter. I can waste all the time they'll let me trying to find something that isn't falling apart.

"What did I say about staying on schedule?" The old woman's voice hisses into the room and a chill runs down my back that has nothing to do with my lack of clothing. "Get dressed and keep moving. You've got lots more to do and they won't hold dinner for a bunch of lazy, no-goods like you."

I grab a green, striped dress and shove it down over my still tender head. The bottom hem is frayed and it's at least three sizes too big, but it isn't missing any buttons and a yellowed ribbon lets me cinch it around the waist. Looking around the room at the other girls, I could have done worse.

We move as a sad-looking group down another hall into yet another room. I blink in the blinding bright lights after the dimness of the hallway. Plain metal chairs sit around the perimeter of the whitewashed hall with small, draped stands next to each one.

Another burly guard barks for each of us to find a chair and sit down. His booming voice echoes off the high ceiling and we scurry off like ants to find a seat as if we're playing the children's party game. When the music stops, the child without a chair is out. Only there isn't any music and I don't want to learn what happens when you're "out" in the PIT.

A middle-aged man bustles into the room and nods to the guard like an old friend. Without a word he walks to the first chair and flips back the thin sheet covering the tray. I crane my neck to see what he's doing. On the little tray a row of needles glint in the overly bright lights like something from a history museum. I drop my eyes and focus on keeping my breaths even, trying not to think about what is happening to the girl across the room. It doesn't take long for him to reach my chair.

"Put your hand on the reader. I need to make sure you aren't bringing any nasty diseases into the PIT. I've got enough to deal with without having to treat an epidemic." The doctor's words are breathy and monotone. He must have given this same speech to each girl in the room.

For the second time today, I put my hand on a reader. At least this one I'm familiar with. I was just at the doctor a few months ago when I turned sixteen. The reader that day came back with a clean bill of health. No sign at all of the apparent evil I've been fostering inside.

The scanner beeps a single shrill note. "You're clear, but I'm not taking any chances." He picks up the biggest of the needles. A pale-yellow liquid sloshes inside the barrel of the injector. "This should kill off anything you've got and inoculate you against most of the filth in there. Though I'll never understand why we waste the medicine on a bunch of Rejects."

I want to yell that this is all a mistake, the Machine malfunctioned, I shouldn't be here. But I don't, because the Machine doesn't make mistakes. Instead I sit perfectly still and take the old-fashioned injection intended to kill off the hidden diseases I must be trying to smuggle into the PIT like contraband bobby pins.

I say nothing because it won't change anything. I'm not Rebecca Collins of 47 Terwilligers Lane, MidWest Territory. I'm nobody scum, worse than dirt on the bottom of this doctor's buffed-leather shoe.

I sit in my chair, rubbing at the injection site. A small lump lies just beneath the skin. The last girl gets her shots and we're led to another room. We started our assembly-line initiation keeping a safe distance from each other, but we've found a certain comfort from bunching up together. It feels safer standing huddled together shoulder to shoulder, though I'm probably not the only one who realizes how false that sense of security is.

A slim girl near the front of our pack is the first to be shoved down into a single chair. I should be worried about what will happen next, but I'm not. If they were going to kill us, they wouldn't have wasted the medicine.

A tall man with the sleeves of his red uniform rolled up to his elbows puts down his Noteboard and walks to the chair. The other guard shouted, but not this one. The dead look in his eyes says we aren't worth yelling at. He grabs the long, dark hair of the shaking girl in the chair, and with one swift snip of scissors I didn't know he had, her hair is gone. He grabs an electric razor and cuts it so close to her scalp there's nothing left but tiny dark pieces that cling to her head in fear of being the next victims to our emotionless barber.

A girl on the edge of our group lets out a huge sob. She sucks in a ragged breath and then breaks down into uncontrollable wails. Our group moves as one to isolate her. It's wrong. We should move to embrace her, give her comfort. Less than an hour and the PIT has already hardened us.

The crying girl with long, silky black hair collapses to the floor. The barber pushes another girl into the chair and before her faded dress hits the plastic back her auburn locks hit the floor. The black-haired girl is screaming, but I refuse to look at her. I keep my focus on the barber relieving another girl of dark-brown tresses.

There's a blur of movement in the corner of my eye. The panicked girl bolts up off the floor and dashes back to the door we came through. The door slides open and every head in our huddled mass turns to the sound. Two guards march in, each one grabbing her by an arm and lifting her off the floor. Her rail-thin legs kick wildly as her screams smack through the tense air.

They force her into the chair and hold her head while the barber hacks away. He steps back from the chair, a mound of straight, black hair covering the floor. The guards pick her back up and drag her out of the room to who knows where. I should care. I don't.

I want to cry. Not for the girl dragged away, but for me. Crying would be a release for the pressure building up in my chest, but I don't have any more tears to give. The barber finishes off our group and my own blonde curls are added to the piles of hair covering the floor.

"Alright, beauties. Let's move it. Dinnertime."

Four

The dining hall we're led to is nothing more than a long, concrete building with tables and benches running the length of the room. Half the tables are already filled. At the far end of the room, a line of people with torn, dirty clothing and bent shoulders hold bowls and cups, waiting to have them filled.

The guard who brought us here is gone, probably off to herd the next group through the rejection gauntlet. I get in line and grab a slightly cracked bowl and cup from a tin barrel. When it's my turn, I get a scoop of thin stew from a woman whose dead stare tells me she's given up. Another similarly discouraged woman plops a crusty slice of bread down into the middle of my bowl. I dip my cup into a barrel of what I assume is water and face the crowd of tables.

The other girls from the bus are huddled together at the end of a table in the corner. Their heads are all tucked down with their chins on their chests. Several of them wrap trembling arms around their torsos as if they fear without the support they would fall apart. Their blubbering mass makes me sick to my stomach. I'm not strong or brave, but my mother would die a million deaths of shame if she saw me collapse into a wallowing puddle of incompetence on my first day. Keeping my distance, I make my way to a mostly empty table against the opposite wall.

I stare into my bowl. Despite my growling stomach at the ceremony, I'm not hungry anymore. Still, I don't know when or how I'll get my next meal. There aren't any spoons so I lift the bowl up to my mouth and sip at the watery broth. It's a struggle to keep from spitting it right back into the bowl.

My mother isn't exactly known for her cooking, but even her worst meal tastes like a king's feast next to this sorry bowl of stew. I push out painful thoughts of my mother and prod a finger into the slop to investigate, but nothing inside is recognizable. It tastes like rotten potatoes. It probably is.

A small boy, maybe eight or nine, covered in grime from head to toe shuffles up to the table next to me. His baggy clothes hang off his thin frame making him look even smaller. I had no idea there were children in the PIT. What kind of place is this?

"Excuse me, miss. If you aren't going to eat your bread, I was wondering…maybe…"

"Of course." My response is instinctual as I fish the hard slice out of my bowl.

The boy grabs the thin bread from my hand and scurries away to the other end of the room without a backward glance or a mumbled 'thank you'.

"You shouldn't have done that." A woman's voice calls out above the soft din of conversation filling the room.

I follow the sound to my right where a young woman sits at the table a couple seats down with a few others. Her clipped, strawberry-blonde hair sticks up in all directions giving her an off-balanced look.

"Are you talking to me?" I'm not sure if I'm supposed to respond to her statement or not.

"Do you see anyone else sitting next to you?" The girl slides down the rough bench until she's right next to me. Three additional strangers repeat her movement until I find myself in the center of a mob of new faces. None of them are smiling. I sweep the room for a sign of the red guard uniforms, but if they're there, they're lost in a sea of washed-out blandness. Not that it matters. I don't get the impression the guards care what happens to us in here. "You just wasted your bread. We only get one of those a day."

"I didn't waste it." I focus on making my words strong, but even I can hear the slight wobble at the end of my sentence. "That little boy looked like he was starving."

"That little boy won't see a crumb of that bread," the girl says. "The Unders all work for one of the bosses. They look for suckers like you who don't know any better to scam for their bread. It all goes to the boss who couldn't care less if one of them fell over from hunger."

"Unders?"

"Some kids never make it to their Acceptance ceremony. They get picked up, usually for something small like stealing bread so they don't starve to death. The Cardinal doesn't take any chances and sends them straight to the PIT."

"How...how do you know this?" Locking up criminals is one thing, but some of these kids look like primary-grade students. I don't want to believe her, but I might. Her voice commands authority...like the Cardinal.

"Three years in here is an eye-opening education." She grins wildly, her yellowed teeth menacing behind her stretched lips, and flashes me a small wink. "Name's Elizabeth, by the way."

I'm not sure if I should be introducing myself to Elizabeth. She looks like the kind of person who could go from friend to fiend in a heartbeat. But my mother would be horrified if a couple hours in the PIT undid all those years of social etiquette training. I stand up and hold out a shaky hand. "Pleased to meet you. I'm Rebecca."

"Alright then, Becca." Elizabeth jumps up from the table and dips down into a deep curtsy. "Let us be the first to welcome you to the PIT."

"Okay, Elizabeth, I think that's enough teasing for one night," one of the guys says. His black hair is even shorter than Elizabeth's, but not by much. I've never seen anyone so dark in my entire life. His skin is as black as night, making the whites of his eyes shine brighter than everyone else's. "I'm Daniel," he says, extending his hand across the table.

"Hi." I sit down and shake his hand, but I can't pull my eyes away from his dark face. His smile is wider than Elizabeth's. It isn't scary, but he makes me uncomfortable in a different way. Like all of a sudden my skin doesn't quite fit right.

"I'm Molly," the other girl calls from next to Elizabeth. Her dark hair hangs no longer than Elizabeth's but has the good sense to lay flat against her tan, petite face.

I finger what's left of my own light curls and glance around the room at all the other short haircuts. Looks like we won't be allowed to let our hair grow back. This is hardly the worst thing that's happened to me today, but it's more than I can handle running on so little food. The rims of my eyes flood and threaten to spill over.

"Don't worry, you'll get used to it." Molly reaches across Elizabeth and hands me a yellowed handkerchief that looks ancient, but clean. "The monthly cuts aren't as hard as the first one."

"So," Elizabeth pipes back in. "You don't look like much of a threat to society. What are you in for?"

The others lean in closer to hear my answer. I feel the pressure of four sets of eyes staring into my face.

"Isn't it obvious?" I dab at my eyes. The last thing I intend to do is cry in front of these strangers. "I failed Acceptance. I've been Rejected."

"Yes, yes, Becca," Elizabeth says, dismissing my answer with the flip of her hand. "But that doesn't answer the question of *why* you were Rejected."

"I..." I don't know how to finish. If I say it out loud, it makes today real, but I can't ignore the truth. "I'm bad."

"Dress me in red and call me the Cardinal, we've got a live one here," Elizabeth says, slapping the table and leaning back on the bench.

"What Elizabeth means," Daniel says, shooting Elizabeth a look I can't read, "is that you can hardly classify someone as only good or bad. Do you really think you're a bad person?"

"I must be," I answer without a pause. Now that I've said it out loud, it's easier to accept. "The Machine is never wrong."

"And before the Acceptance ceremony?" Daniel asks, leaning across the table and holding my gaze with his dark-brown eyes. "Did you think you were bad before the Machine?"

The intensity of Daniel's stare makes it hard to concentrate, but I don't need to think about my answer. I never considered myself bad, never. I'm not perfect, not by a long shot if you ask my mother. I'm not bad, but isn't that exactly what the Machine said I was? The lights flashed red and told everyone in Cardinal City that I can't be trusted to live with them anymore.

Daniel takes my pause for an answer. "How could you go your whole life and not realize you're a bad person?"

"But that's why we need the Machine. Because you can't tell if someone is bad or not just by looking at them. The Machine protects us."

"Correction," Elizabeth cuts in. "The Machine protects them." She hitches her thumb over her shoulder at some invisible group. "But what exactly it's protecting them from is the real question of the day. Have you ever had a desire to hurt someone else?"

"What? Of course not. What kind of person do you think I am?" I slide farther down the bench, but Elizabeth moves along with me, like we're attached by an invisible string.

"We don't know," Elizabeth says. "That's what the questions are for. Have you ever taken something that wasn't yours? Tried to cheat on a test? Wanted to kiss a girl?"

I can't answer her; I can only shake my head back and forth. She thinks I'm some kind of petty thief or sexual deviant.

"Hmmm…a tough one," Elizabeth says, tapping her finger against her chin. She glances at the others, her eyebrows raised. A silent conversation passes amongst them. Tilted heads, grimaces and shoulder shrugs take the place of words. Elizabeth turns her attention back to me. "When was the last time you thought something bad about the Cardinal?"

I slam my hand against the table, and my uneaten bowl of mystery meat clatters against the dirty top. "No, honestly, this is too much. The Cardinal is a wonderful man." Except when he creeps me out by knowing more about me than I know about myself. "He's leading us into the future."

"Said like the perfect little student," Elizabeth spits out from behind clenched teeth. "And everything the Cardinal does is just wonderful, is it? You agree with everything he's done?"

I open my mouth to say 'yes', but can't get the word out. I don't agree with everything. No one can argue that things aren't better since the revival orchestrated by the previous Cardinal. Crime was out of control back then. People lived in constant fear for their lives. With cooperation between the scientific and psychological communities, the Machine was invented, weeding out the criminals. When he died and the current Cardinal was elected to take his place, the important work of rebuilding our nation continued. The Territories are safe to live in again.

But I don't think all the new rules are as great. The mandatory marriage age is something I've always struggled with. I know why it's in place. A strong marriage creates strong families. Children grow up in a stable environment. Plus, the responsibilities of a family keep weaker men from sliding into less-than-desirable behavior. But the idea of forcing people to get married when they don't love each other has never sat well with me.

And if I'm being honest, I'd rather go through Assignment than get married. Not that I don't want a family, but I know I could do more.

"Did you do well in school, Rebecca?" Daniel's voice is soft now. He isn't pushing like Elizabeth. This isn't a test. It's almost as if he already knows the answer to his question.

"I did well, not the best, but not the worst. What does that have to do with anything?"

"But English, that was your best subject, right?"

I don't know how he knows it, or even why it matters, but Daniel is right. I am—was—top of the class in English. Sewing and patternmaking are enough to drive me crazy, but writing an essay is easy. There's freedom that comes with words that don't have to fall into perfect measurements or even stitches. A light tremor runs down my spine and I'm suddenly overexposed on this bench, surrounded by strangers who know more about me than they should.

"Everyone has doubts about the Cardinal, Rebecca. There's nothing strange or bad about that." Daniel's words soothe me a bit.

"But if that doesn't make me bad, then what am I doing here? Does this mean there's a mistake? I need to tell someone. I need to get back home." My voice threatens to escape the tenuous hold I have on my control. They probably think I'm crazy, but I don't care. If there's even a tiny chance of getting out of here I have to take it. I swing one leg over the bench, but a new voice stops me from getting up.

"There was no mistake, and you won't be going home." The boy next to Daniel speaks for the first time. There's something familiar about the lightness of his voice, but I can't place where I've heard it before. "Other people might share your thoughts, but they'd never do anything about it. You're different, smart. You can articulate your thoughts, convince people that the Cardinal isn't right and they should do something about that. And that makes you very dangerous."

I stare into his sad blue eyes, struggling to remember how I know him.

"You don't remember me. I assure you, you aren't looking the same as you were yesterday at lunch either, but there is no hiding beauty, even in a truly ghastly dress."

My mouth drops open and my hands raise to cover up my surprise. Eric. Eric, whose name is inked onto the first line of my dance card. Eric, who my mother referred to last night as a 'perfect catch'. Eric, who should be the last person I would see here.

"But why are you here?"

"I could ask you the same thing, Becca," his blue eyes focusing in on mine, "but I believe we just answered that question and I'm afraid my response would sound rather redundant."

And there it is; my one last glimmer of hope. Eric is the son of a doctor, certainly a respected member of his community. If the Machine rejected him, then it must be broken. I stare at the others, waiting for one of them to come to the same conclusion, but they don't say a word.

"We don't belong here, Eric. We need to go." I swing my other leg around and stand up. It feels like I could simply walk out the doors and ask for a ride back to Cardinal City.

"Oh, I agree that we don't belong here." His sagging shoulders tell me the same story. "I would gladly follow you wherever you'd like to go, but we won't be leaving the PIT."

His words evaporate the small bit of hope I latched on to. He's right. There must be guards somewhere and they'd never let us out. "I don't…I don't understand. How did this happen?" I sit down and drop my head and arms onto the table. Dewy drops collect in the corner of my eyes and dampen my arms.

Eric's shuffling feet move around the table and stop next to me. The bench creaks under his weight and his warm arm covers my shoulders as if he can hide me from the horror of our new reality.

"I know. None of it makes sense, but this is what it is. You can't go back. Even if you could get out, you couldn't go home."

I sit up and wipe away my traitorous tears with a dry corner of Molly's handkerchief. I look him in the eye and ask my silent question. Why can't I go home?

"Your parents are well on their way home now. And when they get there, they'll take down all the pictures of you and put them in a box or burn them in their neat and tidy fireplace. Your clothes will all be donated and your room will be turned into an office or sewing room. Your parents will remove any evidence that you lived there and when people ask them about their children you won't be included in the conversation about spelling bees and piano recitals. You no longer exist out there."

I'm bursting with the desire to slap him across the face if it will get him to shut up. I roll my shoulders to dislodge his heavy arm. Elizabeth and Daniel exchange a knowing look. They think they know me, but they don't. None of them do.

"How do you know? My parents love me." My voice cracks with the force of my words. "How can you say they'll just forget about me, pretend like I was never their daughter? Who are you to tell me what will happen?"

I wish I had his strength. We were both free this morning, but I'm the one melting down. Eric closes his eyes and takes one deep, calming breath. He exhales, a mix of pain and resolution carved into his firm jaw and drooped eyes. "Because that's what my parents did when Elizabeth was Rejected."

Eric's crystal-blue eyes hold my focus, but a quick glance at Elizabeth's identical eyes confirms his story. I can't breathe. Every sound in the room disappears and I can only hear the deep booming of my own heart. It beats out the remaining moments of my life, all of which will be spent here, in the PIT. My arms are freezing, but my hands are warm. Eric is still holding them. He's still staring at me. His lips are moving and he might be saying my name, but the drumbeat inside my head drowns out his words.

A wave of sound pounds into my head and I sway a little on the seat with the force of it. "Rebecca?" Daniel's voice isn't much more than a whisper, but it pulls me out of the downward spiral I was falling into. His dark eyes have so much compassion. My own must be blank. There is nothing left to me. "I think that's enough for tonight, guys. Let's get out of here and give Rebecca some time to think."

Eric squeezes my hands again before standing to follow the others. I should be grateful for a familiar face. I'm not. Eric is a living, breathing reminder of life outside of here, wherever here is.

Alone and tired, I need sleep and a good meal. My dinner bowl still sits mostly untouched on the table, but I don't have the energy to force myself to eat it. There's nothing left for me in the dining hall, so I leave, not sure where I'm supposed to go or if anyone even cares.

Outside, the sun dips behind row after row of squat, plain-faced buildings. The ugly structure to my left has two doors and smells like a bowl of milk left out in the sun on a hot day in July. I head in the opposite direction down a dusty aisle between the hedges of depressing buildings. The guards from earlier are long gone.

There's still enough light to see where I'm going, but I don't want to be caught outside when the sun is gone. There isn't much activity where I am, but three shrill screams have pierced the dusk since I left the dining hall. I need to find a place to spend the night, and fast.

Only a few of the structures have doors, so I poke my head into the others looking for a place to sleep. They're all identical inside, sparse square rooms with rows of rusted metal beds, some occupied, some not. Halfway down the street I find a room with only a few motionless forms inside.

I sink down onto a thin mattress and the bed creaks, the useless springs sagging beneath me. I cover up as much of myself as I can with a threadbare, scratchy blanket. Lying down, I will myself to get some rest, but my mind refuses to shut down for the night. If what they said at dinner is true, the Cardinal thinks I'm a dangerous person. It's almost enough to make me laugh. How could a man with that much power be afraid of me?

If only I could get a message out. Convince him I'm not a threat. My parents could tell him. Cheryl knows I'm not a criminal. He would believe them. He would have to.

I roll about in vain to find a comfortable spot on my dingy pillow. Something scurries in the corner and I pull the blanket up under my chin.

My chest tightens. I'll never have the chance to send the Cardinal a message. I only exist to the rats.

Five

Pale sunlight streaks through a cracked, mud-caked window. My first morning in the PIT. I sit up and stretch my muscles, but they protest against the cool morning air. Everyone else in the bunk is still asleep, looking much too peaceful, given our circumstances.

A low rumble in my stomach tempts me into the brisk air outside and back toward the long building where dinner was served last night. The sharp smell of something burning guides me in the right direction. Now that the sun is up, I get my first good look at my new home. The view does nothing to raise my spirits.

Row after row of single-story, concrete buildings are the only landmarks on the way to the dining hall. Some of them with small, dirty windows like the bunkhouse I slept in and others with only a small, rusted door or a hole where the door should be. The only peek of green is the occasional weed poking up amongst the mud and gravel that serve as roadways. Everything about the place is untended and rundown.

I push through the door of the dining hall and a dry mist sprays down from tubing above the door. It smells like rubbing alcohol, just like the disinfectant shower at the hospital back home. Last year, when my grandfather got sick my family went to visit him. Before we could go inside, we had to pass through an outer room that sprayed us down so we wouldn't bring any germs into my grandfather's room.

Rubbing at the filmy layer left on my arms, I grab another bowl and dunk my cup into the water barrel. No one covered it and small flecks of dirt and tiny insects float at the top of my water. I slump onto the bench and take a slurp of what looks like overcooked oatmeal. I push down a few mushy mouthfuls and set the bowl back down. I'm not hungry anymore.

Instead, I stare across the empty room and pretend I'm not here. I close my eyes, and I'm back in my kitchen at home. My father is at the table, reading the morning news on his Noteboard. Mother is at the stove and the smell of bacon and eggs fills the small room. The loud pop of hot grease in the frying pan pulls me out of my daydream. I look around, eyes wide with anticipation. My shoulders sag. There is definitely no bacon here. The noise was nothing more than a girl with a cough. She lets out another sharp cough and walks up to me.

"Is anyone sitting here?" the skinny, freckled girl asks.

"No," I say, even though I don't really want company. It's the polite thing to do. "You can sit here."

"Thanks," the girl says, sliding onto the bench. "I'm Susan."

"Hi, Susan. I'm Rebecca." Susan's shoulders are slim under her dress, like she doesn't eat enough, but she doesn't have the disheveled look shared by the other people in the room. "Are you new here, too?"

"Me?" Susan giggles behind a mouthful of congealed oatmeal. "No, I've been here a few years. I've just managed to figure out how to survive a little better than most." She glances around the room, then dips her head closer to mine the way Cheryl does when she wants to tell me a secret. Or, the way she used to. "In here, it's all about who you know."

So far I know a skinny girl with a cough and a table full of people who think I'm some kind of Cardinal-hating rabble-rouser.

More people are making their way into the dining hall for an early-morning bowl of mush. Some of them slump onto benches and eat mechanically, their glazed eyes staring at nothing. Halfway down the hall, a small group are chatting over breakfast, laughing at an older man at another table who appears to have fallen asleep in his bowl. Others rush in, pushing to get to the front of the line. They wolf down their meal in seconds before flying back out again.

Across the room is a familiar face. I don't remember his name, but the red hair and freckle-covered, pale face are unforgettable. The last I saw him, he was hauled up between two guards dragging him off stage. I felt bad for him as I stood there with my assumed acceptance.

He sits between two much older boys, evidence of a recent fight scratched across their faces and knuckles. I still feel sorry for him.

The room is full of people now, but all traces of last night's guards are gone. There's no one here to tell me where to go or what to do next. "So, what exactly are we supposed to do here?"

"Well," Susan says, wiping bits of oatmeal from the corner of her mouth with a scrap of cloth she tucks back into the fitted bodice of her dress, "that depends."

"On what?"

"On what kind of life you want to have. You don't have to do anything," she says, gesturing to a few people with their heads down and snoring loudly. "But that means you're stuck with whatever the PIT throws at you. Lumpy bed, too bad. Burnt breakfast, eat it anyway." Susan pushes her bowl away and a thin smile spreads on her face, her freckles stretching across her nose. "Now, if you're interested in trading up, a soft bed, a real breakfast, you have options."

Susan stands up, and despite her frail-looking frame she moves with a purpose and confidence that I've seen only once before when Ernestine Baker strode across the stage at the Acceptance ceremony. Her long legs dance in a small circle as she smooths the skirt of her dress. There wasn't anything like what Susan is wearing on the table for me to pick from last night. Susan's dress still has most of its original color and the hem is even and straight with hardly any wear. The bodice fits against her thin frame, snug along her waist and chest. It almost looks like something I might have worn back home, if not for the revealing neckline exposing more than is prudent in polite circles of society.

I don't have any idea who Susan knows or what options she has, but it has to be better than sitting around here waiting for an inedible lunch. I stand up and try to mimic some of Susan's confidence as I follow her back out into the dim morning light.

"Where are we going?" I ask as we pass the building I slept in and venture into unknown territory.

"You'll need to meet my boss." Susan says, not bothering to look back at me.

"Rebecca?" A deep voice spins me around, and I smash my nose into the faded shirt of Daniel. He's just as handsome in the light of day as he was at dinner. "What are you doing?" he asks, casting a sneer over my head at Susan.

"Rebecca is coming with me. She decided she's interested in the finer things the PIT has to offer." Susan steps up next to me and links her arm inside my elbow. This close, she smells like sweat and lemons. "Isn't that right, Rebecca?"

Daniel turns his attention back to me and the intensity of his stare makes me take a faltering step back. His eyebrows are raised, clearly waiting to hear what I have to say.

"I…I guess so." I want to sound confident, like I know what I'm doing, but my voice comes out wispy and breathless.

"Rebecca," Daniel says, his voice taking on a warm tone, waiting until I look him in the eye. "I need for you to trust me. This is not what you want."

"Wow, you are tense, big man," Susan slips her arm out of mine and steps forward until she's less than an inch from Daniel, her head tipped back to look up at his face. "When I'm done here, maybe we can meet up and I can help you with that."

She's way too close, the bodice of her dress brushing against Daniel's chest with every deep breath. The way her voice drops when she speaks to him makes me instantly uncomfortable. They both turn to me, waiting for my answer. If my mother was here, I would ask her what to do. She knows the appropriate response for every social situation imaginable.

For as long as I can remember, my mother stood next to me, whispering words of instruction in my ear. *Stand up when making an introduction. Always show appreciation for a compliment, but remember humility is a desirable trait in a wife. Always refuse an undesirable offer with politeness in case a better offer doesn't come along.*

My mother isn't here now, and I'm on my own for how to handle myself. I meet Daniel's eyes, searching for a sign. I want to trust him, but I don't know him any better than I know Susan.

Daniel nods his head and stretches a long arm around Susan, holding his hand out to mine. I reach for my grandmother's necklace, but my clammy fingers find only the scratchy material of the dress I slept in. Susan opens her mouth, but before she can get the first word out I put my hand in Daniel's. I sigh with the relief of his warm fingers wrapping around mine. With the slightest of motions he tugs me around to stand beside him and eases an arm around my shoulders.

"You're making a mistake, Rebecca," Susan calls out as we walk back toward the dining hall. I turn to answer her, but she's already walking away in the opposite direction.

We walk by several rows of dilapidated buildings before Daniel finally breaks the silence. "I realize you're new here, but you need to learn to be a better judge of character, and fast. You may not be a hardened criminal, but this place is crawling with them and they can't wait to eat an innocent thing like you alive." His tone is warm, but his words rip at the wounds still fresh from everything that happened yesterday.

I bite my lip. With each step I chant the promise silently to myself. I will not cry. My shoulders tremble from the effort of holding my breath to fight the tears. My lungs are ready to burn through my chest. I suck in a huge breath and a lone sob escapes from inside.

Daniel sighs and pulls me to the side of the pathway between two plain concrete buildings. "Look, I know this is a lot to take in. It wasn't easy for any of us, but you can't let them see your weakness. The time for tears has come and gone. If you want to survive in here, you have to let those insecurities go."

I nod and wipe away my last tear. Daniel's right. I can't afford to wallow in self-pity. It won't change anything.

"So what are you going to do now?" Daniel's face is so serious.

I don't know if he's asking what I'm going to do right now, or what my plan is for the rest of forever in the PIT.

Either way, I have no idea. I always have a schedule. Every day I wake up and know exactly what's planned. I have school and homework, piano lessons, and spending time with Cheryl. Now, there is no plan; just a long stretch of unmarked time between horrible meals and lousy sleep. I shake my head back and forth. I have no idea what I'm going to do.

Daniel looks around as if the answer to my future is written on one of the barren walls around us. "I might be able to help you."

Now I'm the one standing too close, but I don't care. The sleeve of his shirt is worn and soft under my hand. "Please."

"I can't make any promises." He takes my hand off his sleeve, but doesn't let go, which makes me feel a little better. "Come with me and try not to sound like a liability when we get there."

Tugging me behind him, Daniel winds his way through so many side streets and alleys that I lose track of where we are in minutes. We move farther into the maze of buildings. I have no idea where we are, but I'm certain it's nowhere near the dining hall or the building I slept in last night.

The longer we walk, the more spread out the buildings are, but they all look like they should be condemned. Few of these buildings have windows, though several of them get plenty of light through their missing roofs. I'm worried. I barely know Daniel. He could be a rapist or a murderer and I've just let him lead me to a deserted stretch of the PIT where no one can hear me scream and I'd never be able to find my way back out. If he was lying about helping me, I'm as good as dead.

He stops suddenly in front of a run-down building that looks identical to the others in the alley. Without a word, he pushes open the door, pulls me in and slams the door behind us. Inside is dimly lit by a tiny window that's almost completely covered in dirt and grime. I can only see part of the room, but the soft rustle of cloth indicates we aren't alone.

"Becca. I was wondering if we would see you today." Eric walks out of the dim shadows, and his welcoming smile makes my empty stomach flip. "I see you found Daniel."

"Just in time, too," Daniel tells him, plopping onto a nearby bunk. "I stopped her from joining up with our favorite harlot."

Is Daniel suggesting Susan is a…? I can't even think the word.

My eyes adjust to the lack of light and I can make out more of the room. Elizabeth and Molly are here as well, sitting together on another bunk. The room is mostly empty, other than a few beds pressed up against the cracked walls.

Elizabeth jumps up and pulls Daniel over to a dark corner. She drops her voice, but the room is much too small for whispers to stay secret. "I'm glad you found yourself a little pet, but what is she doing here? Now is not the time to start picking up strangers."

"E, Becca is hardly a stranger." Eric envelops my hand in his and my skin tingles where we touch.

"Somewhere in a trash bin at her parents' house my name is signed in her dance card. We're practically engaged."

I appreciate him standing up for me, but the way he stands so close makes it hard to concentrate on the conversation. My brain is focused on each millimeter of skin touching his and the way my hand fits perfectly in his. And did he say engaged? My heart is pounding so loud, it's practically drowning out the conversation. I barely know him. We can't be engaged yet.

"Eric, you need to stay out of this. You're my brother, but you don't get a say, yet. And I say that five is too many." Elizabeth's voice has an authority I've never heard from a girl before. Part of me is scared to death of her, but the other part is in awe of her confidence.

"You aren't the only one with a vote, Elizabeth." Daniel walks back over to me so I'm flanked by two very attractive men. "Now that Eric's here, Molly said she'd prefer a fifth. Don't pretend this isn't an option."

"For crying out loud, Daniel. Why don't you just tell her everything?" Elizabeth throws her hands into the air. "We don't know anything about Little Miss Dance Partner. She could put us all in jeopardy."

I have no idea what they're talking about and zero inclination to ask. My mother once told me that in social gatherings, how much you should speak is dependent on your rank in social standing. I think she was talking about bridge games at the club, but it applies here, too. Elizabeth is clearly running this show and I am the lowest rung on the ladder, as my mother would say.

"The longer you drag your feet on this, the more likely we'll all grow old in the PIT." Daniel stares back at Elizabeth, refusing to back down. I'm suddenly reminded of the arguments my parents had when the lights were turned out and they thought I couldn't hear them.

"I have a suggestion." Molly's calm voice breaks up the staring contest going on between Elizabeth and Daniel. "Daniel's right. You know I'd be happier single and a fifth would make that possible." She raises her hand up to stop the argument Elizabeth is about to make. "But I agree that we need to make sure she can be trusted."

"So where does that leave us?" Elizabeth asks, her voice calmer than before.

Molly looks me straight in the eyes when she answers. And even though she was friendly last night and doesn't seem opposed to me now, I can see in the hardness of her eyes that she would cut me out in a heartbeat. This is her family and she won't let me put them in danger. "It means we need a test."

"A test?" Daniel's voice is tense next to me, but the rest of the room eases into a more relaxed state.

"Yes, a test." Elizabeth actually smiles, though it doesn't make me feel any better. "It's perfect. If Becca can prove she's trustworthy and won't be a thorn in my side, then I'll think about letting her join our little party."

"What kind of test?" Eric takes the words right out of my mouth, that is, if I had the guts to ask Elizabeth a question.

"I don't know yet." She pulls away from the group and rummages through a sack on one of the bunks until she comes up with a wrinkled piece of paper and the nub of a pencil. She sits down and starts scratching away. "I'll need a few days to work out the details. Until then she can lay low," she says as she writes something else down on the paper, "somewhere else."

"Why can't she—?"

"No. Elizabeth's right." Molly's voice once again calms the room. "She can't stay here until we're certain. She'll be fine on her own for a few days."

"Come on, Rebecca." Daniel loops his arm through mine and leads me to the door. "I'll walk you back to your bunkhouse."

"No. I'll take her." Eric flashes me another smile, but there's a tightness behind his eyes that wasn't there earlier. "Becca and I have some catching up to do."

And then everyone goes back to normal. Daniel joins Elizabeth on the bunk, their heads close together, looking over her small bit of paper. Molly is on her bed fixing the hem on a very old-looking dress. I pause at the door, thinking someone will say good-bye, but it's like I'm already gone.

Eric pushes the door open and motions his hand for me to pass through.

"Do you know how to…?" I turn to face Eric, but he's back in the room, leaning down to talk to Elizabeth.

I have no idea how to get back to my bunkhouse on my own, so I wait outside for Eric to come back. It doesn't take long for him to join me, though his face is pinker than a minute ago.

Eric laughs, a light chuckle that instantly puts me at ease. "Sorry about that. I don't exactly know my way around yet. According to Elizabeth we head west, and all roads lead back to the courtyard. If I get you back to the dining hall, can you find your way from there?"

"I think so."

Eric and I walk in silence through the never-ending maze of side streets and alleys. I stumble a few times over the garbage covering the dirt pathways, but Eric is right there with a sturdy arm every time. I have a million questions running through my head, but I don't have any idea how to start a conversation with a boy. Especially a boy who makes my hands sweat and my tongue swell.

Instead, I try to keep track of the twists and turns we make on the way back to the small bunk I slept in last night. I'm not sure it really matters if I sleep in the same place, but it's the closest thing I have to a home base at the moment.

"Tell me about home." Eric's words startle me in the silence and I trip over a broken crate half buried in the dirt. I'm inches from hitting the ground when strong arms grab me around the waist and pull me back to my feet. "All right, then. Are you okay?"

"I'm fine." Eric still has his hands around me and his breath on the back of my neck makes all the little hairs there stand on end. I've never been this close to a boy before. I like it, and I'm terrified. What in the blazes am I supposed to do now? I lean over to brush a fine layer of dust off my skirt and Eric steps back a few paces.

When I turn around, Eric is still looking at me, but there's a trace of disappointment in his gaze. Eric telling Elizabeth we're practically engaged rings in my ears. I did see him as a potential suitor back before the ceremony, but so much has changed in just one day. Can he really still see me that way?

I always thought falling in love would be easy. Add this to the list of things I can't manage. What I wouldn't give to have Cheryl here right now. She'd know exactly what to say. 'Stop being so nervous. This isn't a test on afternoon-tea etiquette. Just be yourself.' I can do that. "There isn't much to tell."

"Much to tell about what?"

"About home." I take a deep breath and hold out my hand to him. It's the bravest thing I've ever done and I'm completely exposed, standing there waiting for him to join me.

Eric hesitates for only a fraction of a second, then takes my hand. I'm rewarded with a smile that's becoming both familiar and comforting.

"I'm glad you found your way back to us today." Eric pulls me around a pile of discarded rubbish into yet another alley. "Of course, I wish we were reuniting under different circumstances."

"Me, too. I don't want to think about where I might be right now if Daniel hadn't found me." I smile up at him, but Eric is staring off into the distance.

He doesn't respond to my comment. Did I say something wrong? My mother is right; I'm not very good at knowing how to act in social situations.

"You don't have to worry about Daniel protecting you."

"What?"

"I'm just saying it was nice of Daniel to rescue you, but you have me to take care of you now." Eric squeezes my hand.

I squeeze back. This isn't so hard. Eric just wants to protect me, and clearly I need it. "Do you think you could take care of this test?"

"If by 'take care of', you mean, 'make go away', no. Once Elizabeth gets an idea into her head, there's no stopping her."

I use my free hand to massage my temple where a headache threatens to take over. "That's what I thought."

"Don't be nervous."

"Easy for you to say. You get an auto-pass since you're Elizabeth's brother." He has the good sense not to argue the point. "She'll probably want me to spin silk out of spiderwebs before I'm allowed to eat another meal with you guys."

"Come on, she's not that bad."

"To you, maybe, but it doesn't take a genius to see that she likes me about as much as a hole in a new pair of gloves."

"Elizabeth was never a fan of gloves."

"You know what I mean."

"Yes, but I also know Elizabeth. She's just a little overprotective. If she didn't like you there wouldn't be a test at all. Besides, I don't think Daniel will let her get carried away."

"The two of them are close then?"

"Elizabeth says adversity has a way of bonding people. They've been together since Daniel was Rejected."

"Oh." The way he says "together" confirms my suspicion that Elizabeth and Daniel are more than just good friends. And it makes sense. If we weren't in the PIT, they would be old enough to get married. Do people get married in the PIT?

For the life of me I can't picture Daniel and Elizabeth holding hands in front of their white picket fence. Then again, I can't really picture me and Eric either. The image of Daniel holding my hand earlier this morning flashes in my eyes, but I quickly shake it away. My brain is more muddled than ever and being here is sucking away what's left of my dreams for the future.

But Eric is kind and attentive. Not to mention incredibly handsome with his clear, sky-blue eyes. If I can get over how nervous he makes me, we might actually have a future together. Whatever that looks like.

We finish the walk to the dining hall in silence. There aren't many other people outside. A rancid smell in the air alerts the few of us out in the streets to something burning in the dining hall. I take the lead and head in the direction of where I slept last night. When we get to the rotting door, all my insecurities about my pending future come tumbling out.

"When will I see you again? How will I know the test is ready?" I took Eric's presence for granted on our walk, but now that he's about to leave I'm terrified.

"Deep breaths, Becca. We can probably eat meals together, but you'll need to sleep here. I'm sure it won't be long before the test is ready. I'll find you in the dining hall or here in your bunk." He raises our linked hands and gives the top of mine a light kiss before leaning in close to my ear. "Try to stay out of trouble until then."

His warm breath tickles my ear and I lean into him. He's the stability I need right now. "Do you have to go?"

Eric rests his chin on my shoulder. Maybe he'll stay and I won't have to face the lonely bunkhouse by myself. The thought doesn't last long. "Elizabeth will be looking for me. I promise I'll be back before you know it. As long as I don't get lost on my way back to the others."

He gives my hand a quick squeeze and then he's gone, disappearing in a swirl of people moving toward the dining hall.

Six

Long shadows cover the rocky courtyard outside the open doors of the dining hall. Other than a few older men dozing on the filthy tabletops, I'm the only person lingering after a disgusting dinner of rotten-carrot broth. Despite his promise that we could still eat together, I haven't seen Eric or any of the others all day.

I'm tempted to mimic the men and sleep here, but I have to go back to my bunk. Eric might come to get me for the test tonight. I'd hoped he would come for me during one of the meals. No such luck.

A piercing scream stabs through the doors of the dining hall. I cover my ears, but my hands aren't enough to block out the sound. Some of the older men wake up, their bleary gazes searching the room. Most of them lay their heads back down as soon as they realize the danger isn't inside.

One of them stands, stretches and ambles down the hall toward my table. He sits down and I take my hands away from my ears, though the shriek still pulses outside.

"It used to be worse, ya know."

I stare into his tan face, lined with decades of hard living. How could it possibly be worse than this?

"Ya don't believe me. It's cause you were livin' soft till ya got here. Never seen what a bad seed can do when it's given time to plant and grow."

Another scream punctuates his statement, but it's farther away than last time. "This whole place is full of bad seeds."

"Nah. Not like it used ta be." He shakes his head. There's a deep sadness behind his eyes. "When I got here, complete chaos. Sure, they cleared the streets outside of all the gangs and militants. Put 'em all right here is what they did. Chaos."

"You were here when they opened the PIT?"

"A few years later. Got picked up before my Acceptance. Can't remember now what I did."

His eyes glaze over and he stares somewhere behind me. I'm losing him, but I need to keep the conversation going. He's been here forever, probably longer than anyone else. He has answers I need. Like how to survive in here. "What was it like? Was it that different than how it is now?"

His eyes return to mine and his head tilts to the side as if he's surprised I'm sitting across from him. He bows his head until his chin hits his chest.

"Every morning was a scene right outta the history books. The ones with pictures of the wars. Bodies piled up, crowding the alleys so much you couldn't get past. Guards could hardly get em all burned before they had to start all over the next day." His head jerks up, and I jump back on my bench. His eyes are wide, and he leans in across the table so close I can smell the burned remains of dinner on his breath.

"Back then ya knew who to watch out for. Everybody was crazy. Now it's worse."

"But—"

"Oh, I see. Ya think 'cause they don't stab ya in the eye they ain't that bad. They still out there, the mad men. But ya never see em comin'. Best watch out, girly."

I rub my hands up and down my arms. He might have answers, but I don't want them anymore.

"Thank you for talking with me. I should get back to my bunk now."

I stand up, but his gnarled hand reaches out and grabs my wrist. I pull my arm back, but his grip is stronger than I expected. His rough skin chafes against my arm and tears spill over my eyes that have nothing to do with pain. "Let me go. Please."

He jerks my arm across the table until my face is within inches of his, hot rancid breath soaking into my skin. I close my eyes, but it can't block out his gruff, raspy voice.

"Ya never see 'em comin'."

His grip loosens and I pull my arm away, not looking back as I push through the doors and run all the way back to my bunkhouse.

Several of the girls who rode the Airbus to the PIT with me are in the bunk. Their chatter fills the silence, but I have no desire to join in their discussion of the dresses they wore to the Acceptance ceremony. I can't forget about that day fast enough.

As the sun finishes its retreat beneath the horizon, their animated talk dies down and everyone finds a bed. I scoot farther down under the rough blanket on my bunk in the back corner. The walls hedging two sides of the bed give me a small sense of security. After spending all day alone, I'll take every small comfort I can.

I close my eyes and soak in the noise of the other girls shifting on their bunks. I have never felt so cut off. Even Elizabeth's snide remarks would be welcome if it meant having someone to talk to. All I can do now is get some sleep and hope tomorrow brings news from Eric.

* * *

A grating noise pierces the silence of the dark room and puts an end to my nightmare. I can't remember anything about it except for the red. Everything was red. Keeping my eyes closed, I wait for the uncomfortable girl to stop moving so the room can return to silence. I count to thirty, but the noise doesn't stop.

I edge open one eyelid and scan the sparse room. It's barely visible in the moonlight filtering in through the dirty window. Bunks of motionless girls spread to the door, except one. Close to the door, one of the girls sits up, thrashing on the bed. I open my mouth to yell at her, but snap it shut before I utter the first word.

The girl by the door isn't alone. Another figure sits on the bed with her. By the silhouette, it looks like a man. A man attacking that poor girl.

Her whimpers are muffled by the huge hand covering her mouth. The man pushes her down against the mattress and I turn my head from what happens next. In the bed next to mine, another girl lies awake, her white eyes wide in the darkness. We should go together to help the girl by the door. I jerk my head and use my finger to point between us. Her eyes widen even farther, and she shakes her head back and forth in jerky movements.

The rustling from the attack gets louder and the victim isn't the only one crying out. What will happen when he's done with her? We're a room full of girls with an obvious unwillingness to protect each other. I'm not willing to lie around and find out.

Taking care to make as little noise as possible, I roll off the bunk on to my hands and knees. I grab my filthy pillow and blanket and shimmy under the bed. The ground is hard and cold, but staying hidden is my only defense.

I push my back against the wall and wait for the horrific noises to stop. There's nothing I can do to help her, not by myself. It doesn't stop the searing tightness in my chest.

The screeching bedsprings quiet down, and the beast slams the door shut behind him. I thought his moans and her screams were loud. I was wrong. Her quiet sobs, suffered alone in a room full of girls too afraid to act is the loudest sound on earth.

There is no more chance at sleep. Instead, I wait under my bunk until the sun paints the room in light pinks and oranges. Other girls move through the room so I roll out of my hiding spot. Several girls circle around the scene of the crime, but I keep my eyes on the door. I can't look into the face of a girl I left to the hidden bad seed.

The disinfectant spray chills my skin as I walk through the door of the dining hall. If only it could clean away my memories from last night. The tables are still mostly empty except the men who haven't moved since dinner. I grab a bowl of mushy oats and find a spot alone.

"Well, look who's here." Elizabeth sets her bowl down across from mine and swings her legs over the bench. "You're looking a little rough this morning, Princess."

Daniel and Molly join her, and Eric sits down next to me. I should be relieved to see them. I'm not. They weren't there last night and they won't be there tonight. I wasn't the one defiled a few hours ago, but I could have been. It could have easily been me or any of the other girls in my bunk. We are alone, and without protection, and this is permanent.

I can't breathe. I open my mouth to suck in air, but my lungs flatten behind my ribcage. Strange gurgling sounds come out of my throat and I can't stop them. I reach my hands up to cover my mouth, but my arms are shaking so much I can't control their movements. I'm not breathing and the room is spinning and I'm going to die.

Eric's warm hands cover the sides of my face and turn my head until our foreheads are touching and our eyes are no more than an inch apart. "Look at me, Becca. I'm right here. Look at me." His voice is calm and even, but his eyes are wide. "I need you to breathe."

I open my mouth again and a shallow trickle of air spirals down my throat. The others must think I've lost it. Maybe I have.

"Good. That's good. Now take another breath."

I obey. More air flows in and the room stops spinning as much. I'm able to focus on his eyes while we lean against each other, taking slow breaths. My heart rate slows down and my arms stop twitching.

"Are you okay, now?" Eric leans back, but his hands stay planted on my face like he's afraid to let go. I'm afraid for him to let go.

I nod my head. If I try to talk, I'll start crying and that's only going to make the whole situation worse. Eric nods back and lets his arms drift down away from my face.

"Do you want to talk about it?" Eric's voice is whisper soft, but that only makes it worse.

I shake my head and turn back to my bowl. When Daniel saved me from Susan he said I couldn't let them see my weakness. He had meant all the dangerous people, but it still applies. I need to prove my worth to Elizabeth. That means pulling myself together. No more breakdowns.

Eating is the last thing I want to do, but after barely getting anything down yesterday my stomach is crying for food. Even of the barely edible variety. We're having the same mushy oats they served yesterday. It reminds me of the glue my mother used to put the new wallpaper up in the dining room last spring.

I choke down a few bites, still keeping my eyes on the table. I can't stand the idea of looking up and seeing their pity, or worse, their disgust. It would be better if they were talking, but all of my breakfast companions are slurping their mush in silence.

Minutes tick by and the dining room fills up with a boisterous crowd of Rejects, but our table stays silent. It's so quiet I can practically hear the looks they must be sharing, the ones questioning my sanity.

I want to jump up and run out the door, but I can't. There's one thing last night made crystal clear; I need this group. The four silent Rejects sitting around me represent my only chance at surviving in here. Without them, I won't last a month.

"I need to get to work." I jerk my head up at Molly's unexpected words. After such a long silence, her voice is like a splash of cold water on my face. "Rebecca, why don't you walk with me?"

Elizabeth doesn't bother to look up, but Eric and Daniel both flash me an encouraging smile.

Molly leads me in silence to the warmth outside. I have no idea what to say to her, but Molly doesn't seem the type who needs small talk.

"I'm sure you found the bathhouse already," she says, gesturing to the small building that smells like cow manure. "Inside are barrels of semi-fresh water you can use to rinse out your hair and wash off some of the dirt. The disinfectant spray at breakfast kills off the germs and diseases, but it doesn't do anything about the grime."

An opportunity to wash off some of this dirt sounds perfect, but Molly heads in the opposite direction, across the courtyard to another small building. She pushes the door open and I'm hit with the smell of musty cotton. Not at all pleasant, but an improvement over cow manure.

Inside, a petite blonde girl stands behind a rough, wooden counter, folding stacks of clothes that have seen better days. A curtain hangs from the ceiling blocking off a small corner. Another girl steps from behind it and hands a dirt-covered dress to the girl behind the counter.

"This is where I work. You can come here to trade in your dress and undergarments for clean ones. Sometimes you can get new shoes, but they're harder to find."

Molly pulls a plastic card out of the front of her dress and scans it against the small black box along the wall. The lights flash green and another door leading to the back of the building clicks open. Molly walks through, an abrupt end to our one-sided conversation, but turns around before the door closes behind her.

"I know being on your own isn't easy." Molly shuffles her feet and stares at a spot on the wall behind me. "I'll see what I can do to speed things along." She heads into the back room and disappears behind the closing door.

What does Molly know about being on her own? She has Elizabeth, Daniel and Eric. All I can do is head back to my bunk and hope I get to join them soon.

Seven

Exhaustion weighs down my eyelids, but I can't fall asleep. Every time I nod off, squeaky bedsprings fill my nightmares. So much worse than the red. At the front of the bunkhouse the door squeaks open, the rusted hinges protesting against the movement. I jerk up, my back pressed into the corner. The sliver of moonlight at the door disappears for a moment and a dark shadow slips into the room.

Please no, not again. He bends over, searching the bunks. He won't find anyone there. Everyone is packed into the bunks at the back of the room. Several girls whimper. No one is sleeping tonight.

The dark form moves to the other side of the room, still searching for his next victim. One of the empty beds screeches across the floor and the attacker grunts out a string of profanities.

"Becca?"

I throw my thin blanket aside and leap out of bed. In three giant steps I crash into Eric, almost taking us down in my haste to reach him. He wraps his arms around me, and I lean in to him, my heartbeat still racing.

"It's okay, Becca. I'm here." He pulls back enough to look me in the eye, the small sliver of moonlight reflecting off his short blond hair. How could I ever confuse him for a monster?

"It's time."

I nod. He's finally here. Am I ready for this? Too late to worry about that now.

Eric loosens his hold, and I do my best to smooth the wrinkles out of my dress. After wearing it all day yesterday and sleeping in it half the night, I can't imagine what I look like. Cardinal knows I don't smell any better. The disinfectant spray each morning before breakfast is the closest thing to a shower I've seen in almost a week.

I tried using the dingy water in the bathhouse, but I'm pretty sure I'll never be clean again. Not that Eric seems to mind, but I wouldn't put it past Elizabeth to dock points for sloppy dress.

We slip outside and pick our way through the narrow paths by the moonlight. Summer isn't far away, but the nights are still cold here. I wrap my arms around my torso and walk faster to keep up my body heat.

"Once this is all over, we'll have to find you a sweater." Eric is trying to be comforting, but right now I can't think about sweaters or staying warm. The test is everything. I will not spend another night lying awake waiting for the monsters to come out.

The others are waiting outside the bunkhouse when we arrive.

"Are you ready?" Elizabeth's arms fold across her chest. Whatever the test is, she's already convinced I'll fail.

Molly is silent by Elizabeth's side, so close their shoulders brush together. It's clear how close they are, but I don't understand why Molly puts up with her. Sure, Elizabeth is a strong person and smart enough to take care of herself in the PIT, but she's a bit mean-spirited. Of course, that could be something special she saves for me.

"We better get started if you're going to have enough time. Your test tonight is a scavenger hunt." Elizabeth hands me a wrinkled scrap of paper with a list scrawled on it. "You have until dawn to find every item on the list and bring it back here without getting caught. Any questions?"

I take a second to scan the list. Bicycle tire, dinner bowl, one sock (not my own). Random items, but nothing that should be too difficult to find. The PIT is littered with cast off items smuggled in by the guards. I start to fold the paper to tuck it into the pocket of my dress, but an item I didn't see before catches my eye. The last item on my scavenger hunt list is a Noteboard.

"Is this a joke? Where in the world am I supposed to find a—?"

"If you think the list is too difficult," Elizabeth says, her eyes gleaming with the thought of my failure, "you're welcome to quit now."

"No," I answer instantly. Elizabeth isn't my favorite person, but if there's one thing I learned in the last several days, it's that I need these people. The PIT isn't like outside where a stranger will help you without batting an eye. Here you can get beaten for an extra slice of stale bread. Or worse. If I'm going to survive, I need friends and these are the ones I want.

"Let me see that list." Daniel holds his hand out, and I give him the scrap of paper before Elizabeth can stop me. His eyes flare as he gets to the bottom. "Cardinal on a cracker, Elizabeth. We talked about this."

"We talked about it." She grabs the list back and thrusts it into my hand. "I made a decision. I'm doing what's best for all of us."

"I've been trying to get my hands on a Noteboard for the past year. We both know it's not possible."

"We don't know that. And we don't know if we can trust her." Elizabeth holds her hands up, palms facing Daniel to stop his argument before he can get the first word out. "If we're going to trust her with our lives, we need to know how far she's willing to go."

Daniel opens his mouth, but shuts it again, his lips pressed into a hard line. He nods once and it's done.

"You have until dawn, then." Elizabeth turns to head inside, but spins back to me before she takes a step. "Make sure the guards don't catch you."

"Are we not supposed to be out here? Is it against the rules?" I glance around the dark alley, my eyes darting to every hidden shadow.

"There aren't any rules in the PIT."

"Then why do I need to watch out for the guards?"

Elizabeth's mouth pulls into a thin line and her eyes droop, almost as if she feels sorry for me. "Because the guards don't have any rules, either." She doesn't wait for my response and heads inside the relative comfort of their bunk with Molly following hot on her tail.

I just assumed the attack last night was another Reject, some low-life criminal taking advantage of a room full of girls. What if he wasn't one of us? My pulse beats against the side of my neck. I take a few deep breaths to calm myself down. Panicking now won't do me any good.

"You'll need this," Daniel says slipping a cord around my neck. His arms brush against my skin and a light tingle runs down my back, followed by a hard splash of guilt. What is wrong with me?

"What is it?" A slim plastic card like the one Molly used hangs from the end of the cord, but other than a black scan line, it's blank.

"It's the PIT version of a OneCard. You'll need it to get into the Admin building."

"Wait, what? Why in the world would I want to go in there?" The scavenger hunt seemed difficult a few minutes ago, but going into a locked building in the middle of the night sounds dangerous.

"Admin is the only place you stand a chance of finding a Noteboard. It's the tall building behind the dining hall. They keep all the computer gear on the fourth floor." Daniel takes a step forward like he might hug me, but stops with his arms only slightly extended and turns to follow Elizabeth into the bunkhouse.

Eric is the only one left outside with me. I am completely unprepared with nothing but a scrap of paper and a borrowed OneCard to help me.

"You can do this, Becca." His eyes flash to the closed door before turning back to me, a devious grin on his face. "Elizabeth doesn't want me to do this, but I'm going to anyway."

Eric takes a worn bag from around his shoulder that I hadn't noticed he was wearing and loops it over my head. "We don't have many of these, but you're going to need a way to cart all those items back here. Elizabeth won't let me go with you, but at least this way I can help."

"It's perfect, Eric. Thank you." The bag, still warm from his back, makes me feel less exposed out here in the night air.

"Just be careful. I've become quite fond of you and I'd hate to see you come back with even a scratch." Without warning, Eric leans in and places the softest of kisses on my cheek. I'm thankful for the darkness because my face must be five shades of red. This is different than a kiss on the hand. His face that close to mine is more personal, more intimate.

My mind flashes back to the first time we met, when Eric asked for a spot on my dance card. It's a golden moment from before everything changed. The memory strengthens my resolve. I want to make more memories like that. Good memories to erase the bad ones I've already made since getting here. In order for that to happen, I need to find all the items on my list.

"I can do this," I whisper, hesitant to break the spell of our tender moment.

"I know," Eric says, kissing my hand one last time before turning to join the others.

* * *

I'm lost. The PIT is bigger than I imagined and it didn't take long to get turned around on the deserted dirt paths running haphazardly between the rows of identical buildings. The patched bag across my shoulder is heavy with the items I've already found, but I still have several to go, including the Noteboard. I'm saving that one for last.

Before that I need to find a sock and a piece of food.

Somewhere to my right, raging shouts soak into the dark air. I can't make out all their words, but it's clear two men are having some kind of argument. Their deep voices echo off the buildings, pushing me forward. I want as much distance as possible between me and their angry shouts.

A panicked scream stops me mid-step. My heartbeat muffles the screaming. Is there anywhere in the PIT where women are safe? I lean against a cool, concrete wall, hidden in the shadows. I need a minute to pull myself together. The voices grow louder and their words ring out clear in the still night air.

"It's mine; I found the little bitch fair and square."

"The Cardinal can have what's fair, I'm taking the ginger and anyone who wants to stop me will find out what my blade feels like between his ribs."

I'm not waiting around to find out who'll end up with the girl. Whoever she is, she'll be in trouble either way and I don't really care. What is this place doing to me? I dart into an alley hidden in the darkness on my left and fall forward, my face pushed into the rocky soil. I hold my breath. Did they hear that? My lungs ache with a need for oxygen. Please don't come over here. Their angry voices move into the distance, and I let out a painful gush of air.

I run a quick hand along my elbows and knees to check for any scrapes or cuts. Other than a skinned right knee, I'm fine. I could use a bandage, but I'm as likely to get one as I am to finding everything on this stupid list. The raw skin burns, but I can keep going. I have to. Favoring my stinging knee, I shuffle back to the mouth of the alley to investigate what tripped me.

I stare into the almost complete darkness and scan the rocky ground. My foot lands on something squishy and I jerk back. Squinting I can just make out the form in front of me. It looks like a thick stick. Except it's not a stick because it's soft and there's another identical shape right next to it.

I stick my hand out again and bite back a scream. I tripped over legs. The bulk of the body is clear now that I know what I'm looking for. By the size, it's a man, his back leaning up against the concrete wall of a bunkhouse, arms hanging limp by his side. Holding my breath, I listen for sounds of breathing or snoring. Don't be dead. Please be an old man who fell asleep outside.

The night air is quiet. Unable to hold my breath any longer, I let go of the stale air in my lungs and suck in fresh air. Only, this air isn't fresh. It's putrid. I bury my nose into the crook of my elbow, but it doesn't help. Whoever this was, he's long gone now. I need to get as far away as possible before I toss up my dinner.

Keeping close to the other side of the narrow alley, I pick my way back out to the main pathway. Staying in the shadows, I pull the crumpled list out of my pocket. Sock, food, Noteboard. I know where the Noteboard is, though getting it will be an issue. The other items have me rattled. I need time to think, but by my best estimation there's less than an hour before sunrise. I stare at my scuffed shoes and force my mind to focus, but I'm coming up with nothing. I pull my foot back and kick at loose pebbles on the side of the path.

I snap my head up and charge back into the rancid alley. My stomach churns, but I have to do this. I need everything on the list. Holding my breath, I grab the bloated foot of the dead man and peel a damp sock off his foot. I can only imagine it smells as bad as the decaying body it came from, but that's Elizabeth's problem now. I stuff it into Eric's bag and dash out of there before my breath runs out.

Back in the open, cloudless sky, the black air has a purplish hue. The sun is still somewhere under the horizon, but dawn can't be far away. I sprint west down the dirt path. Elizabeth had better be right about all roads leading to the dining hall. The dumpsters behind the building are my best chance at finding a piece of food and it puts me right next to the Admin building.

The structures in front of me close in tighter, a sign I'm running in the right direction. A cramp pinches my side and I'm wheezing with every jarring step, but I can't stop now. Not with so much riding on tonight. I turn another corner and the concrete walls open up to a square patch of dirt I've heard others refer to as the courtyard.

Every other courtyard I've seen was full of thick oak trees, soft, green grass and carefully tended flower beds, but this is the PIT. The courtyard here is nothing more than an empty square of dirt and rocks.

Directly in front of me is the dining hall, and behind it, looming like one of the Cardinal's red uniformed guards, is the Admin building. My heart rate jumps at the sight of the eight-story building. My future rests on the slim chance that somewhere inside that imposing structure someone has left behind what I so desperately need. I push away all thoughts of the Admin building. Before I even try getting in there, I need some food.

Behind the dining hall, dumpsters line the chipped concrete wall. I scan the dusty ground, but I'll never find anything without climbing into the huge, foul smelling containers. There isn't a graceful way of getting in. What would my mother say if she could see me diving headfirst into a giant box of refuse? I could laugh if I wasn't fighting back the urge to be sick.

Holding my nose, I pick through piles of potato peels and empty sacks of oats, but there's nothing Elizabeth will accept as food. The smell is overwhelming and the sky above me is growing lighter every minute. If I'm going to make it into the Admin building before it starts filling up with workers, I need to leave now. I grab a handful of potato peels, shove them in my bag and throw my dirt-smeared legs over the side of the dumpster.

I dash across the open ground between the dining hall and the Admin building, my heart pounding in my ears. I chant "I can do this, I can do this" under my breath over and over as I run. I'm almost to the door, but stop dead in my tracks. Daniel didn't mention anything about a security camera, but there it is, pointed directly at the main entrance. Video evidence of me sneaking into a building I'm not supposed to be in using a OneCard I'm not supposed to have is probably one of those things that can land a girl in Quarantine. I can't do this.

I turn around and jog a few feet back toward the dining hall dumpsters, my failure a sour taste on the back of my tongue. A scavenger hunt is all they asked of me to be accepted. Difficult for sure, but hardly life-threatening. I couldn't even do that. Over my shoulder, the glass-fronted building taunts me; physical proof that I'm not capable enough to be a contributing part of their group.

Back at the dumpsters, I bend over, my hands braced against my knees while I gulp down a dozen ragged breaths. I stare back at the building, scouring the façade for another way in, but the front door is the only entrance. I can't do this…but…what if I can? What if I can get that Noteboard?

My mother's voice in my head is practically screaming at me to run back to the bunkhouse as fast as my tired legs can carry me. It's one thing to pick up random garbage lying around the PIT. It's gross, but not against any rules. Breaking into a government building crosses a line I've never even seen before. If I go inside, I will officially break the law, no matter what Elizabeth says about the lack of rules. I'll be a criminal in more than just name. For the first time ever, my mother might be wrong.

Using my last store of energy, I sprint to the main entrance. Please let me be too fast for the camera to identify me. I grab Daniel's card and swipe it along the reader by the door. The little black box emits a high pitched beep and the door slides open enough for me slip inside and catch my breath. I can't rest long. There are four flights of stairs to climb if I have any chance of finding this blasted Noteboard.

I scan Daniel's card on the fourth floor landing and dash through the door before it even slides all the way open. Breath pours out of me in loud wheezes. If I get out of this, I need to do something about getting into better shape. Hemming skirts and baking cakes were great practice for becoming someone's wife, but not-so-great preparation for life in the PIT. I don't care who hears me now. If my face is on that video camera, I'm as good as caught. I just want to find the Noteboard and get out.

To my left, a wall of glass separates the main floor of cubicles from another area. That must be where they keep the computers. I dash around the corner and plow right into the open entrance of a cubicle. The desk chair catches me before I fall on my face, but my scraped knee is on fire. Whoever sits here left their coat hung over the back of the chair and the cheap wool grated right over my cut. I'm probably bleeding, but I don't have time to stop and inspect it now. A wall of glass is straight ahead, separating me from the room containing exactly what I need.

A backlit sign next to the door reads Technology Room. I send Daniel a silent thank you as I once again scan his card, but there is no reassuring beep and the door doesn't slide open. I scan the card again, but the door stays stubbornly closed. Noteboards by the dozen sit out on long tables, mocking me through the thin layer of glass.

I'm tired and frustrated and I just want to sit down on the floor right here by the door and wait for a guard to catch me where I don't belong. Breathe, Rebecca. Breathe. It doesn't matter if I leave now anyway. The camera downstairs probably caught my picture. If I leave, red uniformed guards will show up at breakfast, or worse, the others' bunkhouse, and cart me off to Quarantine.

I have no idea what Quarantine is like, but it can't be good. Conditions in the PIT are barely livable. How do the guards in there treat criminals considered too dangerous to interact with other convicted criminals? A bead of sweat runs down my spine like a spider scrambling to escape the crush of a boot.

It's time to get out of here. The least I can do is head back to the bunk so Eric can have his bag back. Elizabeth will be irate if I get caught and the guards confiscate it.

My hand is on the door to the stairs, but a prickling feeling on the back of my neck holds me back. The forgotten coat on the desk chair isn't the kind worn to stay warm. I run back to the cubicle. This is a suit jacket. Not as nice as any from the Acceptance ceremony. More like the kind my father wears to work. What if the owner didn't mean to leave it here? What if that isn't all he forgot?

Losing your OneCard is a big deal, but it still happens. My father lost his a few years ago, somewhere on his way home from work. He always kept it in the inner pocket of his suit jacket. My mother figured he dropped his card after swiping it for the transport. He spent all morning the next day at the Cardinal Territory Outpost getting a new one and got a reprimand at work. The wasted time at the CTO probably bothered him more than the black mark in his file. Is there a chance the owner of this jacket keeps his OneCard in the little inner pocket, too?

I'm almost too nervous to check, but at this point I don't have anything to lose. I'm already pushing my luck with each passing second. Any minute employees are going to come up here and turn on the lights. And there I'll be, with my hand in the cookie jar and nowhere to hide.

I slide my hand in the satin lined pocket and pull out a white rectangle of plastic with a black scan line running the length of it. First I break into a government building and now I'm stealing someone's identity. The irony of becoming a criminal because of the PIT isn't lost on me, but I don't have time to doubt or justify my actions.

I throw myself at the Technology Room and whimper with relief when the scanner beeps. The door slides open and I rush inside. There isn't time to be picky. Noteboards, cables and hardware cover every open surface. I grab the nearest Noteboard and shove it into Eric's bag. Taking too much stuff is sure to set off alerts in inventory numbers, but at this point I'm most likely already going down. If I'm going to get caught, I might as well go out with a bang. I grab another Noteboard and a handful of cables.

Kneeling down on the floor, I shove the extra equipment in my nearly full bag, a tight fit with all the other items I collected tonight. Sweat drips down my forehead. I lean back to wipe it away and find another precious gift staring me in the face. Stuck to the side of the cold steel garbage can is a half-melted piece of chocolate. I don't have time to find something to wrap it in. Scooping it into my palm, I stand up and make a mad dash to the door.

I need to get out of here, but my conscience won't let me leave with a stolen OneCard. There are lines I won't cross, and pulling an innocent man down for my crimes is one of them. Using only my fingertips, I pull back the corner of his jacket and slide his card back into the inner pocket. I get as far as the next cubicle when the stairwell door slides open.

"I really appreciate this, John. My wife would kill me if I lost another card."

"Emily and I just celebrated fifteen years. Trust me, I understand."

Footsteps echo down the empty rows and I dive under the nearest desk sucking in a moan when my knee bangs against the chair. Two pairs of legs march right by me, stopping only a few feet away in front of the desk I was just at.

"Oh, thank the Cardinal, it's here. I was starting to worry I'd have to scour the Airbus station."

A man wearing the distinct red of a Cardinal uniform rocks back on his heels and a booming laugh bounces around the cavernous room. "Now you'll have time to make it home for a couple hours of sleep and Cindy won't make you crash on the couch."

"I think I'll pad my luck with a quick stop at the bakery. Nothing says 'please forgive me' like a butter croissant."

"For a man only married six months you've certainly caught on fast."

They share a good laugh and I use the sound to cover up a slight shift in position. My legs are desperate to stretch out of this tight ball, but fear freezes everything but the slightest of movements.

"Alright, let's get you out of here and back home to that new wife."

They turn and walk past my hiding spot again, adrenaline exaggerating the loud boom of each footstep. The stairwell door opens again, followed by the soft click of it closing.

The floor is deadly silent, but I can't move yet. What if that guard is still close by? If Cheryl was here, she'd know exactly what to do. She'd tell me to get up and run. Hesitation never held her back from anything she wanted.

I summon my last reserve of strength and pretend Cheryl is right next to me, running through the office, down the stairs and out through the lobby.

Outside, the sky is showing the first red-and-orange signs of dawn. I dash across the courtyard, ignoring the camera. I'm resigned to getting caught, but I'm going to get these computers to the others first. The narrow alleys leading back to Elizabeth's bunkhouse are empty. It's still too early for anyone else in the PIT to be stirring for breakfast.

Breathless, but giddy with success, I push against the rusted metal door of the bunkhouse. They're all here, sitting on the bunks, waiting for me.

"She's back." Eric's smile warms me and helps ease the stitch of pain shooting up my abdomen. He's at my side in an instant, leading me to a bunk so I can catch my breath.

"Yes, thanks for the obvious." Elizabeth doesn't move from where she's scowling on a bunk in the corner. "Cutting it awfully close, aren't we, princess?"

"She's here," Daniel's voice cuts in and Elizabeth bites back another hurtful barb.

"It doesn't mean anything unless she's got everything on the list." Elizabeth walks across the room until she's standing right in front of me. "What do you say? Did you get everything?"

"It's in there, but there isn't time. I need to get out of here before you all get in trouble." I toss the bag to Elizabeth and move past her to the door. What I wouldn't give for a few minutes to say goodbye to Eric; to thank him for what he's done for me. There isn't time. Guards could be on their way here right now, and every minute I stay risks putting them all in danger.

"Whoa, you aren't ready to go anywhere." Eric links his arm through mine and tugs me back toward the bunk.

I shake my head, but don't have the energy or strength to fight him. "I have to go. The cameras."

"What cameras?" Elizabeth moves closer to the bunk. A flicker of concern passes over her face. She may not care what happens to me, but I won't be thanked for putting the others in danger.

Eric rubs my back and, after a minute, I'm breathing steadily again. "There's a camera in front of the Admin building. I didn't have time to find another way in, so I had to run in front of it. If it didn't catch my face on the way in, I'm sure it got me on the way out."

Eric stiffens next me and I can't blame him. I'm a human ticking time bomb that could go off any minute. "Elizabeth, we have to—"

Elizabeth doubles over, grabbing her stomach, and laughs out loud bursts of air.

My confession of imminent demise has sent her over the edge. Daniel starts laughing, too. He has my bag full of scavenger hunt loot in one hand, but the other is covering his mouth in a vain attempt to keep his giddy laughs inside. Even Molly is chuckling lightly from her spot in the corner.

"Why are you laughing? This isn't funny." I don't understand their laughter, but it makes me feel better. Elizabeth would risk everything to protect the short list of people in this room. If they were in danger, she wouldn't be standing there laughing her head off.

"I'm sorry," Elizabeth says, wiping a tear from her eye and standing up straight to catch her breath. "It's just…the look on your face…absolutely precious." She takes a deep breath and manages to get her laughter under control. "Those cameras haven't been on in ages."

There are no words. The cameras didn't record my face. Guards aren't hunting for me. I'm safe; we're all safe. And Elizabeth is a jerk for letting me sit here in a panic.

"What in the world?" Daniel has my open bag of loot in both hands, holding it as far away from his face as possible. "Why does your bag smell like rotting garbage?"

"Oh." I smile at Daniel's wrinkled nose. That's what he gets for laughing at me. "That's the sock and potato peels."

Elizabeth doesn't waste any time dissolving her smile. "If you think a handful of peels are going to cut it as—"

I hold out my hand before she can finish her sentence. The leftover piece of chocolate is almost completely melted and unrecognizable, but the sweet smell is unmistakable.

"That's chocolate," Eric says, grabbing my wrist and holding my palm up under his nose. He closes his eyes and breathes in deep, taking advantage of his first glimpse of sugar in almost a week.

"Cardinal on a cracker." Daniel springs up from the bed, a Noteboard in each hand. The smile on his face reminds me of my cousin on his birthday last fall. He'd been asking his parents for a new Noteboard game for months. When the brown-paper wrapping revealed just what he wanted, his face almost split in half with the size of his smile. "There's two Noteboards, plus a ton of cables and connectors."

Elizabeth grabs the bag and pulls out the remaining items one by one. They all get tossed into a small pile on the floor except the potato peels which she flings out the door. I enjoy the look of disgust when the stench of the dead man's sock hits her. Serves her right for what she put me through.

"That's it, then. She did it," Daniel says, clutching the Noteboards like his firstborn child.

No one else says a word. The others look to Elizabeth standing in the middle of the room with the empty bag. I'm waiting for her to disqualify one of my finds and by the look on her face she's looking for a way to do it.

Molly gets up and lays a light hand on Elizabeth's shoulder. The tension leaves her face and she tosses the empty bag back at Eric.

"We'd better get moving if we want to get breakfast." Elizabeth turns on her heel and walks out the door, with Molly following close behind.

Eric and Daniel stand. I'm not sure if I'm supposed to stay or go or run away. "What does that mean? Am I in?"

Eric offers a hand to help me off the bed. "Welcome to the club, Becca."

Nine

Breakfast is a quiet affair. Even though I passed the test and Eric assures me I'm 'in', I'm still the outsider. Brand new and separate from the group, like the Noteboards in the technology room. I can't hear the unsaid words layered beneath comments about burnt mush and cracked cups.

"So, now what?"

Elizabeth inches her gaze up from her bowl to glare at me. "Now nothing. Eat your breakfast."

I swallow back my fear. Elizabeth might be ready to bite my head off, but I didn't risk everything getting those Noteboards last night for nothing. "I want to know what's going on. I know there's something you're not telling me."

Elizabeth stands up, slamming her empty bowl onto the table. "You won't know anything until you learn to keep your mouth shut."

She marches to the door, but not before glaring at Eric and Daniel.

The rest of us follow her out, and the awkward silence of breakfast extends to the walk back to the bunkhouse. Elizabeth and Molly, leading the pack, pass by the bunk where I've slept the past several nights. I thought once I passed, I'd move in with the others, but now I'm not so sure. Elizabeth doesn't even try to hide her dislike of me, but Eric acts like I'm supposed to be with him. That's where I want to be, but I don't know where I should be.

I pause by the rusted door of my bunk, but Eric grabs my hand and gives it a small squeeze. He tugs on my arm, guiding me back to the dirt path. His smile is enough to keep me with the group for now.

Back in the isolated bunk, everyone takes a seat on one of the flat mattresses. Elizabeth flounces down on the bunk in the corner, ignoring us all. Daniel and Molly sit together, their eyes never leaving my face. Eric pulls me down on the bed next to him, and the four of us stare at each other, waiting for someone to start talking. The minutes stretch on before Daniel finally breaks the silence.

"Elizabeth—"

She stops him with a raised hand, but doesn't look away from the corner that's held her attention since we all walked in.

"She passed the test."

"Don't you think I know that, Daniel?"

"Elizabeth?" Molly's soft, tinkling voice leeches the look of anguish from Elizabeth's face. "Our shifts start soon, and this can't wait."

"Molly's right," Daniel picks up, not giving Elizabeth a chance to cut him off again. "Summer isn't far off, and we need to be ready to go."

"Fine." Elizabeth finally looks up from the corner and gives me all her attention. Her expression is far from friendly, but lacks its usual contempt. "We're going to break out of the PIT."

"Wait. What?" The pounding of my heart makes it hard to think. No one breaks out of the PIT: that's why the Territories are so safe. Why people can sleep at night with their windows open and doors unlocked. Rejects breaking out of the PIT would send all the Territories back into a state of violent turmoil. It can't be done. But their serious faces tell me this isn't a joke. "It's impossible. What makes you think you can do what hasn't been done in the eighty years since this place opened?"

"Because we aren't criminals," Daniel answers, pounding a fist against his leg. "We aren't in here because of homicidal tendencies or a need to steal or hurt people. We're here because the Cardinal is afraid of us. He thinks he can stick us in here, and we'll just lie down and roll over." His eyes are alive with conviction. "He underestimates us. He forgets just how dangerous a smart man can be when he's pushed into a corner."

My heart is dancing inside my chest. I've never heard Daniel speak like this, so sure of himself, so sure of us. I want him to keep going, but he takes a deep breath and resumes his calm demeanor.

"So you have a plan?" For the first time in almost a week I feel something besides despair and loneliness.

Daniel told me to forget about home, block out those memories, but now wisps of hope break through and swirl in my chest.

"Of course we have a plan, Blondie," Elizabeth cuts back in. "Molly and I have to get to work so I'll leave Daniel and Eric to fill you in on the details."

Elizabeth and Molly stand to leave, but before the door closes behind them, Elizabeth stops it with the tips of her fingers. Her short blonde hair is silhouetted by the slot of sunlight streaming through the partially opened door.

"We're trusting you, Becca. This isn't a game."

"I know—"

"No, you don't. If you betray us…we aren't in here for being violent, but people can change."

Molly tucks her head back inside and tugs on Elizabeth's arm. Elizabeth slams the door closed. Her words hang in the air, sucking out all the oxygen and making it hard to draw enough breath into my lungs.

Daniel stretches and moves to another bunk, closer to where Eric and I are sitting. "You can't let Elizabeth get to you."

"She didn't get to me." I jump up, shaking off Eric's comforting hand. How can I not let her threat bother me? Elizabeth doesn't like me, she doesn't trust me, and she certainly doesn't want me here. And why would she? She and Molly are as close as sisters. They don't need a tag-along.

"This isn't easy for her," Daniel says, cutting into my thoughts.

"And it should be easy for me?" I yell at him, my hands shaking. "Or Eric, or any of us?"

I take a deep breath. I don't want to shout; don't want to take my anger and fear out on Eric and Daniel, the only people who've shown me kindness since I got here.

"No, it's not easy." Daniel's soft voice is a stark contrast to my yells. "But things were worse for Elizabeth. She's been here three years, but Molly and I only got here two years ago."

Three days of living on my own almost pushed me to my limit. What would an entire year be like? No one to talk to; no one to share my meals, my fears. How different would life in the PIT be if I were completely alone? "I didn't…I…"

"When Molly and I got here, the connection was instant. Elizabeth made us her family. For the past two years, it's been the three of us looking out for each other. She cried herself to sleep the night before the Acceptance ceremony this year." Daniel looks at Eric the way someone might look at a wounded animal. "Watching you walk into the PIT was her worst nightmare come true. And yet, a small part of her, a part she doesn't let people see very often, was glad to see you."

Eric winces and his shoulders droop. I reach for his hand at the same time he reaches for mine. This is Elizabeth's family; her brother, her best friend, her boyfriend. Who am I? No one. No, worse than no one. I'm a threat to the family Elizabeth created. "Tell me what the plan is."

"It's simple," Daniel says, the tension in the room erased. "We don't know exactly where the PIT is, but we know we're on a coastline."

I've never been to the ocean, but I've seen pictures. Long stretches of snowy-white beaches and an eternity of water crashing into a golden sunset. I haven't seen anything close to those pictures in the time I've been in the PIT.

Daniel smiles at my disbelief. "You can tell by the smell of the air. It's the salt. Plus, I've seen it."

And now he has all of my attention. "You've seen the ocean?"

Daniel nods. "At the edge of the PIT, there's a fence that surrounds the whole place. It's way too high to climb and the barbs at the top could slice a man in two, but I found a spot where the bottom is pulled out of the concrete. About a mile out is the coastline."

"So that's how we're getting out? We just duck under the fence and follow the coastline until we get somewhere else?" The plan sounds overly simple. Surely someone has tried this before.

"It'd be nice if it were that easy, Becca." Eric joins the conversation. "But things in the PIT are rarely simple. It may take a few days, but eventually the Cardinal guards will know we're missing. You can only skip so many work shifts before they start looking for you."

"Then why have jobs?" I'm not a genius, but this seems like an easy hurdle to get around. "If that will tip them off, you should quit right now."

"We can't quit," Daniel explains. "Jobs equal OneCards. We'll need them on the outside. Plus, they give us access to the supplies we need. Elizabeth works in food preparation, which lets her sneak out with cans we can use for taking food and water with us. Hopefully she can get food when the time comes. Molly works sorting and repairing clothes. We'll each need a nice outfit for our first appearance in whatever Territory we end up in. Molly will get those."

"What about you?"

"I'm retired," he says, a goofy grin spreading across his face. "Now that I have this lovely new Noteboard, I'm in charge of making sure the Cardinal can't find us. Tomorrow we'll head over to the Admin building and get you signed up as my replacement."

Eric shifts his weight next to me and asks the question I've been wondering. "Elizabeth was vague when she explained this part to me. If we can't follow the coastline, where will we go?"

"Oh, we're still going to follow the coastline," Daniel says, "just not in the way the Cardinal Guards will be expecting. No one will be looking for a boat."

"You have a boat?" I can't believe it. A boat changes everything.

"Not yet. And we don't really expect to find one. But the plan is to find what we need to build a raft. Elizabeth has experience sailing with her dad." Daniel jerks his chin at Eric. "I assume you know your way around the water, too?"

Eric nods his head in confirmation.

"We'll get ourselves far enough from the shore that the guards can't see us, then follow the current south until we're in the clear."

The plan is simple, but brilliant. And more than that, I see how it might work. Closing my eyes, I picture all of us rowing into the ocean and letting the waves carry us to a new life. For the first time in what feels like ages, I feel hope. "So what do you need me to do?"

"Whenever you're not working, you need to keep an eye out for anything that can be used to help build the raft. We'll need paddles and something to corral the food and supplies. Everyone is scouring the entire PIT for materials to make the raft out of."

Daniel smiles again and I can appreciate why Elizabeth likes him. When his smile is genuine, it lights up his whole face and his eyes sparkle with mischief like a little boy. Before the Acceptance ceremony the girls must have been dying to have him on their dance card. Afterward, they would have pretended he never existed.

He exists now. We all do. The Cardinal thinks he can keep us locked up in here, but I'm not going to spend the rest of my life looking over my shoulder. I smooth down what's left of my curls and lift my chin.

"When do we get started?"

Ten

Daniel leads me past the dining hall. The Admin building is the only one in the PIT that isn't made of concrete and the area outside is mostly free of garbage. I didn't notice any details of the building when I was here last night, but I take them all in now. Etched in the large glass door is a ring of olive branches, the symbol of the Cardinal. My whole life I was taught that the Cardinal represented peace and stability. Now, the symbol brings back those few moments of standing on stage, red lights flashing while my life was stripped away.

"This is where all PIT business happens. The workers in here coordinate the clothing donations, food shipments and our monthly haircuts." Daniel tugs on one of my short curls. His smile brings me out of my bad memory. "It's also the best place to get a job."

"You do realize I have absolutely no skills…at all. Unless the Cardinal is looking for someone to braid his hair or make a casserole." I'm not trying to be modest. In school, boys attend business classes to prepare them for Assignment after graduation. Not the girls. I learned how to bake a pie, sew a button and diaper a baby. Hardly useful skills in the PIT. English is the only class everyone takes, but only so the girls are able to read recipes and notes left from our husbands.

"That's not a problem." Daniel uses the OneCard I returned to him and the glass door slides open with a soft whoosh. "It's not as if they would let you do anything important. Let me do the talking and I'll get you a good job."

I follow him in and we're immediately stopped by a guard dressed in a red Cardinal uniform. Behind him, several other red-suits are stationed throughout the room. So this is where they've all been. Daniel flashes his card before tucking it into his pocket.

"Just signing her up for a job," he says, thumbing toward me. The beefy guard grunts in response and nods toward the enclosed counter.

The room reminds me of the bank with its serious men sitting behind the desks, keeping an eye on everyone's money. Except the pudgy man behind the protective glass doesn't look serious; he looks bored and disgusted. Does he go home every night and complain to his wife about the filth he has to talk to every day?

"I want to quit my job and let her take over." Daniel's voice is confident, but sounds muddled echoing off the glass divider.

"Fine, give me your card."

Daniel makes a big show of searching his pockets and coming up empty. He turns around, scanning the ground behind him and gives me a wink the sour man behind the counter can't see. "I must have left it in my bunk."

"Cardinal help me," the man grumbles under his breath. "I can't believe they trust you swine with cards anyway. Put your hand on the reader." Daniel obeys and waits for the lights to stop flashing before lowering his hand.

The grumpy official stares at his Noteboard, and scratches his chin. "Daniel Whedon?" Daniel nods, his face expressionless. "That sounds familiar. Is your—?"

"I'm no one." Daniel's voice is polite, but it's clear the conversation is over.

"You don't have to tell me that."

I hate this man behind the counter, judging us like he knows who we are. I know exactly what he's thinking, because it's the same thing I thought until recently. The PIT is for the worst of the worst. Scumbags, slime, destroyers, filth; that's who lives in the PIT.

The man turns away, done with us, but we don't have everything we need yet.

Daniel taps on the glass and a nearby guard gives him a warning growl. "What about the job for her?"

It's a lost cause. This man is done dealing with us. I can tell from the blank look on his face, almost as if he's looking right through us.

"I'll vouch for her, if that will help." My chest swells with gratitude. Daniel has only known me a few days. Since then, he's saved me from a life of prostitution, introduced me to my only friends, and trusted me with information that could get him and everyone he cares about tossed into Quarantine or worse. So far, I've been nothing but a pain and a burden. I need this job so I can contribute to the group. I refuse to be the weak link.

"Humph, like the word of a Reject means anything to me." The man behind the counter gives both of us a look of loathing and disgust. "Still, someone has to do it." He nods his head at me. "Put your hand on the reader."

The lights flash just like the readers from the Machine, but there's no life-ending red this time. He types something into his Noteboard and shoves a plastic OneCard through a small slit in the glass. "Here's your card. Bring it here tonight after sunset if you can manage not to lose it. A guard will be in the lobby to give you your assignment."

"Thank you, thank you so much." The man behind the counter looks at me like I've just asked to marry his son. I take it as a sign to get out and fast.

"Hold up just a minute," Daniel says as soon as the glass door slides closed behind us. He swings a bag identical to Eric's off his shoulder and sifts through its contents. After a minute he holds up a long piece of string. On closer inspection, I realize it's actually a dingy shoestring. One that might have been white long ago, but had been dragged through the dirt enough to take on a sickly yellow-brown color that matches everything else in the PIT.

I have no idea what I'm supposed to do with a dirty shoelace.

"Here." Daniel strings the lace through a small punched hole in my card and ties the ends together to create a necklace. "Now you don't have to worry about losing it or having it stolen. You'll need to protect that card."

He hangs it around my neck and the card hits my chest in the same place the silver knot of my grandmother's necklace did. I force back the sour lump rising in my throat.

"Thanks." I'm not sure of the proper sentiment when given a dirty shoelace necklace. I don't have a frame of reference for anything that's happened in the past few days. "Why are you being so nice to me? It's not just this. You're the one who first brought me to the bunk and you always stick up for me with Elizabeth."

"Honestly?" Daniel slides the strap of the bag over his head and walks back toward the dining hall. "I'm not sure. I don't say that to be mean, but favors are not something one usually hands out around here." He stops and looks at me like he's really seeing me for the first time. "Yes, I do know why. I have a sister back home. Well, at least I did have a sister, not that she'd acknowledge me now. When I look at you, I see a lot of her; innocent and naïve, too trusting for your own good." Daniel looks away and starts walking again. "If the tables were turned and it was her in here instead of me, I'd hope someone would look out for her."

I stand rooted to my spot and picture Daniel back at home doting on his sister. She's still out there somewhere with his parents, all three living their lives. Does she still care for him as much as he cares for her? Do my parents still think about me? My hand clutches at empty fabric where my grandmother's necklace should be and a lump clogs my throat. Eric is wrong. She would never forget about me.

Daniel turns around and motions his hand for me to follow. "Come on. It's time for lunch."

The others are already at one of the long tables in the corner when we walk into the hall.

"Look who's got a shiny new OneCard." Eric scoots over to make room for me next to him.

"Thanks to Daniel. I'm now officially employed." It sounds weird to say it out loud. I always pictured my future as someone's wife, raising a family, taking care of a home. I push those thoughts out. Right now, I need to focus on being a part of this family and that means doing what I can to get us ready to leave.

"And what will the princess be doing for our illustrious leader?" Elizabeth chimes in from across the table.

"Garbage detail," Daniel says puffing his chest out in a pride that leaves me baffled.

"Whoa, you never said anything about garbage detail."

Daniel looks at me with wounded eyes. I look away and smooth down the bodice of my dress. Nothing says class like insulting the person who's done the most to help me so far. I smile at him and soften my tone.

"Not to sound ungrateful or anything, but you said you'd get me a good job."

"I did. Garbage detail is the best job here." Daniel sets down his bowl and gives me his full attention. "You're not going to find a lot of perks in the PIT. The Cardinal makes sure we have housing, clothes and food. It isn't good, but that's what we get. Everything else is considered above the needs of criminals like us."

"But that's not to say we don't have our ways of getting what we really need," Elizabeth adds, using her index finger to scrape the last remnants of today's attempt at stew from her bowl. "Some of the guards can be bribed, but that's as likely to get you Quarantined as anything else. You can bargain with the bosses, but you'll give more than you get for certain. The best way to find the little extras is taking on a job."

"Are you serious?" I pull my hand away from my gaping mouth. Do they really expect me to find hidden treasures in the trash?

"Molly works in the clothing room." Elizabeth nudges her lightly with her elbow. "Whenever a shipment of donations comes in, Molly and the other workers get the first opportunity to go through it and hold back the best clothes for themselves."

"And the people we care about," Molly whispers next to her.

"My job doesn't come with as many fringe benefits for you guys. On the days I work in the kitchen, I get to eat before the stew is a burned mush."

"Those jobs make sense," I say, poking at my uneaten bowl of something foul smelling. "What's the hidden bonus of taking out the garbage?"

"The people who work in the Admin building don't live in the PIT. They have normal lives where they can get anything they need." Daniel leans in to the table, a huge smile on his face. "With that luxury comes a willingness to part with it."

"And?" I choke down another bite of stew. I slide what's left across the table to Elizabeth and her eyes light up.

"Think about the things that might have ended up in your trash can at home. Scraps of paper, the nub of a pencil, random buttons, boxes or cans with just a bit of food left in the bottom. In your old life, all of that was considered trash, but here it's like finding a piece of gold."

"Becca," Elizabeth mumbles between bites of stew, "what would you do if I laid half a hamburger in front of you right now? Would you question where I got it, or what happened to the other half?" She doesn't wait for an answer, but she doesn't need to. Any one of us would devour the whole thing before we had time to question its origin. My stomach growls at the thought of it. She wiggles her eyebrows as if she's about to tell me a really juicy secret. "Mr. Jones in office 203 orders out for lunch almost every day, but rarely has time to finish the whole meal. And what does he do with what's left? Right into the trash bin where Daniel collects it four times a week."

"She's right," Daniel says with much less dramatic flair. "You wouldn't believe what you can find in the trash bins. Of course, you're going to need a bag. Elizabeth?"

The two of them face off in a staring contest, but eventually Elizabeth caves, throwing her head back in defeat. "Fine, fine, we have another back at the bunk." She finishes off the last bite of my leftover stew and points a greasy finger at me. "But don't think this makes us best friends or anything."

She winks at me and I think she might not hate me, after all.

Eleven

After lunch Elizabeth and Molly head off to search for materials, leaving me with the boys.

"So what now? What are we supposed to do all day?" Other than eating disgusting food and collecting garbage a few nights a week, I have no idea what goes on inside the PIT. I doubt the Cardinal hosts monthly social gatherings.

"Whatever we want, really." Daniel takes off across the courtyard, and with nowhere else to go, Eric and I follow. "If you have a job, you go to it. If not, you do something else. I'd say the only rule around here is don't kill anyone, but that's not true. They couldn't care less if we killed each other."

"Then why don't they?"

Daniel stops walking to face me. "Why don't they what?"

I look away so I can voice the thought that's been sitting in the back of my head since I got here. "Why don't they just kill us?"

Eric stiffens beside me, but Daniel only nods.

"Because the Cardinal needs us." He motions to our pitiful surroundings. "You've got guards, administrators, and the laborers. Not to mention the manpower needed for the logistics of transporting spoiled food and donated clothes. The PIT is a mini city, employing who knows how many men. With so many jobs becoming automated, the Cardinal needs us alive. But just barely."

As if I needed more motivation to get out of here. "What are you going to do today?"

"I'm heading out to my secret lair to see if I can find some accessories for the fun new toy you brought me. You're welcome to come with me."

"We'd love to see your secret lair." Eric threads his arm through mine, but it feels more possessive than romantic.

Daniel looks like he regrets the invitation, but it's too late now. "Come on, then. Just try not to draw any attention. A secret lair isn't a secret if the whole PIT knows about it."

Daniel leads us through a part of the compound where the buildings are packed one right next to the other until we reach an outer area where the buildings are older and more spread apart.

My feet are throbbing and I'm about to suggest a break, but he stops and gestures around us. "This is the southern edge of the PIT. And that," he points straight ahead, "is the fence."

I've never seen anything like it. A steel, chain-link fence at least two stories high, towers above us. I shade my eyes from the sun and peer up at the top. Even if someone managed to climb up, the five foot overhang would require impressive acrobatic moves in order to avoid a twenty-foot free-fall and several broken bones. Getting to the overhang would be a challenge by itself considering the amount of barbed wire crisscrossing the last several feet of fence. No wonder there are hardly any guards. With a fence like this, the Cardinal doesn't need them.

Outside the fence is nothing but an endless open plain as far as the eye can see. On the very edge of the western horizon miniature mountains dot the landscape. I stare out and imagine running through the waist-high grass until I'm nothing more than a tiny dot in the distance.

"You okay?" Daniel's hand on my arm pulls me out of the fantasy.

"Yeah, I'm fine." I'm not, but there isn't anything more Daniel can do. I won't be okay until we get out of here.

"Let's keep going. We're almost there."

We walk past a few more abandoned buildings and Daniel stops in front of one that stands out a bit. The roof is metal instead of rotted wood like the others. I don't know anything about architecture, but this building looks sturdier than the ones around it, like someone put a bit more effort into it. Daniel pushes open the door, his hand just below the circle of olive branches still visible against the faded red paint.

"This is an Admin building," Eric says pausing outside the threshold.

"It was, though it hasn't seen a red uniform in decades." Daniel holds the door open and waves his empty hand. "It's safe, I promise."

It's dark inside, but dirt-filtered sunlight from the windows provides enough light to walk around without tripping on anything. The one-room building looks almost exactly like the Technology room I broke into last night. The only difference is dozens of monitors lining the walls here.

"What is this place?" I ask, running my finger across a desk and removing a thick layer of dust.

"The old security building." Daniel is beaming. This room is a techno-savvy dreamland. "Back when all the cameras around the PIT were still active, this is where the guards monitored everyone's movements. When the cameras went offline, they abandoned the room and left their equipment behind."

"So just like that, they gave up watching us?" It doesn't make sense.

"This was a while ago. Back then the PIT was smaller, easier to control. As the population grew it became harder and harder to watch what was going on." Daniel runs a hand over his short, dark hair. "It required too many guards to monitor the cameras. The Cardinal needed those resources elsewhere."

"Why? What did he need them for?"

A thunderous crash pulls my attention away from Daniel. I spin around to find Eric standing in a pile of boxes and a cloud of dust.

"Too bad all they left behind is a bunch of outdated garbage." Eric picks up a cable that's split down the seam, its colored wires spilling out.

"Outdated, yes. Garbage, only to the untrained eye." Daniel takes the ruined cable from Eric. "There are gemstones hidden in here and it's my job to find them."

This place looks like a cemetery for hardware. Empty shells of computers cover most of the workspace and one corner has been taken over by a family of rodents.

"So what are we looking for, exactly?" Not that I have any idea what any of this is, but I can at least pretend to be helpful.

Daniel holds out a hand and counts off his wish list on his fingers. "A network chip, connection cables, a storage drive and a card reader."

"What are you going to do with all that?" Eric asks, sifting through the contents of a drawer.

"That's what I need to hack into the Cardinal's system."

I giggle, a tiny burst of mirth that gets cut short. He's serious. "What? You can't…how will you…what?"

"Unless we plan on living in the woods and eating tree bark, we'll need new identities once we escape." Daniel pockets a gadget and flashes me an unsettling grin. "I promise it sounds much more complicated that it really is."

Sure, nothing at all complicated about breaking into what has to be the most secure network in the world. So much for our simple boat ride to freedom.

* * *

The darkened Admin building gives me the chills. Even though the cameras aren't working, I can't shake the feeling that I'm under constant surveillance. I swipe my card across the reader and the doors swish open to my first night of work.

A guard stands by the main desk, a Noteboard in hand. He doesn't look up at me, but he must be the one I get my assignment from.

"Hi, my name is Rebecca—"

His right hand shoots up and cuffs me on the side of my head. Bright spots of light flash behind my eyelids.

"What in the Cardinal's name makes you think I care what your name is?" He grabs the card dangling on my makeshift necklace and drags me closer. A beep sounds from the computer and he pushes me back a step. "Sixth floor. Put the can back in the hall when you're done and hurry up about it. Think I want to be here all night waiting on you lazy swine?"

I'm still a little dizzy from the hit to my head, but I rush to the stairwell door. The overhead lights are out, leaving only the emergency lights and exit signs to guide me up the stuffy stairs. Apparently PIT workers aren't worth the energy to leave the lights on. No doubt we're not worth the energy to heat it, either. Thank goodness we'll be long gone before I have to work in the cold of winter.

As promised, Elizabeth pulled out a dusty bag from under one of the mattresses when we all got back to the bunkhouse. It looks like someone's dog used it as a chew toy, but Molly sewed up all the big holes. Anything the group would find the least bit useful will be tucked away inside and turned over to Elizabeth after my shift. She's coordinating supplies for the escape. Of course, food won't make it back. According to her, walking around the PIT with food is like asking to be attacked.

After another sub-par dinner, food is what I'm dreaming about. Only a week ago I would have been disgusted by the idea of eating someone's half-eaten lunch from the garbage can. Not tonight.

Pushing the large, wheeled can down the thin rows, I empty desk cans and look for hidden treasures. Daniel gave me tips on things to look out for. Food is at the top of the list, along with paper and writing instruments. I'm also supposed to keep an eye out for any discarded clothing, especially outerwear like gloves or scarves. I doubt I'll find anything like that given the warm spring weather, but you never know.

His last suggestion was to look for things that can be made into weapons. Letter openers, scissors, paperweights; anything sharp or heavy. But nothing from the desks. Daniel was adamant about it. Other workers might steal from the desks, but according to him, "we don't." Elizabeth rolled her eyes when he gave me the speech, but I couldn't agree with him more. We aren't criminals, and just because we live with them doesn't mean we have to act like them. The makeshift weapons are only a last resort if something happens during the escape. We don't plan to use them to build a reign of terror in the PIT. I've never even held a weapon, but after everything I've seen in here, having one would be nice.

A few rows in, I fall into a rhythm. Stop at the desk, empty the contents of the can onto the ground. Look for food first and eat it right away. Then sort through the rest, tucking anything useful into the bag and tossing the rest into the can. Elizabeth drilled home the point that I have to do a good job of cleaning up the mess. If I leave any garbage on the floor, even a little, I might lose the job and all the perks that come with it.

By the time I'm done with the floor, I have a decent bag of loot. Several scraps of paper and two broken pencils join a discarded headset and a plastic knife. I'm not sure the plastic knife is worth saving, but I don't want to risk Elizabeth yelling at me for leaving it behind.

The large can I push back toward the stairwell is mostly full of empty food containers and pencil shavings. Everything from candy wrappers to dehydrated-noodle cups combine to create a collage titled "Food I don't get to eat." I reach in to check the inside of a candy wrapper one last time, but freeze at the swish of the stairwell door.

The guard in the lobby didn't mention anyone else working this floor, and there was only one can waiting on the landing. There's no reason for another worker to come in here. Moving as quickly and silently as possible, I half crawl, half wiggle to the nearest cubicle and duck down under the desk. I hold my breath and listen for footsteps on the industrial-grey carpet. Either no one is moving and I imagined the door opening, or whoever is out there moves with stealth.

I count out one hundred deep breaths, but there are no other indications that anyone is there. Someone must have been confused about the floors and realized their mistake when they opened the door. I uncurl myself from the tight ball under the desk. When I stand up my shoulder bumps into the desk and knocks over a picture frame. It's a photo of his wife and two young children sitting outside, smiling up at the camera, happy to know that all the criminals are locked away.

The last thing I need is trouble on my first day. Thankfully, the frame isn't broken. It only takes a second to set the photo back in its spot. I turn to leave and spin right into a firm, warm chest.

I scream as loud as I can, arms flailing at my attacker. Strong arms wrap around my torso, pinning my arms to my side. The only free part of me is my legs, so I kick at his shins and stomp on his feet. Anything to get away.

"Where do you think you're going?" Massive hands push me into the desk, knocking picture frames everywhere. Fingers weave into my close-cropped hair, jerking my head back and throwing me onto the floor. I don't get a chance to see my attacker's face before his knee digs into my spine, pinning me to the sterile grey carpet.

He grabs the bag from my shoulder and everything I've collected tonight dumps on to the floor.

"Where's the food?" His heavy knee digs harder into my back, pushing my trembling torso into the floor. Any second my ribs are going to crack.

"There isn't any." I can't get enough air into my lungs and my shaky voice comes out as barely a whisper.

"Don't lie to me," he says, grinding the side of my face down until my cheekbone is about to cave in.

"Not lying." I shake my head a fraction of an inch, the carpet burning my skin. "Food is gone."

The weight lifts from my back and he throws the burlap bag at my face. "Next time, you better have something better than pencils." His worn shoe connects with my elbow, but I bite my tongue against the pain stabbing up my arm.

I'm frozen in place as the door whooshes open and closed behind me. Tears I've been holding back choke out of my throat. Huge sobs shake my shoulders, adding to the pain in my arm, chest and face.

"Becca?"

I spring like a cat back under the desk, clawing to get away from whoever is here to hurt me again.

"Becca, it's me, Eric."

I stop thrashing long enough to find Eric crouched down in front me, his eyes narrowed in concern.

"Eric?" One nod from him and I'm up and in his arms.

"Look at your face. What happened?"

I can't find my voice to answer him. Instead, I pull him closer, desperate for protection against the darkness that can't get me with him here. Hot blood pounds in my ears, my body still tensed to fight. I don't understand what he's doing here, but the relief of being safe overwhelms my other emotions.

He holds me, rubbing small circles against my back until I stop shaking and can tell him what happened. Eric moves gentle fingers against my cheek and arm. Light presses on my ribs bring a hiss to my lips, but Eric proclaims nothing broken. He helps me gather my collection into the bag and put all the tossed picture frames back in place, staying silent the whole time.

When everything is back in place Eric lifts my chin until I meet his gaze. "Are you okay?"

I nod and force a small smile. "I'm glad you're here now. But…what are you doing here?"

"Well, this *is* the best job in the PIT, and I needed something to get my OneCard. I came here after dinner when the rest of you were talking about garbage tactics. The troll of a man in charge tried to put me in the kitchen, but I talked him into janitor duty." He runs a hand through his shortened blond hair and smiles down at me. "I thought it might be nice if we got to spend more time together. Now, I'm never letting you out of my sight again."

"We have to get out of here." I grip his hands so tight it hurts, but the pain lets me know I'm still alive. "I can't do this, Eric. I'm not strong enough to live in here."

"We're going to get out. Before you know it this place will be nothing more than a bad dream."

"Promise?"

Eric holds out his arm as if we're at the Acceptance ball and he's about to lead me out on to the dance floor for a romantic waltz. "Promise. Now let's go home."

I thread my arm through his and pretend I'm back in the blue satin dress and new white gloves. For one blissful minute I'm the pampered princess walking on the arm of the prince who can make all my dreams come true. But then the moment passes. Eric shoves my trash bin back in place in the stairwell and we make our way out of the darkened building, a bag of priceless junk hanging on my shoulder.

Twelve

"Nothing at all down that way." My sixth alley search of the night wasn't any more successful than the others. "Unless you count the quartet of…ladies."

I shiver at the memory of how they called after me, their suggestions far from ladylike.

"The same for me, minus the ladies." Eric smiles and marks off both alleys on our hand-drawn map. Weeks of searching and our only escape supplies are a few old poles and a burlap sack. At this rate, we'll never have everything we need before the end of summer. I do my best to stay positive for the others, but with Eric I don't have to pretend.

I slump onto a busted box, my feet burning from hours of walking, searching through piles of junk no one in the PIT has any use for. Eric sits down next to me and grabs my hand. When we first got here, his palms were smooth and unmarked. Now the pads of his fingers are callused, and a small scar runs across his palm from a run-in with a stray nail. "Come on, Becca. Don't give up."

I tilt my head back and soak up a minute of the cool night air. With my eyes closed, I can pretend we're sitting on the front porch swing at my parents' house.

"I think I smell burnt rice. Are you ready for dinner?"

"Wow, Eric, when you say it like that, it sounds like a dream date." I smile up at him, ready to move past my sour mood, but Eric isn't smiling.

"When we get out of here, I'm going to take you on a real date." He grips both of my hands and his face is more serious than I've ever seen it. "As soon as we get settled, we can go out for a fancy dinner and dancing. I'll buy you a fancy dress, ten times nicer than the one you wore to Acceptance."

"I'd like that." And I mean it. At first, the way Eric acted so familiar made me nervous, but now it's a comfort. I could love him.

"Good, but for now it's burnt rice in the dining hall." His smile is back and we walk in silence toward another unsatisfying meal.

A light breeze blows through little pockets of weeds growing between the buildings. Spring is slowly fading into summer. Back at my parents' house, flowers of every shade of the rainbow are blooming in window boxes and tended beds. The closest thing to color we have here is an occasional dandelion.

There's one poking up near the corner of a building and I tug Eric over so I can pick it. Its yellow petals are pale, almost sickly, but compared to dust, rocks and dirty concrete it's a thing of beauty. Pinching the stem at the bottom I pluck it from the sandy soil.

"Here, let me." Eric takes the stem and tucks it behind my ear. "Beautiful."

The side of my cheek will be stained yellow from the pollen, but I don't care. "Let's find one for you, there must be more around here." The flower has done more than lift my spirits. My legs aren't as tired as they were just minutes ago. I skip around the side of the building in search of another flower.

"Becca, come here, quick." Eric's voice cuts through the early evening air, louder than it needs to be.

I rush back to the other side of the bunkhouse, my thin soles sliding in the dust. In the dimly lit alley, Eric pulls long, thick, coils of rope from under a moldy wooden crate.

"Rope. You found rope!" I run to his side and help him wrap the thick strand around his shoulders so we can carry it back to the bunkhouse. A find like this needs to be hidden away as fast as we can.

"You found it. Now put it back."

I spin around with my heart lodged in my throat. Eric freezes next to me. The deadpan voice belongs to a tall woman holding a rusted pole like a baseball bat.

She swings the pole around until its pointing at the dead center of my chest. "I don't know who you are or what you're doing, but that's my rope."

"We didn't know. I'm so sorry." I glance at Eric and shift my eyes toward the crate, silently pleading for him to put the rope down.

"Well, now you know."

Eric doesn't move and she waves the pole for emphasis. I nudge him with my elbow. We need to get out of here before one of us gets hurt.

Eric hesitates. Please don't take off and leave me here with the crazy woman holding a blunt weapon. We need that rope, but I'd rather not be left to deal with the consequences of stealing it.

"What proof do you have that you own this rope?" Eric's voice swells with confidence. I wipe damp palms on my dusty dress.

"I'd say the business end of this pole is all the proof I need." The woman takes a step closer, but jerks to a stop, staring at me. "Well, if it isn't little Rebecca Collins. Didn't think I'd ever see you here."

My muscles go rigid and the bodice of my dress fills with ice cubes. "What?" I turn to Eric, but his eyes are wide. He doesn't know who this is either.

"You probably don't recognize me. It's been over six years, but I'd recognize that curly hair and button nose anywhere." She smiles at me, but only the very edges of her lips curl up. "Do they remember me at all back home?"

I step back into Eric, who wraps his arms around me instantly. His embrace is the only thing keeping me on my feet. "Constance? Constance Berger?"

"Then they do remember me. Or at least one of you does. Although, you're in here, so I'm not sure that really counts anymore." Constance leans the pole against the side of the building, but she doesn't look any less dangerous. "Well, come on inside then, we have a lot to catch up on."

She waves her hand around for us to follow and flaps us through the door like a mother hen.

My shock in the alley is nothing compared to the shock waiting for us inside. Constance's bunk looks nothing like a bunkhouse in the PIT. It looks like a home; one that belongs to someone very poor, but still a home.

Two beds are pushed together in the back corner and made up the way my mother used to with the corners all tucked under. In the other back corner, a tall crate is set up with a bowl on top and a cracked mirror hanging over it. A rectangle table made from an old door and four unmatched lengths of wood dominate the central space. Constance offers us a seat on wooden crates around the table.

"If you don't mind," Constance says to Eric, "you can set the rope down over in that corner."

Eric tightens his grip on the loops around his neck and eyes the door. Without the threat of a rusty pole, there's nothing stopping him from leaving. Constance shakes her head and releases a sigh that turns into a light laugh. "I'm not saying I won't share, but for now why don't you take it off so you can be more comfortable."

Eric nods his head and lays the rope down without a word. He takes a seat, and Constance strikes up a conversation as if we're old friends meeting for a cup of tea and gossip.

"Now, Rebecca, you must tell me what naughty things you've been up to that earned you a spot in this delightful home away from home." Her tone is light and airy, nothing like it was outside. I can't tell if she's serious or making a joke.

"I could ask you the same thing." I want to trust her, but I'm not about to let her make fun of me.

"That's fair. I've known I would end up here since I was fourteen." She lifts her lips in the same smile that isn't a smile and continues her story in a more relaxed voice. "I was sick. I don't know if you would remember that. You were so young and our families weren't exactly close."

It's true. Our fathers both work at the same office, but unlike my own mother, Constance's mother was content to socialize with others in the same economic situation. She never forced her way into club bridge games and exclusive teas. I nod, acknowledging the words she isn't saying.

"I collapsed one day in school and my mother took me to see Dr. Harold. He rushed me into surgery. I had tumors…on my uterus." Constance is still facing us, but her eyes are somewhere else. "He told my mother afterward that he tried to get them out without damaging anything else, but they were too advanced. He had to remove too much."

Constance's eyes are dry, but she swallows deeply. Her eyes dart back to mine, a range of emotions flashing across her light-green eyes. "When he told my mother I'd never have children, he didn't look at me. Not once. He looked right through me like I didn't exist anymore. That's when I knew I didn't."

"Didn't what?" I'm afraid to know.

"Exist."

"I don't understand. What does that have to do with the PIT?"

Her hands bang sharply against the fragile table, and both Eric and I jump in our seats. "Don't you get it?" Constance walks over to the small bowl in the corner and splashes a bit of water on her face. Her shoulders rise with a few deep breaths. She walks back to the table, her face still damp. "I can't have children. That's what women do; they get married and have babies. That's our role in maintaining the stability of our society."

"Are you saying the Machine rejected you because you can't have children?" I grab Eric's hand under the table.

"No. The Machine rejected me because the Cardinal has no use for me. Because any man I married wouldn't have the obligations of a whole family depending on him."

Please don't let this be true. The Machine rejected me for having doubts about the Cardinal. If it rejected Constance for not fitting into her role, where does it stop?

"Which brings us back to you. You were a goodie-goodie last time I saw you, but it's always possible you found your dark side after I left."

Constance has been completely honest with me and she clearly doesn't harbor any love for the Cardinal, but I don't want to tell her. It's my dirty secret to take to the grave. Constance leans farther on to the table, her eyes completely focused on me.

The door opens and a huge man walks into the room. Other than Daniel, he's one of the tallest men I've ever seen. His long legs and arms are thick with muscles under his hand-me-down clothes. Everything about him screams strength, except his face. The left side is alive and bright, but the right side belongs on a corpse. The edge of his lips hangs down, giving him a half-frown, and his right eyelid droops like he's falling asleep.

Constance bounces up from her seat and rushes into an embrace and deep kiss that leaves my neck flushed.

"This is my husband, Thomas." Constance is absolutely beaming. She lifts up on her toes and balances there for a minute before tugging him over to the table. I guess that answers the question of marriage in the PIT. "This is Rebecca. We're old pals from the MidWest. And this is…actually, I didn't catch your name."

Eric stands and holds his hand out to Thomas as if we've all run into each other during a night out on the town. "I'm Eric."

"Go ahead and ask me the question I know you want to ask." Thomas's deep voice vibrates through the mostly empty square room. Paired with his height, he's an imposing figure, but his lopsided smile puts me at ease.

"Are you really married to Constance?" The words blurt out of my mouth before I can clamp a hand down over my lips.

I wait for Thomas to start yelling, but he throws back his head and roars with laughter that bounces his broad shoulders. He wipes away a tear from the corner of his good eye. "Everyone else wants to know what's wrong with me, but you want to know about the one thing that's right. I suppose you think we're crazy, but the PIT actually gave us both the only chance we had at finding real love. Our situation could be a lot worse."

This time I'm able to get my hands up to my mouth before I blurt out the words swimming in my head.

Thomas makes it sound like he's happy the Cardinal rejected him.

"Don't be so shocked." Constance gestures an open hand to the table and we all sit back down. "Even if Thomas and I had found each other and been allowed to marry outside, our life would be dismal at best. Thomas survived a horrible illness when he was just a baby, but the muscles in his face never recovered."

"Before the PIT, I was the Territory pity case." Thomas's words don't carry any resentment, but there's pain in the stiff lines of his face. "Everyone treated me like I was dimwitted. As if the disease that ruined my face claimed my brain as well."

"Your face isn't ruined, my love." Constance runs her hand down his slack skin, caressing every flaw like a treasured work of art before turning her gaze back to us. "Outside, I'd have to deal with constant judgment. I'd be labeled as something less, but the PIT is the great equalizer. What harm is there in being barren in a prison where no one can have children?"

"But surely people..." A remaining sense of decorum keeps me from finishing the sentence out loud, but they all know what I mean. Girls in too-tight dresses, their cleavage thrust up to their chins, prance through the alleys and make sauntering laps around the dining hall.

"The Cardinal puts sterility drugs in the food and water," Constance says as if she's commenting on the color of her dress. "Everyone has to eat."

I clutch at the waist of my dress. When we get out of here, eventually I'll get married, but I've never given much thought to children. They were always an assumed part of my future. What if the drugs in here don't wear off when we leave? What if I can never have children?

I hate the Cardinal and the thought doesn't make me shameful the way it should. He isn't protecting anyone by forcing us all in here. He's cultivating some kind of perfect society that the four of us aren't good enough to be part of. The Cardinal took my freedom, and now he may have taken away part of a future I'd yet to even dream of.

"I know what that look means." Constance is grinning at me and this time it's a full smile. "What are your plans for that rope?"

I work to unclench my fists and relax the tightened muscles of my shoulders. Eric takes one of my hands and rubs his thumb in a soothing circle along my knuckles. He sits straight as a board beside me and somehow he makes his words forceful without being demanding. "We need it."

"Clearly." Constance's fingers drum out a steady rhythm on the old-door-turned-tabletop. "The question is really the nature of your need. It's much too nice of a rope to be turned into anything as mundane as a clothesline." She leans back on her makeshift seat, her fingers arching on the table, then relaxing to draw lazy circles along the worn surface. "Now, if I could trust the rope to have a...higher purpose, I can see letting it go."

I stand and drop Eric's hand. Leaning into the table, I meet Constance's easy smile with one of my own. "We don't need a clothesline."

"And little Rebecca Collins is all grown up." Constance stands, pulling her lumbering husband up with her. "I smell dinner calling." They walk arm in arm toward the door, but Constance pauses before they leave us to collect our trophy. "Do watch that you don't get yourself tangled."

She can't possibly know our plans, but Constance's words carry a weight far heavier than the coil we carry back to our own bunkhouse.

Thirteen

The last hours before sunset are my favorite time of the day. It's the only time all five of us can sit together in the bunk with no other obligations pulling us away. When the sun is up, Molly and Elizabeth are usually at work. Eric and I don't start until after sundown. We still have our meals together, but decided that we shouldn't discuss any part of our plan where there's even the slightest chance someone can overhear us.

Right now, no one has to be anywhere and the freedom to talk openly without the threat of discovery always makes me feel more alive. There's a sense of comfort about us in the evenings, and even Elizabeth feels like a friend. Tonight we're using a small basin of brownish water to scrub out some empty tins that Elizabeth collected at work.

Molly is using the remaining hours of daylight to secure a few loose buttons on Eric's outside shirt. We'll have to get new clothes as soon as we hit dry land, but until then, Molly's patched up shirts and dresses will have to pass the non-PIT standard.

"Did you find anything new today, Eric?" I cringe at the undisguised hope tinting my voice. I don't really expect good news. Lucking into Constance's rope a few days ago was a major find, but we still have a lot more to collect before we'll be ready to go. Earlier today, Eric went out to an older part of the PIT we didn't have marked on our map yet. I offered to go with him, but he declined on the off chance that he ran into any trouble.

"Not really. I spent most of the time taking note of building locations so I can update our map." He gets up from where he's been laying down on the bunk and brings the newly updated paper over to show me. The dozens of lines and dots barely fit on the ragged paper. The PIT is so much bigger than I ever could have imagined. "We've searched everything west of this area," he says pointing to a roughly drawn row toward the edge of the wrinkled paper. "And here is the workshop."

It feels a little premature to call it that, but eventually the remote building the guys searched out yesterday will be where we build our raft. For now, it's empty.

"I went out from there to plot our evacuation route to the fence. We'll need wide alleys to haul the raft without making too much noise." On the map, Eric drew a dark black line with his broken pencil to show the fence that protects the rest of society from us riffraff inside. A small 'x' indicates the weak spot where we can get through to the coast. "I thought we could check out some of these remote areas after our shift tonight."

I set the last cleaned-out can in the bag with the others Elizabeth washed. "As long as we have enough moonlight to make sure we don't miss anything."

"It's a date." Eric stands to tuck the map back under his thin mattress and flashes me a flirty smile. "One moonlit stroll by the beach."

Elizabeth and Daniel snort at Eric's attempt at romance, but I think it's sweet that he's trying. He's always doing little things like holding my hand or helping me up from the benches in the dining hall. Elizabeth and Daniel are more like my parents, never touching or showing their affection for each other where other people can see.

Elizabeth rolls her eyes and carries the bag of clean tins to the corner where no one will trip over them once the setting sun sinks the bunkhouse into darkness.

"Come on, you stupid thing." Daniel is camped out on a bed with one of the Noteboards, his face buried in his hands. "Ayesocose."

"What?" His words are muffled by his hands. I know it's not polite, but I giggle at his dramatics anyway.

"Sorry," he says, lifting his head up. "I said, 'I'm so close.'"

"Close to what?" I plop down on the bunk next to him. My elbow brushes against his and I'm suddenly aware of just how close we are, the warmth of his dark skin radiating out in the cooling air to lift goose bumps along my arm. I adjust the skirt of my dress to give me an excuse to scoot and create some distance between us.

"I found this old card reader out at the deserted security building. I'm trying to connect it to the Noteboard so I can recode our OneCards."

"This is a card reader?" I pick it up and let the metal cool my heated palms. It does nothing to ease my racing pulse. Why am I acting this way? It's just Daniel.

The heavy box is like a brick in my hand. The readers in the Admin building are all slick grey squares no bigger than my palm. The huge black box Daniel tinkers with is almost as big as the Noteboard it's linked to.

"Don't judge my reader." Daniel says harshly, taking the box back. "Unless you'd like to grab a new one off the wall during your shift tonight." He winks at me, destroying my minimal success at controlling my heart rate.

Eric calls across the room from his spot on another bunk. "Two Noteboards and half a dozen cables aren't good enough for you?"

Daniel raises his hands in surrender, making all of us laugh.

It's easy to joke around with him when I don't think about how handsome he is. I shake the thought out of my head. Eric is handsome. "What exactly does re-coding our cards include?"

"Really, princess?" Elizabeth pipes up from the corner where she's storing our newly cleaned cans. "Are you prepared for an hour-long dissertation on the intricacies of the Cardinal's network?"

Daniel frowns at her, but Elizabeth just sticks out her tongue and turns away. They both chuckle, and Daniel picks up our conversation as if there wasn't any interruption.

"Well, besides removing our Rejected status, I'll need to give us new names and new backgrounds." Daniel taps the face of the Noteboard and an official-looking site pops up. "Here's the national marriage register I hacked into last week."

The collar of my dress is tighter than it was a minute ago.

"See, here is where I'll set up the licenses and backdate our documents." He taps again and the screen flashes from one page to another. "You and Eric still look pretty young so I won't have to backdate yours very far."

"Backdate our what?" Even with the sun almost set, the room is growing steadily warmer.

"Your marriage date." Daniel looks up from the screen and his face drops. "Didn't you know?"

I can't say anything. If I open my mouth I might spew my meager dinner. I close my eyes to keep the room from spinning. Marry Eric…now? Can I do that? I picture myself wearing a formal gown and making the marriage pledge to Eric. My stomach rolls and saliva fills my mouth.

Eric's sad eyes meet mine from across the room and there's not enough air to breathe. I get up, but blood rushes to my head and I sway on my feet. Eric rushes over and guides me back to his bunk, rubbing my back. I'm a horrible person.

"I'm sorry, Rebecca." Daniel sounds far away, even though he's just across the room. "I assumed you already knew about the marriages."

I shake my head and the squirming in my stomach subsides some. I force deep breaths in through my nose. I have to calm down.

"We can't go back to our own Territories because everyone knows us there. I can set it up for Eric and me to get a Cardinal-assigned Territory Transfer. That way, no one will be suspicious when we show up." Daniel's words tumble out almost faster than I can digest them. "The only reason for the rest of you to move with us is if we're married."

I nod my head, because everything Daniel says makes sense. A transfer is the only reason for people to show up in a new Territory. If the girls and I are going with them, we'll need to be their wives.

Daniel stands up and looks to Elizabeth and Molly for support, but they're tucked in the corner, heads together, lost in their own conversation. "It doesn't mean anything; a name change and a checked box in the Cardinal's system."

"I'm okay, really. I understand." I stretch my mouth into the best smile I can muster so Eric doesn't think I'm upset about marrying him. My teeth grind together; I'll be fine. "I just didn't put it all together until now. I thought we had more time."

"It'll all work out, Becca." Eric's face is filled with understanding. My throat fills with sand and I fight the tears stinging the back of my eyes. Here I am, having a panic attack about marrying him, and he's trying to comfort me.

"Eric, I didn't mean…please don't think."

"You don't have to explain anything to me. Your reaction was perfectly normal, but time isn't a luxury we have anymore." His hand is warm on mine and puts me at ease. "We're going to make this work."

"I trust you. I'm…" A new thought interrupts my apology. Two guys, three girls. "We don't have enough people. What about Molly?"

Molly's head lifts up at her name, her face completely blank in the dimming light. "I'm going to be a widow traveling with her sister. Of course, I'm heartbroken and you all feel horrible about my loss." She winks at me and smiles. "I'll wear black."

Molly, the girl who rarely says more than four words to me and only in response to asking her a question, just made a real joke. Not a good one, but a joke all the same.

A small chuckle bubbles up from inside, trailed by a louder giggle, and followed by side-clenching laughter. My amusement is contagious and soon the others are laughing right along with me.

It isn't nearly as funny as we're all making it, but it's been too long since we had something to laugh about.

"Maybe we should find an urn and fill it with a little PIT dirt?" Daniel barely gets his words out between loud guffaws.

"Yes, it's the only proper way…to honor the memory…of your late husband…PITrick." Elizabeth laughs so hard at her own joke, she snorts after the last word.

Tears roll down my cheeks and my side hurts, but I never want to stop laughing. "He was a fine man," I get out between gasping breaths, "but an awful cook."

Molly holds a pillow across her stomach in a losing attempt to hold back her laughter. "Don't talk about my fake dead husband that way!" She tosses the pillow at my head, but misses me in the darkening room and hits Eric, instead. "He was only looking for a little Acceptance."

We laugh until each of us is exhausted. The room is filled with heavy breathing and wide smiles I can barely see in the fading light. Even back home, I never felt so much like part of a real family as I do in this minute. With strangers I dismissed as monsters little more than a month ago.

I can't agree with Constance that life inside the PIT is better than outside, but it has given me something I didn't know was missing. What will it be like once we're back in the real world? Life will be different, better, but will we still have this? How much will our freedom really cost?

Eric's hand finds mine in the dark and squeezes tight. "Come on, Becca, time for work." He hands me my dusty shoulder bag and we head out hand in hand for another night of picking through trash.

* * *

"Here, you should finish it." I hand the greasy container back to Eric so he can fish the last bite out of the bottom. The mostly full take-out box of noodles was our best find yet. Eric found it resting at the top of a garbage can on his floor and saved it for us to share.

I lean back against the cool concrete wall behind the dining hall and savor the taste of salt on my lips. These noodles are the first thing I've eaten in weeks that doesn't carry the distinct burnt taste that flavors everything in the PIT. The sixth floor cans aren't as generous as I'd hoped.

The smell from the dumpsters we're hiding between doesn't enhance the meal, but walking around the PIT with food is a fast way to find trouble. Last week an Under got a broken arm when he carried a piece of bread out of the dining hall. A band of slightly older boys was on him in the blink of an eye and he was left holding crumbs and an arm bent in the wrong direction.

Eric throws the empty container into the darkness. It's a small thing, but it bothers me. Lately, I'm bothered by more and more of Eric's little nuances. That's probably how it is for most couples the more they get to know about each other. It doesn't make me feel any better about our future together.

I stand up from my spot in the dirt and toss the noodle box into the dumpsters.

"Really?" he asks, pushing up from the ground. "I hardly think one more piece of trash is going to matter in this dump."

"We may be Rejects, but that doesn't mean we have to live like barbarians."

Eric only shrugs before wiping his hands on his dusty pants and pulling our wrinkled map out of his bag. He points to a spot on the grid close to the dark line of the fence. "I think we should go out to the edge tonight. I didn't run into anyone else while I was out there earlier so it should be safe."

The walk out to the area Eric selected will take us at least half an hour. Even though summer is nearly here, the heat of the day fades as soon as the sun sets. It's already much cooler than it was when we walked into the Admin building. I'm not at all excited about a long walk out to search in a new area, but we can't avoid the edge forever.

"Well, we aren't going to find an escape boat sitting around here." I slide my bag back on and take Eric's extended hand on instinct. I don't even bother to brush the dust off the back of my dress. My mother would die a thousand deaths of embarrassment if she could see me now.

It's peaceful this time of night when almost everyone is tucked away in a bunkhouse, huddled against the cool air. The only people out on a night like this are those up to no good. Eric fills the silence with information he's gleaned from Elizabeth.

"According to E, the edge of the PIT is the original site. There weren't as many Rejects then. As the Machine rejected more people, they just kept expanding the fence to include more land."

We turn the final corner leading to the last row of buildings and it's clear why no one lives out here. If the bunk we live in is run-down, the ones out here are dilapidated. Some of them have tin roofs or small porches, but most are little more than three walls leaning against each other. An air of desolation hangs around everything like a thick layer of dust.

We have ten buildings to search tonight so long as I don't freeze first. I'm keeping an eye out for any item that could be useful, but the main search is still for anything that floats.

Without flashlights, we have to depend on the moon filtering through the glassless windows to see. It takes forever to search each building, creeping from one spot of light to the next, sticking hands into unseen corners. Outside the cracked walls, the wind blows through the holes of missing doors and windows, stirring up dirt into the air.

We're only in the third house, but it feels like we've been out here for hours already. My thin mattress and stained pillow call to me, making each step harder to take. The room looks deserted, but we have to walk through and make sure we aren't missing anything in the dark. This would be a much easier task during the day, but we can't risk someone seeing what we're up to.

"Let's split up so we can go faster." Eric's voice cuts across the silence and I'm torn. Half of me thinks Eric is brilliant because anything that gets us done faster is wonderful. The other half thinks he's lost all his marbles. I can't walk into a pitch-black room by myself, feeling around for useful objects.

Eric shuffles to the door, but pauses when I don't answer him. "Come on, it's freezing out here and I'll only be one building away."

My desire to get out of the cold wins out over my fear. "Okay, just don't go far."

Eric takes off for the next house and I creep into the darkened room on my own. I slide my feet along the wall, taking my time so I don't trip. A soft shuffling freezes my steps. The dim light makes it impossible to see the source of the noise. I open my mouth to call out to Eric, but my throat is dry. I can't force out any sound. The noise sounds again, and this time two eyes stare out of the dark corner, glaring right at me.

I take one tentative step back, and then another. A crash from the corner echoes through the room and I don't wait to find out what it is. I turn and run for the door as fast as my frozen legs can carry me. Whoever is back there doesn't sound like he's following me, but I'm not taking any chances.

What are we doing out here? This place might have been deserted during the day, but not anymore. For all we know a deranged lunatic could be in the corner, lying in wait for a defenseless victim to come wandering in.

I burst through the door of the next bunk and collide with Eric. I know it's him from the familiar curve of his chest. My nails dig into his arm, desperate to cling to the safety he offers.

"Becca, what's wrong?" Eric's hands rove over my shivering body checking for injuries. "Are you alright?"

I nod. My lungs are burning from my sprint and I can't catch my breath to tell him what happened.

Eric eases me back out of the building and we sit on the remains of its wooden porch. He pulls me closer as I work to calm my breathing.

"Someone…inside the house." I finally get out enough words to explain why I barreled into him.

"Okay, you're fine now, Becca. No one followed you over here. It was probably just an Under hiding out for the night."

I'm sure he's right. The warmth of Eric's arm around my shoulders brings a relief both from my fear and the bitter cold of the ocean wind. We haven't made enough progress, but I'm certain I can't go back inside another building tonight. Eric must sense my defeat as well.

"What do you say we take a break from scavenging for one night?"

I nod and Eric guides me up till we face each other, his strong arms wrapping me up in comfort. "Come with me, I want to show you something."

Eric leads me few streets away to a building that doesn't look any different from the others. Hopping up on a tottering crate, he reaches down for me to join him. I hesitate. I'm not afraid of heights, but I really just want to go home to the comfort of my saggy bed.

"Trust me, it's worth it." And because I do trust him, I hold out my arms and let Eric pull me up to the flat roof of the old bunkhouse. "Now look," Eric says pointing out to a spot far in the distance.

At first I can't see anything but a field of darkness, like an artist has painted the scene with thick, black paint. But then I notice small shimmers in the midst of the obscurity.

Moonlight glimmers off the ground in a way I've never seen before. Beneath the sparse light, the ground unfurls, like tall blades of prairie grass in the wind. It hits me.

"Is that the…?"

"Magical, isn't it? When the waves crest, the moon catches the surface and puts on a light show." His arm spreads across the cool air and mimics the undulations of the water in front of us.

"I've never seen anything like it." No one I know has ever seen the coast, and it certainly isn't something I ever thought I'd see. It's like the PIT is giving us a little present; a consolation prize for living with grey drab every day. "It's beautiful."

"I agree."

I turn to Eric, but he isn't staring at the rolling ocean any more. Reaching up, he tucks a strand of short hair the wind has blown loose back behind my ear. All of Eric's features are highlighted in the white light of the moon. His strong chin and broad mouth. Even his nose, which looks a little crooked this close. There's no denying that he's handsome.

Eric steps closer, taking both of my hands in his own. I have no experience in situations like this, but I'm almost certain he's going to kiss me. Pretty soon we'll be married, even if it is only a document. I want him to kiss me.

I slide forward the tiniest bit, unable to resist the draw of his warmth. His eyes close and his head dips down towards mine, so I lift up my face to meet him.

His lips are warm and salty against mine. His mouth pushes down into mine, sending a flood of warmth through my body. Familiar hands move to the small of my back, finding a perfect spot to rest, pulling me closer. I'm not sure what to do with my hands, but they find a natural place on Eric's shoulders.

Cheryl and I spent countless hours imagining the fateful moments of our first kisses. I always pictured it happening while sitting on my parent's front porch, rocking on the hanging swing. Crickets would serenade me and my future husband while lightning bugs created the perfect atmosphere. We'd be sipping tall glasses of lemonade and holding hands because the thought of a firm hand holding mine always sounded perfect.

My dream man would lean in and whisper 'I love you' in my ear and I would smile back and say 'I love you, too.' And then, because we both know that kind of declaration is always followed shortly by an engagement, he would kiss me. Our lips touching for the first time would be a brief, but sweet promise of years of kisses to come.

Eric's kiss doesn't hold any of that promise. He's never said he loves me and I wouldn't be able to say it back. But maybe that doesn't matter anymore. I wrap my hands around his neck and deepen the kiss, pushing myself to feel…more. This is my future. Eric is my future.

Porch swings and lemonade belong to Cheryl now. My first kiss is a rundown rooftop and ocean waves crashing in the background. The PIT has taken too much. I'm claiming this moment. It owes me this first kiss.

I squeeze my eyes tight against the flood of emotions fighting to claw out of my chest. Every touch of Eric's lips telling me this isn't really what I want. An unbidden picture of Daniel pops into my mind, his strong dark arms a stark contrast against the faded green of my dress as he holds me close. A sharp pain blossoms in my chest and I struggle to push it back down. Much too soon and yet not soon enough, Eric pulls away, his forehead resting against my own.

"I've wanted to do that since I first met you in that restaurant."

That day feels like a lifetime ago, but only a few months have passed. I've changed so much in such a short period of time. But some things don't change and I'm suddenly uncomfortable with how close Eric is standing and how familiar his arms feel around my waist.

Guilt sweeps through me when I think of Daniel back in the bunkhouse with Elizabeth. I've tried to push my feelings for him away. I convinced myself it was nothing more than admiration, maybe an innocent crush, but I can't pretend that's the case anymore. Elizabeth should hate me more than she does. I step back from the contact with Eric, needing a blast of the chilly night air to clear my head.

Eric's eyes show the hurt at my reaction. I should apologize, explain that I don't know how to do this. But how can I tell him that kissing him feels wrong because we aren't on my parents' porch, and I don't love him, and that I really just want to kiss his sister's boyfriend.

"Eric—" I focus over his shoulder so I don't have to look him in the eye. A reflection of light interrupts the bland monotony of the hundreds of black rooftops. "Look." I spin him around and rush to the edge of the roof. Right behind the house next door the moon highlights row upon row of metal barrels.

Eric helps me scramble down off the roof and I'm too distracted by the blue barrels to be bothered by the way his hand lingers on my waist. Adrenaline pumps through me, warming my hands and feet as I bend to examine each barrel. Some of them are hopelessly cracked or have big holes from who knows how many years of sitting outside in the salty air. It'll take a while to go through all of them but there are enough that even if over half aren't usable, we'll still have a decent-sized raft.

"What are they doing here?" I've seen plenty of junk on our scouting trips, but never anything like this.

"They're oil drums," Eric says from his inspection a few rows over. "The PIT was probably one of the last places to convert over to full solar and electromagnetic energy sources. When the Territories stopped using oil they probably couldn't get a regular supply line here anymore and had to have it shipped in barrels like the stone-age until they converted over."

"Cardinal on a cracker." It's a phrase I've heard Daniel use and it sounds fitting. The PIT really is the place where all things come to die. "These barrels are probably fifty years old."

"Or older." It's darker back down on the ground, but the moon shines enough light for me to see Eric hold out his hand to me. "We need to get back and let the others know what you found."

I take his hand, because I know he wants me to. Maybe someday I'll hold his hand because I want to. For now, I let his warm touch guide me back home while I try not to pretend it's Daniel leading me home.

Fourteen

"Ow!" The sharp jab of another pin pokes into my waist for the fourth time.

"I'm sorry." Molly pulls the fabric tighter and weaves the pin in. "This would be easier if you would hold still."

Molly has been altering my dress for the past half-hour and I'm not sure she's making any progress. She found my 'outside' dress weeks ago, but when I tried it on for a fitting this afternoon it was at least three sizes too big.

My mother would be so pleased that I finally lost all that baby fat she always complained about. Stingy meals spiced up by the occasional bag of chip crumbs aren't enough to maintain a healthy weight.

Daniel is the only other one in the room today. Eric is out at the workshop, and Elizabeth is at work. Normally, Molly would be with her, but she quit yesterday so she could get our new outfits finished. Now that the raft is in construction mode, everyone is feeling the excitement and pressure of getting ready to leave.

Daniel looks up from working on the Noteboard just as I bite my lip against another pin prick. He shoots me a wink and my knees buckle. Molly drops her needle for at least the tenth time.

"I think that's enough for today." Molly straightens up and hands me my PIT dress from the bed next to her. "You're fidgety, and I'm tired. We'll work on it again tomorrow."

Daniel turns around so I can change. His presence in the room while I'm undressing kicks my heart rate up another notch. I give myself a mental face slap. I have to stop thinking about him that way. He's Elizabeth's boyfriend and future husband. And even if he wasn't, I'm as good as engaged to Eric.

Molly helps me with my last button and sits down to work on the tiny stitches she pinned into my escape dress. What am I supposed to do with myself now? We still have a few hours left until dinner and I hate the idea of sitting around doing nothing. This is usually the time when Eric and I talk.

Learning more about each other is an essential part of our cover outside the PIT. Even couples who marry early spend a few years getting to know each other. Eric and I have only a fraction of that time. I like hearing his stories of growing up in the NorthWest Territory, but he's been too busy to share them lately. Every extra minute is spent working on the raft. I offered to help, but I'd just be in the way. It's not like I know anything about boats.

"Daniel, have you seen the burlap sack?" Molly is on her hands and knees, peeking under every bed in the bunkhouse. "I thought I saw you with it the other day."

Daniel rubs the back of his neck and stares at the ceiling as if he's trying to remember. "The last I saw it, it was in the corner over there. Why?"

"It's not a big deal, really." Molly stands back up and swipes the dust off her hands. "I was going to store extra bits of fabric in there in case I need to make any last-minute adjustments or repairs. I can find something else to put them in." Her voice is as steady as always, but she keeps clenching and unclenching her fists.

She takes our appearances very seriously and I understand why. It's her major contribution to the group. I wish I had something important to do, though Eric claims I'm amazing for finding the oil drums.

Daniel looks just as upset as Molly though I imagine it has less to do with the bag and more to do with whatever he's been working on all afternoon. He keeps wiping his hands on the thin sheet of his bed like he can't get them dry

"What are you working on today?" I take a few tentative steps in his direction. There's nothing wrong with asking a simple question.

"I'm trying to get into the right database so I can make sure Eric and I have Assignments." He swipes a finger across the screen and wipes his hands on the bed again. "Do you want to see?"

"I probably won't understand any of it." I'm trying to keep my distance, but Daniel has the most fascinating job of any of us. The way he can manipulate data from inside the Cardinal's system is amazing. It makes me feel like we're fighting back already.

Daniel pauses his fingers on the Noteboard and rolls his eyes at me. Clearly he isn't buying my 'I'm too dumb to get it' act. He pats the spot on the bed next to him.

I have to sit down. It would be rude not to. Maybe Daniel will be too absorbed in his work to notice the effect he has on me. I wipe my clammy hands on the back of my dress and join him on the bed.

Daniel scoots over so he can rest the left side of the Noteboard on my leg. He's only trying to give me a better view of the screen, but the heat radiating off him warms the entire right side of my body. I resist the urge to snuggle into his shoulder.

"This is a map of the Territories." A quick tap of his fingers brings up a larger shot of the eastern coast. "And here is where we are." He points to a section of coastline east of the SouthEast Territory. According to the last geography class I took years ago, this area is supposed to be uninhabitable.

"How do you know where we are?" The location of the PIT is such a secret back home. I assumed it would be hard to discover, even with Daniel's talent for hacking into places he shouldn't be.

Daniel puts his hand over his heart and exaggerates a painful expression on his face that doesn't detract at all from his handsome dark features. "You wound me, Rebecca. The Cardinal's security measures are no match for my superior skills."

"A thousand pardons," I say in a cultured voice my mother would be proud of if I weren't shamelessly flirting with a nearly married man.

"Now that you recognize the master in your presence, I will share my secrets with you." Daniel winks at me and returns his attention to the screen. Thank the stars he isn't looking at me. If the heat on my neck is any indication, my skin is probably glowing red. "Following the current, I estimate it will take us about three days to reach the coast to the east of the Gulf Territory."

I let out a slow breath to keep my voice steady. "So is that where we're going to live?"

"We could, but I think we'd be better off putting a bit more distance between us and the PIT. Not that they'll publicize an escape, but it doesn't hurt to be careful." He taps away the map of the coastline and another area of the map is highlighted. "We can take a train from the Gulf Territory to the MidSouth Territory and make our home there. I'll have our transfer paperwork set up by then, including Airbus tickets and meal vouchers. Once we're on the train, we should be home free."

"That sounds complicated. Wouldn't it be easier to go to another country? We wouldn't have to worry about anyone recognizing us."

Daniel stares at me like I suggested we move to Cardinal City. "No one leaves the country. Trust me when I say reprogramming our entire identities is much easier than getting documentation to travel abroad. This is basic data manipulation." He bumps his shoulder into mine. "I'll keep us safe."

My shoulder burns where he touched me and tingles run in waves down my arm. His confidence makes it all sound so easy. I know it won't be, but I'm getting excited about the adventure. Traveling to Cardinal City for the Acceptance ceremony was my first time away from home. "Have you ever been to MidSouth before?"

Daniel nods. "I went there with my dad once. It's nice."

"I know it's silly, but I'm going to miss not living in the MidWest."

"What do you think you'll miss the most?" We don't talk about home very much. A few weeks ago we all told Daniel where we're from so he could mark it off the list of possible places to settle. Other than that, it's been almost a taboo topic.

I think back to home. My parents, my grandmother, Cheryl and our friends from school. They were all so important to me, but I feel like a different person now. "The smell of oranges. That's what I'm going to miss."

"I didn't think they grew oranges there." Daniel's brows are knit with genuine confusion. The bubble of laughter floating up my throat is soothing.

"We don't, so they're a special treat." I close my eyes, and I'm back at home, standing on the platform waiting on the Airbus to arrive. In the distance is the low hum of the bus, but long before I can see it, the tangy smell of oranges announces the shipment's arrival. The citrusy aroma takes over the station and I can almost taste the sweet juice on the tip of my tongue.

I open my eyes and Daniel is staring at me, smiling in the way that weaves my stomach into knots. A wave of guilt washes down my spine, and I lower my eyes from Daniel's. It isn't his fault that he gets an adorable little wrinkle between his brows when he's staring at the Noteboard. And he can't be blamed that his smile produces dimples on both of his cheeks. Anyone in the PIT can see that Daniel is handsome, but Elizabeth would kill me if she knew I thought about it. And besides, Eric is handsome, too. In a different way. His good looks feel more deliberate.

I scoot a bit farther away and Daniel clears his throat. "The Gulf Territory grows the oranges. We'll be much closer in MidSouth, so we should be able to get oranges whenever they're in season."

"Did you learn all of that from the Cardinal's files?" Daniel's knowledge seems deeper than the average student. Even in the economics classes, I can't imagine they would spend so much effort teaching the boys about the Territories they don't live in.

Daniel's voice stays even, but his shoulders stiffen at the question. "I grew up in Cardinal City."

"Oh," I say as if that explains everything, even though I have no idea why growing up there would matter. I dig the toe of my filthy shoe into the dirt floor.

Daniel taps his fingers against the leg of his pants a few times and clears his throat. "My father is on the Cardinal's Council."

That's unexpected. It explains why he knows so much about the different Territories, but opens up at least a dozen other questions. I don't want to press the issue on what's obviously a tender subject, but there are so many things Daniel might be able to explain.

"I know you want to ask something else, Rebecca. Go ahead."

The heat on my neck tells me my face is ten shades of red, but I still ask the question that jumps to the top of my mind. "I know the Cardinal isn't being honest about why people are sent to the PIT. I guess I assumed there must be a valid reason behind his actions. That I just don't have the information he does." I rub a drop of sweat off the back of my neck. "You probably know more about it than most of us can even guess at."

"You're right about one thing. I know a lot about the reasons behind the Cardinal's decisions." Daniel turns to me on the bunk and grabs my clammy hand. "It didn't help me understand. It only made it certain I would end up here."

The door flies open and Elizabeth bursts into the room. Daniel and I jump apart. The last thing I want is to stir up trouble between him and Elizabeth, but she doesn't notice our too-close position.

"Elizabeth, what the…?" Molly is up and across the room with a towel and water before I can get a word out. Elizabeth clutches her face, bright-red blood flowing between her fingers.

Molly forces her to sit on a bed and pries her fingers away from the mess. Elizabeth's lips are both split and blood gushes from her nose. Purple bruises shade the skin under her eyes.

"Cardinal on a cracker." Daniel jumps up from the bed, but keeps his distance to give Molly room to work. "What happened?"

"I was trying to—"

Molly cuts her off and then shoots Daniel a watery glare that could peel paint. "Can we hold off on the talking until I stop you from bleeding to death?"

Elizabeth rolls her eyes, but stays quiet so Molly can get her cleaned up.

"Your nose is broken," she says, wiping her eyes with the back of her hands, "but you'll live." Molly throws the rag into the small bowl of water and stands up, stretching her back.

Elizabeth gives her nose a gentle prod. "Thanks, Molly. What would I do without you?"

"Probably bleed to death," she says and opens the door to toss the bloody water out. Molly pauses in the open doorway and sucks in a long, quivering breath.

Elizabeth joins her at the door and pulls her around into a hug. "Hey, I'm fine. I'm sure it looks a lot worse than it is. If anything, this is all the more reason to hurry up and get out of here."

"I know. Just the way you looked. Coming in here." Molly stifles another sob. "Like someone beat you…"

They stand together for a minute and my heart breaks a bit. Molly and Elizabeth are as close as sisters. The way Cheryl and I are…were…should be still.

Molly steps back and slaps her half-heartedly on the shoulder. "Do you have any idea what that was like? To see you walk in here dripping in blood? What happened?"

Elizabeth walks back to her bunk and runs both her now-clean hands through her dirty hair. "A guard caught me sneaking food after the shift. I was trying to bulk up our supplies, but I wasn't as careful as I should have been."

Daniel sits next to her, an arm around her shoulder. "Did he…?"

"He knocked me to the ground with one punch, then came back in with a few kicks to the face. At least I didn't lose any teeth." Elizabeth flashes her still-intact mouth at us all, but freezes with a glance at the bunk next to me.

Molly is sitting back against the wall, her legs pulled up with her knees tucked under her chin. Tear-filled eyes stare out at the room, but she's managed to keep them from falling.

"So who's ready to get out of here?" Eric busts through the door and takes in our somber scene. "Did I miss something? What in the world happened to your face?"

"Never mind my face." Elizabeth pushes up from the bunk and grabs Eric by the shoulders, a huge smile on her face. "Does that mean…?"

"It's finished."

I freeze in the middle of the room. For weeks, Eric and Daniel have taken turns working on the raft, tying the barrels together with Constance's rope and smearing it with tar we found out by the edge of the PIT. I knew they were getting close, but finished? It doesn't feel real.

Eric sits down and pats the bunk next to him. "I coated the last of the rope today. We need a few days to let it dry and then…"

"We leave." I bounce down onto the saggy mattress next to him, my skin vibrating with all the emotions floating underneath.

"Only if we have everything ready." Elizabeth shakes off a questioning look from Eric and sits with Molly on the bunk, giving her a tight hug. "We have a lot to get done before then. Becca, can you help Molly finish up the clothing?"

"Of course. Whatever you need me to do." My arms twitch with the extra energy pulsing through me. Eric squeezes my hand.

"Eric and I can use my card to break into the food storehouse tomorrow night. We don't know how many days we'll be stuck on that raft and I don't plan to starve to death out there."

When I thought about the escape before, my biggest fear was always that we would get caught. But what if the hardest challenge is just surviving outside the fence?

Elizabeth walks over to Daniel. He hasn't moved a muscle since Eric announced the big news. She touches his arm and they hug for the first time I've seen. My stomach twists. I want to look away, but I can't stop staring at them. None of Eric's tender touches ever expressed as much love as the hug between Elizabeth and Daniel. He pulls back and stares into Elizabeth's face, his eyes alive with excitement. "All this time, planning and waiting. Are we really getting out of here?"

"As long as you have us all set up in the network." Elizabeth punches his arm lightly. "Are you almost done?"

"Yeah, everything is set with our OneCards." Daniel taps the screen of the Noteboard so he can show Elizabeth his progress. "I'll activate the changes right before we leave so we don't set off any alarms..." His sentence trails off into an uneasy silence and a frown mars his previously elated face.

"What is it?" Elizabeth grabs the Noteboard, but I doubt she has any idea how to use it.

"Someone else was in my file today." The crease between his eyes deepens and then evens out as he gains control of his emotions. "It's probably just a coincidence. I'm sure the Admin folks run periodic checks on the system."

He takes the computer back from Elizabeth, but she doesn't look relieved by his words.

"Are you sure? We can't afford to take any chances. Do you think something you've done could have tipped someone off about what we're doing?"

"No, we're fine. I'm sorry I worried you." Daniel pulls up another screen. "See, we're all listed as normal. If the Cardinal's guards thought we were up to something, do you really think we'd still be sitting here?"

Eric squeezes my hand a bit too tight for comfort. I'm not ashamed to admit Daniel's words make me uncomfortable, too. Elizabeth nods her head and Daniel pulls up yet another screen.

"I finally got into the Assignment center. There are quite a few open positions in the MidSouth Territory, so we have plenty of options."

Eric stretches his back, wincing a little when his right shoulder rotates. "After these past few weeks I can tell you one thing. I'm not suited for manual labor."

"Gotcha," Daniel says, the atmosphere in the room now lightened. "I'll just mark you down for clerical worker."

"Where's the prestige in that? Sign me up as a doctor, or maybe a lawyer."

Maybe my mother will get her wish of me marrying up after all. Of course, she can never know I'm not still rotting away here in the PIT.

"Nice one, Eric." Daniel shakes his head laughing. "I'll put myself down for ambassador to Cardinal City."

Eric tenses beside me. "That wasn't a joke. My father is a doctor and that's probably what I'd get in Assignment if I wasn't in here."

"You can't be a doctor. An Assignment like that requires years of extra training." Daniel reaches up a jerky hand to pick at the top button of his shirt. "Even if you looked old enough, which you don't, the other doctors would know right away that you didn't complete the extra schooling."

Elizabeth cuts in before Eric can argue. "Daniel's right. You know hardly anything about medicine and that would raise red flags. People would start asking questions and we'd all be in danger."

"So what are you saying?" Eric jumps up and paces back and forth in front of the bed. "We plan to break out of the PIT so we can sit in some office all day answering the phone or filing reports?"

"Yes, that's exactly what we're going to do." Daniel's voice is firm. This is the closest to angry I've seen him since the day I almost became a PIT whore. "And every day, we get to wake up and eat a real meal that doesn't taste like dirt, and take a shower, and come home to a real house with a roof that doesn't leak, and never worry about someone stabbing us in the back when we walk down the street."

He walks across the room until he's right in front of Eric, only inches separating their faces. "Working a boring office job sounds like a fair trade to me, but if you don't think so, say the word now. No one is making you go with us."

"Enough." Elizabeth marches into the middle of the room and slides between them forcing both Eric and Daniel to take a step back. "Eric, stop complaining. The important thing to focus on is getting everything together and getting out of here. And you," she says turning around to face Daniel. "I'm sure you can find something a little less menial than paper pusher that doesn't require years of extra training."

Eric and Daniel slump off back to the beds like little boys sent to time out. "Now put on your happy faces 'cause it's time for dinner. We only have a few more chances to eat this slop so we better get it while we can."

Dinner is silent, and even though Elizabeth ordered everyone to put on happy faces, no one listened. We rush through the goopy potato mush and slump back to the bunk.

Molly seems to be the only one not affected by the roller-coaster mood swings this afternoon. She's in a rare talkative mood. Of course, that could just be how she reacts to tension. "We'll finish measuring your dress for alterations tomorrow. Then while I'm working on that you can hem Eric's pants. You do know how to hem, right?"

I nod. Despite the sour mood in the bunk, I'm still a bundle of excitement. In a few days we'll be leaving here for good. Everything Daniel said replays in my head. Clean clothes every day, a shower and a soft bed, real food, safety; all the things I took for granted before my Acceptance ceremony.

It's hard to imagine walking into a kitchen any time I want for a glass of clean water or a quick snack. Every time I try to picture it, I come up with my parents' house with the square, outdated kitchen. My mother complained a hundred times a day about drawers that stuck or the cracked counter. I used to think she was right about wanting something nicer. Now, I'd give my right eye for a kitchen just like it.

"Where are we going to live?" I can't believe I haven't thought to ask this before. My focus never went further than getting out, but now that our escape is so close, the number of unknowns is daunting.

"I'll get us set up in the system to move into a Temp House. One we get settled, we can look for our own housing." Daniel doesn't look at all concerned. While I was worrying about finding a boat, he was taking care of the details. But what about the little things?

"How are we going to explain our hair?" The boys don't have much to worry about, but Molly, Elizabeth and I haven't had a proper haircut in forever. I don't know what my own yellow curls are doing, but if the other two are any indication, I'm not looking good.

"It's taken care of," Daniel says. "Molly found hats you can wear while we're traveling. Once we reach our destination, we have an advantage. So few people travel outside of their own territories that no one knows what's current in other places. We'll just say your haircuts are the height of fashion this season in Cardinal City."

I have other questions, but it's a waste of time to ask them. I'm sure there isn't anything I'm worried about that Daniel hasn't already considered and taken care of.

"Becca, I was thinking we could take a walk before our shift." Eric has calmed down some from his fight with Daniel, but his eyes still dart around the room. "Not many nights left before we rejoin the real world."

I'm exhausted from everything that happened today, but the last thing I want to do right now is add to Eric's sour mood. "Sure, I'd like that."

Eric twines his fingers through mine and we head back out the door. It's not as cool outside as it was just a few weeks ago. Summer has finally arrived in force at the PIT. Even with the sun low behind the Admin building, there's a mugginess to the air that keeps out the chill.

We walk in a comfortable silence until Eric stops and jumps up on an oil drum. I recognize the spot from the night we found the cache of barrels. The night Eric kissed me. The night I knew I wasn't in love with him.

"It's such a nice view." He reaches down a hand and pulls me up next to him. Above the buildings, the wind from the ocean is cooler. I lean into Eric and let him wrap his warm, sturdy arms around me.

I may not love him, not the way I always thought I'd love someone, but I can do this. I can let him protect me and I can respect him, and with enough time maybe I'll grow to love him. Maybe this is the way our relationship would have been if things had been different.

Maybe in the two years between Acceptance and Selection I would have learned to love Eric for the man he is. Without the luxury of time, I need to learn to love him as my paper husband.

"I know this hasn't been easy for you. Cardinal knows it hasn't been easy for any of us." Eric loosens his hold and turns me around so we're facing each other. "I just want you to know how grateful I am that you've been by my side since day one."

"Eric—" I want to stop him.

"Becca, will—" I have to stop him.

"It's getting cold, maybe we should head back." And it is cold. The warmth from the summer air disappeared in seconds and yet a small bead of sweat runs down the small of my back.

"Will you marry me?"

The air around me isn't warm or cold; it's gone. The sound of waves crashing against the shore vanishes and I'm left in a bubble of nothingness.

Eric drops down on one knee in front of me and grabs my left hand. This is the way it's done, the way I've always imagined it, but I want nothing more than for him to stand up.

But why should he? It doesn't matter what I say because in two days we'll be married, as far as the Cardinal is concerned. This is Eric being the amazing person he is; giving me something he thinks I need. And that makes me feel even worse that this is the opposite of what I want. I thought it was. A few months ago this was the moment filling my nightly dreams. Eric is exactly who I wanted to marry. Someone my mother would be proud to have in our family. But he's not who I dream about anymore. It's hard to have dreams at all inside the PIT.

"Yes, of course." Because I can't say no. It wouldn't change anything.

Eric stands up and cradles my face between his warm hands. He kisses me for the second time. "I don't have a ring, but I'll get one as soon as I can."

I force my lips into a smile and nod as if the overwhelming joy of the moment has left me speechless.

"I know this isn't exactly traditional, but I thought a proper proposal would help to make things more official."

I know Eric expects me to say something. He keeps raising his eyebrows, waiting for me to gush with excitement. "I'm a lucky girl." I know it isn't what he's expecting, but it's the best I can do at the moment.

"Well, I guess we better get going. We have a shift tonight and we don't want to raise any alarms until we have to." Eric helps me down off the roof and we walk in silence to the Admin building. But this isn't the comfortable silence that filled our walk out to the fence.

My legs and arms weigh me down to the point I'm barely keeping up with Eric's pace. He kisses me on the cheek before we separate for our assigned floors. I smile again, but only long enough to reach my floor and cry.

I have never in my life enjoyed sewing more than I do today. It takes me all morning to get the hem straight on Eric's pants, but every pinprick is worth the hard-earned hours of solitude. Each time Eric comes over to see how things are going or just to chat, Molly shoos him away. *Rebecca needs to concentrate. You have a lifetime to chitchat. She's fine, now leave her alone.*

I'd hug her except she might stab me with her needle. Somehow, I don't think she'd appreciate my random display of thanks. Besides, she has no idea how grateful I am every time she makes Eric leave me alone.

I finish the pants and Molly hands over Daniel's shirt, showing me how to crease the fabric along her pin marks to add darts.

Elizabeth and Daniel are busy sorting through the food containers, trying to decide how many to set aside for water. No one is that worried about food. Cardinal knows we can survive on next to nothing, but water is a different story. The washed-out tins don't hold much, and with no way to keep them covered we're likely to lose some of our supply from spills.

I tie off the thread on the last dart and fold Daniel's checked shirt up with the others, running my hand down the row of tiny stitches.

"Break time." Eric is at my side, pulling me up off the floor the second my hands are empty. I look to Molly to save me, but she's no help.

"Go ahead." Molly shoos us off with the fingers not holding a needle. "This is the last piece."

"Where are you going?" Elizabeth calls from the corner.

"A quick walk," Eric says guiding me toward the door. "I just want a little private time with my fiancée."

"Someone's taking the paper marriage a little far, don't you think?" Daniel stands up to stretch, laughing at the joke.

"Didn't E tell you the news?" Eric turns back to the room, wrapping a tight arm around my shoulder. "Rebecca and I made the engagement official last night."

Daniel blinks, his mouth hanging wide open. Clearly Elizabeth hadn't told him. "No. I…congratulations." He sets the tin can in his hand down with the others, knocking several over in the process.

"Don't be long." Elizabeth bends over to pick up the scattered cans. "I want to head out for the food as soon as the sun goes down."

"I want to go with you."

Everyone stops what they're doing to stare at Molly.

"No offense," Eric says beside me, "but we don't really need a chaperone."

"Not you," Molly says. She turns to Elizabeth. "I want to go with you tonight to get the food."

"No, absolutely not." Elizabeth's tone makes it clear the topic is not up for discussion, but that doesn't stop Molly.

"I wasn't asking for permission." She stands up and throws down the skirt she's been working on. "I'm tired of sitting around here like an invalid seamstress while the rest of you take all the risks. I'm going with you."

Molly and Elizabeth stare at each other, the tension seething just below the surface. For the first time, I'm the one grabbing Eric's hand and pulling him out of the bunkhouse.

* * *

The knot in the bottom of my stomach keeps me from sleeping, despite the late hour. They should have been back ages ago. After what Daniel called "the longest staring contest in history," Elizabeth finally agreed that Molly could go with her to steal food for our trip while Eric, Daniel and I waited behind. Giving them extra time to stay off the main pathways and the extra weight slowing them down on the return trip, the whole thing shouldn't have taken more than two hours. When the clock on the Noteboard showed four hours had passed, Daniel and Eric headed out to search for them.

I force my eyes closed and try not to imagine the worst. Tonight's mission had so many opportunities for something to go wrong. They could have been caught and dragged off to Quarantine, or worse. People have been killed here for a lot less than the food they might be carrying. Squeezing my eyes shut, I bury my head into the flimsy pillow.

The door bangs open and I'm off the bunk in a heartbeat. Eric flies in with Daniel right behind him. He's carrying someone in his arms, but it's too dark for me to make out any features.

"What happened?" I rush over to the bunk where Daniel lays down the limp form I now recognize as Molly.

"We don't know yet." Daniel kneels next to the bunk and runs his hands along Molly's limbs.

Eric finds my hand in the dark and I'm grateful for the contact. "We found her crawling back here, but all she said was 'She told me to run' before she passed out."

Molly whimpers at one of Daniel's touches, but doesn't wake up.

"It's her leg, probably broken." Daniel stands running both hands through his hair. "We need to find something to set it."

Eric runs to the corner and digs through the meager supplies we have stored there. "We need a few sticks, as straight as you can find them. Becca, take one of the blankets and tear it into strips." He stands up with the largest of our food containers. "I'm going to collect some mud."

Everyone jumps into action and I'm glad to have something to do. We all work in silence, but there's no avoiding the unspoken question hanging around the room. Where is Elizabeth?

It doesn't take long to gather the supplies. Eric takes Daniel's spot, kneeling by the bed. "You guys need to grab her arms." He indicates the spots on either side of the bunk by Molly's head. "I have to straighten the bones and the minute I do, she's going to wake up in some serious pain. You need to keep her from moving too much."

Daniel and I nod once we're in place. Eric moves like a flash of lightning, using one arm to tug down on Molly's leg near her ankle and the other to guide the middle of her shin bone back into position. True to his word, Molly wakes up the second he moves her leg.

"Elizabeth!" The name screams out of her, the single word filled with undisguised desperation. It takes all my strength to keep her arm from flying up from the bed. "Get off of me. We have to get to her."

"Shh, Molly, please. You have to keep still." I can't see the features of Daniel's face in the dark, but his voice gives away his emotion. He probably wants to run for Elizabeth as much as Molly does. Daniel's words calm her down some, and Eric works to position the sticks around the broken leg.

We watch in silence while his sure hands dip the strips of torn sheet into the mud and wrap them around Molly's leg. She grits her teeth and I offer my hand for her to squeeze. I can't imagine the pain, but Molly doesn't make another sound the whole time Eric applies the makeshift cast.

"I don't know how long it will hold, but it's the best I can do for now." Eric sits back and wipes his forehead with the back of his arm.

"Molly…" Daniel's voice is haggard. "What happened? Where's…where's Elizabeth?"

Molly's arm tenses on the bed and her grip on my hand is painful. "They took her."

"Who?"

"The guards." Molly sucks in a deep breath followed by a few sobs before she pulls herself together to continue the story. "We found the food and were climbing back out the window of the storehouse. They must have heard the noise."

Molly shifts on the bed and as one the three of us rush through the room to gather up pillows and blankets. Taking care not to move her leg too much, we raise her up into a sitting position with pillows wedged between her back and the wall. Once she's comfortable, we all settle down to hear the rest of her story.

"Thank you." Molly lays her head back against the wall. With her eyes closed she could almost be asleep, but I doubt any of us will be sleeping any time soon. "It all happened so fast. They grabbed Elizabeth first. She yelled at me, told me to run. I didn't want to leave her, but…I couldn't…I couldn't help her." Tears run down her pale face and I wonder what gives her more pain, her broken bone or knowing she couldn't save Elizabeth.

"I ran as fast as I could, but it was dark." Her eyes open into bright spots of white in the dark room. "I tripped and must have passed out for a while. When I woke up, I couldn't walk. I tried to crawl back here. That's when you found me."

Eric's voice is no more than a whisper next to me. "What will they do to her?"

"There's no way to know for sure." Daniel's words carry the strain of the night's events. "The best scenario is they take her straight to Quarantine."

"What's the worst scenario?" Eric says it, but we're all thinking it.

The only reply is Molly's whimpering cries.

"Rebecca, stay here with Molly. Try to get some sleep. Let's go, Eric."

I shuffle off to my bunk to lie staring at the ceiling until the first rays of morning light stream through our lone dirty window.

Sixteen

It's been a week since the guards hauled Elizabeth to Quarantine for stealing food. Or at least, that's what we hope happened. We've barely mentioned her name since the guys came back from their search without her. According to Daniel, a week is the usual sentence length. I'm sure the four of us are thinking the same thing this morning, but we're all afraid to say it out loud.

Our supplies are packed and ready in the corner. We all agreed we can't risk breaking in to the food stores again. Instead we've each saved our daily slice of bread. We've also smuggled a can into the dining hall each meal, sacrificing a few spoonfuls from everyone's bowl to contribute to our stores. Our food supply is enough to get us through a few days at least.

"I can't sit around here waiting all day." Eric stands up from the bunk and marches toward the door. "I'll be back to help carry Molly to lunch." The door swings shut, leaving the three of us in silence.

Molly shifts around in her bed. The pain has gone down, but she still can't put any weight on her leg.

"Can I get you anything?"

"No, just trying to get comfortable." She reaches back and does her best to fluff the stack of flat pillows behind her. "You could tell me a story to help me sleep."

I sit down on the ground by the head of her bed. "What kind of story?"

"I don't know. Tell me about something happy from your childhood."

My childhood was filled with a constantly disappointed mother and a father beaten down by a life he never planned and the wife who never let him forget it. Not many happy memories, but there were moments.

"This one time, my mother was so sick she couldn't get out of bed for a week."

"That hardly sounds like a happy memory."

I laugh, but try to cover it up with a cough. "Our house was never as quiet as it was that week. My father and I made do with cold meat sandwiches, but by the end of the week all the food was gone."

"Cardinal knows a man couldn't figure out how to do the shopping."

"It turned out all right. The last night before my mother got better he took us out to dinner. That was the last time the two of us spent any real time together. We ordered steaks and chocolate dessert and talked for hours about everything and nothing. I'd give anything to have another night like that with him."

I swipe the back of my hand under my eye to remove the trace of tears. My father, always so quiet, kind of blended into the background of most of my memories. But I never doubted for a minute how much he loved me.

"That's a nice memory. The only thing my father ever gave me was a black eye or a broken wrist."

I whip my head around to stare at Molly. "What?"

"All my father ever wanted was a son. Instead, he got me and a wife who lost every baby she tried to have after me."

"I had no idea. I'm so…sorry." The words sound weak, even to me.

"Don't be sorry for me. I got out, even if it wasn't the way I planned." Her hands tighten on the blanket tucked around her. "My mother is still in there with him."

I grab her hand and her fingers relax one by one. "I don't understand. If your father beat you, why didn't he end up in here? He's a monster."

"Not a monster. Just broken."

"How can you say that?" Now I'm the one clenching the blanket. "He beat you."

"Yes, and he also donated regularly to the orphan's fund, chaired the civics' day committee and attended every school function imaginable. To others, he was an example of everything right about our society."

Molly wasn't lying all those months ago when she told me she knew what it was like to be alone. How many years did she hide this secret? How long did she suffer in silence?

"He may have put on a good show, but inside he was damaged goods. Shouldn't the machine have known that and rejected him?"

Molly's face is unreadable. "Aren't we all a little bit broken inside?"

"I think that's enough conversation for now." Daniel offers Molly another blanket. "You should try to get some rest."

She nods and pulls the thin blanket up under her chin. Daniel takes my arm and walks toward the door. "Let's give her a bit of quiet."

Outside, a light breeze relieves some of the sweltering heat that's permeated the PIT. Daniel clears away some trash on the shaded side of our building so we have a semi-cool place to sit down. Neither of us says anything as we take our seats. We don't need to. We both know the score.

If Elizabeth doesn't come home today, we'll have to make a decision. Continue to wait for her or assume she isn't coming back and leave. Every day we wait is another day we risk someone fixing the hole in the fence or a guard discovering our raft. None of us want to admit it, but we can't wait forever if we want to get out of here.

"Are you happy, Rebecca?" Daniel's question comes out of nowhere.

"What do you mean?"

"It's not a trick question." Daniel smiles for the first time in a week, though it's not the full smile that shows off his dimples. "Assuming Elizabeth comes back soon, you'll be out on the raft in a few days and on your way to a new life of freedom as Mrs. Eric Dunstan." He turns until our eyes meet and there's a seriousness there that doesn't match the light tone of his words. "Does that make you happy?"

I look away to trace a circle in the dirt with my finger. I am a horrible person. The best-case scenario for Elizabeth is that she's locked away in Quarantine and Molly is lying inside with a broken leg that will probably never mend right, given the level of medical care she received. Daniel has no idea if he'll ever see his girlfriend again, and here I am feeling sorry for myself because I get to marry a really great guy. I may be a horrible person, but I don't have to push my selfishness on to Daniel.

"Of course, why wouldn't I be happy?" I smile at Daniel and hope he can't see the lie hidden in my words. "I have everything I could ever hope for."

"I'm glad." Daniel smiles at me again, and this time his dimples appear on the side of his mouth, pushing my heart rate into overdrive. "I…Your happiness is important to me."

"If you guys are done with this little lovefest, I was thinking we could get out of here."

Daniel and I look up at the same time into Elizabeth's emaciated face.

It takes less than a second for Daniel to get to his feet and sweep Elizabeth into a huge hug, her feet lifting right off the ground. "You're here. I can't believe it. Are you okay?"

"Put me down, I'm fine."

I get a good look at her when Daniel sets her back on the ground. She doesn't look fine. She's even skinnier than usual and the dark circles under her eyes make her face yellow and gaunt.

"Molly?"

"She's here. Inside, sleeping, but—" Daniel doesn't get a chance to finish his sentence before Elizabeth is around the corner and through the front door.

She's kneeling by Molly's bed, grasping her hands, when we enter the bunkhouse. Molly is sitting up and chatting animatedly. Elizabeth's return has brought back some of her color. It lightens my heart to see her smiling, but Elizabeth can't take her eyes off the mud cast covering Molly's leg. A mixture of pain and love radiates from her stiff shoulders and tender touch.

Daniel joins her and the three of them are sucked into a little world I'm not a part of. I'm mad at myself. I can't tell if I'm more upset by Daniel's arm around Elizabeth's shoulders or that it bothers me to watch him and know it will never be me he holds that way.

I step back outside and let the sun beat down on my face. The sharp pricks of light hitting my closed eyelids make it easier to resist the tears. I sit down in front of the door and focus on the noise of the PIT so I don't have to hear the joyful laughs coming through the thin walls of our bunk.

Out here, there is no laughing. Not a lot of others choose bunkhouses this far from the main buildings, so we don't get many visitors, but the loudest voices carry in the warm air. Two women shouting. They're too far away to make out words, but it's clear from their angry shrieks it isn't a friendly conversation. Not more than a few blocks away a sharp slap followed by angry sobs and deep, booming yells bring back the memory of my first morning in the PIT. The day I almost took a course that would surely have led to finding myself as the recipient of a beating similar to the one taking place. Just another reason to care for Daniel; another reason to get out of here.

I shut out the other noises and strain to hear the waves beating up against the shoreline that will lead us to freedom. We're too far away from the coast to actually hear the crush of the foamy waves pounding the sand, but I can pretend. The ocean calling us to a new life.

Footsteps nearby bring me back to the present. Even this far from the masses, it's not safe to sit around with my eyes closed. I jump up from the ground and brush dirt from the back of my dress as Eric comes into sight.

I should run to him, shouting the good news of Elizabeth's return, but I can't muster the energy for that level of forced emotion. Instead, I stand stoically by the door and wait for him to walk to me.

"What are you doing out here?" Eric flashes me a lazy smile and leans in for a kiss, but I angle my face slightly so it lands on my cheek.

"Your sister is back. I thought I'd give everyone a little privacy."

I expect Eric to show a similar reaction to Daniel. Maybe give a shout of joy or run into the room to see her with his own eyes, but instead his face takes on a pained look, his eyes wide with what looks like fear.

"Eric, what is it?"

"Nothing," he says, shaking his head as if to dispel whatever thought had created such a strong reaction in him. He grabs the bend of my arm with one hand and the rusted door with the other. "Guess I'd better go say hi."

Elizabeth turns at the sound of the door protesting against the rusted hinges. Her steps toward us are measured, but the teary grin on her face gives away the emotions she usually keeps locked up tight. Eric lets go of my arm to give his sister a hug and for a moment I can forget about the small part of me that's hurting.

"Welcome back, E."

"It's good to be out of Quarantine, that's for sure." Elizabeth pulls back from the embrace and turns until she can see everyone. She's still smiling, but there's a tightness around her lips. She's working just as hard to maintain her smile as I am. "I don't plan on sticking around here long enough to end up there ever again. We leave tonight."

"But Molly's leg…" Daniel's still sitting down by her bed, his eyes glued to the grey mud cast that blends in with the dingy white sheets.

"Molly's leg is exactly why we have to get out of here." Elizabeth's eyes don't mask the pain when she says Molly's name, but her voice is strong and she's instantly morphed back into commander mode. "The cast Eric made is enough to stabilize her, but her bone will never heal properly this way." She gives Eric's shoulder a quick squeeze. "Dad would be really proud of how well you did with what you had. But outside we can get her real medical care. It's time to go."

Eric grabs my hand and pulls me away toward the door. "We'll be back," he calls out to Elizabeth over his shoulder.

"Don't be gone long. I want to move our supplies into position before dinner."

Eric and I head out into the warm summer afternoon, his guiding arm hurrying my pace. The wider pathways between the buildings are more crowded today. I guess with the arrival of summer everyone plans to spend more time outside. As if we needed more of a reason to get out of here tonight. We head to the mostly empty dining hall. Other than a few older men who have nothing better to do than sit around waiting for dinner, we're alone.

Eric pulls me down onto a bench in the corner. It's warmer in here, but I'm thankful to get off the crowded streets.

"This is where it all started." Eric's heel bounces up and down, shaking the bench. "You didn't recognize me at first, but I knew you right away."

Why is he being nostalgic about the PIT now? I can't wait to forget everything about this place.

"When I asked for a dance, in that restaurant, I knew then I'd marry you someday. Sometimes you just know about people. You know what I mean?"

I nod, but a lump in my throat clogs my words. I know what he means. Eric was exactly what I was looking for, before the PIT.

"I wanted to talk to you alone, before all the craziness happens later. This is our last chance to really talk until we get off the raft." Eric takes both my hands and throws one leg over the bench to face me. I turn as best I can without sacrificing what little decorum I have left.

"Rebecca, I love you."

I know what I'm supposed to say. My mother's voice is practically screaming in my head. *I love you, too.* But I can't say it. I love Eric, but only in the way that I love Elizabeth and Molly. How could I not love the people who are giving me back my freedom?

But that's not the kind of love Eric is talking about. I agreed to marry him, but I won't lie to him.

"Eric," my voice comes out strained, so I bow my head to give me a minute to calm my nerves. I look back up and Eric is staring at me like his whole life is riding on my words. The desperation in his eyes makes it that much harder to say what I have to. "I care for you, very much. And I know in time, as we learn more about each other, I will love you, too."

His smile falters for a fraction of a second and exposes the sadness behind his façade before he fixes his features back in place. "Thank you for being honest. You…you are an amazing person. No matter what happens—" He coughs into his fist. "—I know you'll come out of everything on top. We should get back to the bunkhouse."

Eric holds my hand as we leave the building, but there's less urgency in his touch than was there before.

He pauses in the sunlight, his face pointed up to capture the rays' warmth. When he looks back at me, his face has a quiet peace about it. It makes it easier for me to know that he's okay with our conversation.

"I have one more thing to do before we leave." Eric walks back behind the dining hall toward the Admin building. I have no idea what we're doing here, but I want to get as far away from anything related to the Cardinal as possible.

"Eric, we should get back. The others are waiting on us." I don't like the look of determination on his face. The last thing we need is another one of us getting thrown into Quarantine on the night we're scheduled to leave.

Eric bends down outside the door and picks up a handful of mud from a small puddle. "One second." He reaches up and smears the mud on the door, covering the circle of olive branches etched into the glass. Inside, the red-uniformed guard stares at the grey-brown smears and marches toward the door.

"Eric, let's get out of here." I tug on his arm and he doesn't resist me. I wait until we're back in the courtyard before I question him. "What were you thinking? You could have gotten in trouble."

"I needed to send a message. They don't decide my fate anymore." His voice is flat and absent of the charm he usually uses when he talks to me. This scares me more than the mud. "You won't tell Elizabeth, will you?"

I want to, but I don't see what good it will do now. "No, I won't tell her. Let's just get out of here."

* * *

"Where have you guys been?" Elizabeth is pacing the floor when we walk back into the bunkhouse. "Never mind. Grab a bag and come on. We have to get this stuff out to the fence while there's enough daylight to see what we're doing. And I still want to go over the plan before dinner."

Daniel hands me a pack, his hands covered with sandy dirt. Guilt washes over me that we were outside, risking punishment, while everyone else was here getting ready for tonight.

The walk to the fence takes forever. Daniel and Eric carry Molly between them on a chair rigged from a warped plank of wood, slowing down their pace. It doesn't help that Elizabeth keeps zigzagging through tiny alleys and backtracking to make sure we aren't being followed. "We can't be too careful. Everything needs to go off without a hitch tonight."

Out at the edge of the PIT, we gather up piles of garbage and scatter them randomly to disguise our half-buried bags of loot.

"So here's how it will go down." We all make a small circle around Elizabeth while she uses a stick to draw a rough map in the dirt. "Daniel and Eric will carry Molly over here, to the side of this building." She taps a place on the dirt map. "Becca, you'll be there with her and I'll be on the other side of the path behind this building." She digs the tip of the stick into the dirt to indicate her spot.

"Daniel and Eric will go back to the warehouse and drag the raft out to the broken spot in the fence. It'll probably be too dark to see much of anything, so as soon as you guys have the raft in position, whistle to let us know you're ready." Daniel and Eric nod along with her explanation.

Elizabeth turns her attention to me and Molly. "I'll need to help with the fence. Becca, do you think you can carry Molly on your back from your hiding spot to the raft?" I nod and Elizabeth nods back. A silent agreement to take care of Molly. "When you hear the signal, get here as fast as you can. Molly will get on and the rest of us will push the raft past the fence and down to the shore. It'll take all of us to get it through."

Elizabeth drops the stick and uses her shoe to wipe away the crudely drawn map. "After that it's pretty clear. We push the raft to the water and paddle until we're out of sight. The current will take care of the rest until we're home free."

It sounds so simple when she explains it, but we all know the dozens of things that could go wrong at any point in the plan. We've done everything we can. Now we have to count on having better luck than any of us was given on the Acceptance stage.

"Any questions?" I have tons, but none that Elizabeth can answer. A moment of silence passes through the group as the enormity of what we're going to do tonight hits us. "Alright then, let's go eat."

The dining hall is packed, but the normal background noise of conversations, banging bowls and arguments is quieter than usual. A quick glance around the room explains why. Several guards in their bright red uniforms are stationed up and down the walls around the room.

I turn to run, but Daniel grabs my elbow and steers me to the food line. He leans down and hisses in my ear. "Don't panic. They aren't here for us."

And he's right; the guards don't react to our entrance at all. We grab our food and head to one of the few empty tables.

"Why are they here?" Their presence may not have anything to do with our plans, but it's quite a coincidence. After months of absence, here they are on the night we're escaping.

"Keep your voices down." Elizabeth shoots all of us a threatening look over the edge of her bowl of broth. "They're probably just bringing in a new load of Unders."

It doesn't look like there are any more kids running around than usual, but with tonight's crowd, it's hard to tell.

"E's right," Eric says, though he doesn't give my hand a comforting squeeze like he usually does. "You should eat. It's going to be a long night."

The broth tonight isn't bad and the bread looks only slightly stale instead of hard as rock. It's like the kitchen staff wants to send us off in style. We all slip our slices to Molly who tucks them inside of the only bag not hidden out by the fence. Dinner is quiet. What else is there to say?

Our walk back from dinner is just as quiet, and the silence continues in the bunkhouse. All our supplies are already in place so we don't have anything to distract us from the slow passage of time. I try to get a little rest, but can't relax enough to fall asleep. My brain keeps running through all the things that can go wrong.

Everyone lies down except Elizabeth. She stands, staring out the single window, watching the moon rise in the darkening sky. After what feels like hours of staring at the ceiling, Elizabeth calls out to the room. "It's time."

Seventeen

Everyone sits up without a moment's hesitation or a swipe of sleepy eyes. I'm not the only one who couldn't sleep.

"We all know what to do. No more talking until we're out of here." Elizabeth turns to the boys. "Are you ready?"

They nod, but no one moves. We all know the consequences if we're caught. This could be the last moment we all have together. As if we all have the same thought, we huddle up in the dark, our arms wrapped around the person next to us, our heads tilted into the middle until our foreheads touch.

My chest burns and next to me, balancing on one leg, Molly sniffs back a tear. This is my family.

Elizabeth pulls back and everyone separates. Now is the time for action. I take one last look into the shadows of our bunkhouse before following the others out the door into the dark night air.

Per instructions, we stick to the smaller alleys between the buildings and off the wider paths that provide a direct route to our destination. With so much garbage in our way and only a sliver of moonlight, we move at a snail's pace. Despite the slow movement, my heart is beating uncontrollably, forcing my breaths to come out in ragged huffs. Besides my sporadic breathing, the only sound is the shuffling of our feet on the dusty alleys.

Only a few blocks from the fence an unexpected noise pierces the stillness of our journey. From our left a deep voice booms out an off-pitch rendition of the Anthem of the Territories. Without a word, Daniel and Eric change direction and carry Molly over to hide in the shadow of a pile of garbage. Elizabeth grabs my hand and ducks inside a doorless bunkhouse. I hold my breath, the fear of the moment giving me the strength to keep the burning air locked inside my chest. Counting in my head, I reach sixty-eight and Elizabeth taps me on the shoulder and heads back out into the alley. The shadow of an older man, bent slightly at the waist and heading in the opposite direction, fades with his mock patriotism into the night. I let my breath out in one loud puff.

We travel the last few blocks and hustle to our spots. We're making more noise than we should, but none of us want another run-in. I can't get out of here fast enough.

Eric and Daniel help Molly off her modified seat. Eric pulls me close in the darkness, his strong arms squeezing me tighter than ever before.

"Be safe." His words are so quiet I can barely hear them.

"You, too."

He nods and heads back in with Daniel to get the raft.

Molly helps me adjust the dusty bag of clothes over my shoulder so there's still enough room on my back to carry her the short distance to the fence. This close to the edge the only sound is the constant rhythm of waves washing up on the beach before the ocean sucks them back in.

We sit in silence, Molly's head resting on my shoulder, both of us enjoying the relaxing rush of the waves. Another sound interrupts the night air, almost in time with the water crashing against the shore. I know it instantly as empty oil drums pushing against the dirt. It's almost time. There's a soft rattle and I imagine the raft hitting the fence.

Molly tenses behind me, her slim arms wrapping around my shoulders. I lift up into a squatting position. I don't want to waste a second of time getting to the raft.

An eternity passes while a thousand thoughts of disaster spin through my head. With each crash of waves I expect the whistle and when it doesn't come I picture a hundred red uniforms dragging Eric and Daniel off to Quarantine or worse.

A sharp, high whistle pierces my darkest imaginings. I stand on instinct and lift Molly with a strength I never would have believed possible just a few months ago. Pounding footsteps are barely audible under the steady beat of my heart going off like a drumbeat in my ears.

A shout in the dark draws my eyes but I can only see shadows moving ahead of me. Too many shadows.

"Run, run now!" Elizabeth's panicked voice shouts into the almost complete darkness. She's telling us to run away, not toward the raft.

"No!" Molly's voice is a painful screech in my ear. Before I can stop her she's sliding off my back and half running, half hopping toward the spot Elizabeth's voice came from. I chase after her, desperate to get us both as far away as possible, but she's moving with a speed that ignores her broken leg. I catch up with her in time to see two guards struggling to pull Elizabeth's arms behind her back.

Molly doesn't hesitate before throwing herself toward the wrestling match. "Get off of her." Moonlight glints off a thick black baton and her shout is cut short by a crunching noise. The baton rises up again and flecks of liquid fling into the air, backlit by an almost-full moon. Molly's legs twitch in the sandy dirt, then go still. Sour bile rises up the back of my throat.

Tight arms wrap around me from behind and for a single space of time I think Eric has found me in the dark and I'm safe. But I'm not. Rough hands jerk my arms behind my back and I don't resist. It's pointless to fight back. All those weeks of planning and preparation are ruined in less than a minute. My knees give out and I crash to the sandy soil, still warm from a day in the sun. Something scratchy falls over my head, but before it all goes black I catch a glimpse of Eric trapped between two guards. The look of horror on his face is identical to the way my parents looked the last time I saw them. Once again, my world is ending.

Eighteen

I have no idea what day it is. Day is an assumption on my part, too. Without a window it could be the middle of the night. Either way, it doesn't matter. None of it does. I always wondered what Quarantine is like. Now I know.

After what felt like one hundred days I stopped counting. When I first got here I tried to track the days by the time between meals, but time doesn't hold any meaning anymore. I can't tell if my meals are hours apart or days.

I only eat the cold broth because if I don't, they make me. After the third bowl of untouched soup three guards held me down while a fourth poured the cold, greasy water down my throat. It splashed all over and soaked into the front of my dress, leaving an itchy film on my chest. I still smell like grease.

Of course, that could just be my natural smell by now. I can't remember the last time they sent in a washbasin. Not that it does much good. It doesn't come with any soap or a wash rag, so the best I can do is splash the dirty water on the few exposed parts of my skin.

I spend all my countless hours sleeping. I don't have the energy to do much else. Even with the broth, I'm constantly hungry. My dress that fit perfectly when I got here hangs on me like a sack.

The guards shuffling down the hallway outside my door refuse to talk to me. If the others are here, I can't hear them and they never answer my own screams. Everything is gone. Eric, Daniel, Elizabeth, Molly. The thick, wet crunch of a baton hitting bone forces thoughts of Molly away. I can only hope we can't hear each other. Thinking about the alternative hurts too much. I know none of us got past the fence.

The events of that night are fuzzy, like I'm watching a play from the top balcony without any binoculars. I don't know who was where or who did what, but there was way too much red for any of us to have gotten away. All our dreams of leaving were swept away like loose sand on the beach. We risked everything to get out of here, and it was all for nothing.

They knew we were coming. It's the only explanation for why that many guards were out at the edge of the PIT in the middle of the night. Even if someone had seen one of us out there, we would have been long gone before they were able to track down a guard and get back out there. I've never seen more than five or six guards together and that was the night I got here. There were at least three times that many out at the fence.

It's fitting, really, that I should end up in a cell with nothing but a wafer-thin mattress. The others tried to convince me that I'm not a criminal, but they were wrong. I broke into locked rooms, stole things I had no right to, plotted against the Cardinal and tried to break out. I'm a thief and a liar. I'm not to be trusted. They should lock me up in here forever so I can't hurt anyone else.

Nineteen

Leaving me here would be a mercy, but apparently the Cardinal doesn't believe in it. At least, not for me. This morning, a guard came in and sprayed me down with the same disinfectant from the dining hall. He also brought a bucket of water. I waited for him to leave, but I'm not to be trusted, even with cleaning myself. He stood silently while I used the thin rag to wipe the layers of dirt and grease off my arms and legs.

The water was brown with my filth, but I kept dipping the rag in and wiping what I could from my neck, face, feet. I wanted to strip off my dress and wash my back. A small contingency of insects live in my mattress and my back is a favorite snacking spot. But I couldn't bear the thought of stripping down in front of the guard. After all this time I can still hear my mother's voice warning me to maintain decorum.

It seems like a laughable idea given the fact that I was giving myself a sponge bath in a guarded jail cell. I guess I have to hold on to the few things I have left in this world.

After my bath, the same barber from the night I arrived in the PIT came in to cut my hair. It had grown down past my ears in the time I've been in Quarantine. Now the short curls are flat against my head again.

I've just changed into a new dress that yet another guard brought a few minutes ago. At least he didn't wait to make sure I changed. The clean clothes are a blessing to my chafed skin. I can almost pretend I'm me again, except I'm not sure I can remember who that is anymore.

This dress has long, itchy, wool sleeves and a high collar. We've been here longer than I thought.

Footsteps click outside and pause right in front of my door. As always, the steady staccato beep of the card reader gives me a few seconds of warning that the door is about to open. I'm ready when the windowless metal slides open, but nothing prepared me for this.

Eric is there, a calm, non-expression on his face. I can't think. I'm in his arms in a second. My tears dried up ages ago, so I'm left with empty, wracking sobs that drive my shoulders into his red-clad chest. I bury myself into him and breathe in the scent of aftershave and coffee.

A gut reaction pulls me back. Eric shouldn't smell like coffee. He should smell like sweat and grease. But he doesn't. Eric smells good and his hair is combed to the side where it's growing back.

"I don't… Eric, what's going on?"

"Your Quarantine sentence is up. You're being sent back into the PIT." His voice is slow and emotionless, like he's explaining something very basic to a child. He reaches out for my elbow, but I jerk it back out of his touch.

"Why are you wearing a uniform? Where are the others?" The door of my cell slides shut behind me and I flatten against it, the zipper of my clean dress stabbing into my backbone.

A hulking guard steps out from around the corner. "Is there a problem with the prisoner?"

"No, I'm just escorting her out." Eric waves the guard off and we both watch as he heads back to wherever he came from. "Becca, please don't make this harder than it has to be. If you fight me they might make you stay in Quarantine."

I laugh, an emotionless puff of air that makes my chest heave with the effort. "Do you really think I care? They could leave me here forever."

"You don't mean that," Eric says, reaching for me again. "Let's go."

"Don't touch me. No, you…you never touch me again." My head is dizzy. I haven't stood for this long in ages. The events of that night so long ago play in a loop in my head. There's only one explanation that makes sense now. "It was you. You told them we were leaving."

Eric lays his hands on my shoulders, as if his touch can calm me.

"No," I scream at him dashing a few feet down the sterile hallway and using up all my remaining energy. My voice comes out in squeaks. "You sold us out to the Cardinal. It was you. You did this."

Eric reaches out to pick me up from where I've collapsed on the cold, tile floor, but I refuse to cooperate. He lifts me onto his shoulders and my fists beat limply against his back. "Why? Why did you do it? How? Your family?"

He doesn't answer me and I don't have any more strength to fight him. His arms are tight on my waist but not rough. We walk down several hallways, until a soft beep signals an opening door.

Eric sets me down and I'm instantly blinded by the bright rays of daylight.

"Go back to the PIT, Becca. Go live your life and forget about me. Forget about outside."

The door slides shut and I'm alone.

It was summer when I last saw the sun, but there is nothing left of that warmth. The dirt beneath my thin shoes is frozen and a biting wind stings my bare legs.

My eyes adjust to the light and familiar surroundings come into focus. The cold glass-and-metal structure of the Admin building is straight ahead, about a hundred yards away. To the right of it is the dining hall. I have no idea if a meal is being served, but at least I can find some warmth there.

My legs don't want to move. I want my thin mattress in a bare cell, and a dirty dress and to travel back to an hour ago, when the worst thing I could imagine was that Eric wasn't sent to Quarantine because they killed him, instead. I can't have that, any of that. I could lay down here. And in the morning, the red-clad guards who walk the halls of Quarantine without ever saying a word will find the bony frame of a girl, frozen in front of the door.

That's what I want to do, but I can't do that, either. I can't give the Cardinal, or the guards, or Eric, the satisfaction of one less prisoner to worry about. I can't lie down and not know what happened to the others. Daniel, Elizabeth and Molly might already be in the dining hall and I need to see them. I need to see that the sickening crunch I heard was a boot coming down on a crate and not the smashing of bones.

One foot trudges in front of the other until enough footsteps take me to the dining hall. The only people inside are the old men that never seem to leave, but they're still handing out watery bowls of soup for lunch.

I need to find the others, but I won't make it far without eating something first. It's a struggle to get the soup down. I have to chew every overcooked piece of vegetable down to mush to keep from being sick. My stomach threatens revolt with every bite. It doesn't know what to do with so much food.

An older man shuffles by the table. I recognize him from my first week in the PIT. I needed answers and he'd been here so long. What was it he told me? "Ya never see 'em comin'." He's smarter than I gave him credit for.

I push my bowl away. Only half the broth is gone, but I can't force any more down. The urge to lay my head on the greasy table is calling to me. I have to get up or I'll spend all day here.

Outside, the sun is still high in the sky, but none of its warmth reaches me here in the PIT. I wrap my arms around my rail-thin torso, but only get a few steps. A blast of freezing wind pushes me back to the door.

"Rebecca?" Like a welcome shadow in the too-bright sunlight, Daniel is in front of me, opening the door and guiding me back to an empty table. This is Daniel, but not the one I know. The light is gone from behind his eyes. It's like staring into two black holes. This, this deadness staring back at me from a face that held so much life, is what breaks the final piece that was holding me together.

I draw my knees up under my chin and wrap my arms around the bones of my legs. The rocking keeps me from screaming. I'm going to become the crazy lady who walks the alleys at night, looking for a family she lost a lifetime ago.

Daniel says nothing. He lets one hand rest on my knee and waits for me.

I can breathe again, and the questions come. "Do you know about Eric?"

Daniel nods. "He let me out a few minutes ago." For a split second, life flashes behind his eyes, cold and angry, before disappearing back down into the place where I can only hope a small part of the old Daniel lives. "He tried to talk to me, but I wouldn't let him. He doesn't deserve a chance to ease his mind."

"What about Elizabeth, Molly?"

"I don't know about anyone else. I saw you and came over. That's as far as I've gotten."

"Do you think we can go back to the bunkhouse? Do you think they'll be there?" I wince at the undisguised hope in my voice. If there's anything I've learned in the PIT, it's that hope will kill you here.

"Let's go." Daniel holds out a hand. His presence gives me the extra bit of strength I need to get up and keep moving.

Outside, the dirt roads are covered in a light frost and we pass no one as we trudge along them. From the outside, the bunkhouse looks the same as it did the day we all stood inside and said a silent good-bye we hoped we didn't need.

Elizabeth's red-rimmed eyes stare at us as we walk through the door. She's alone in the nearly empty room, and it's clear she's been crying into the thin pillow. I've never seen her cry before. It's like we've all been broken open, emptied out, and filled back in with doppelgangers that aren't sure how they're supposed to act.

Elizabeth sits up, but doesn't bother to wipe away her tears. "Eric?"

I nod. She's not asking if he's okay, but if we've seen him. If we know he's the traitorous backstabber who stole our chance at freedom.

"Molly?" Daniel's word is quiet, like a whisper he's afraid to say.

Elizabeth implodes, crumpling in on her diminished frame until she's nothing more than a ball of fabric and cropped blonde hair. She isn't crying; she's howling like a wounded animal.

Daniel is at her side in an instant, but his words of comfort don't seem to penetrate her cocoon.

I don't make it to a bed. My legs crumple underneath me as the weight of Elizabeth's cries pound against my head. And then I can't hear her anymore. Over and over again, I hear Molly crying out and the wet, crunching sound that silenced her.

It's too much for my agitated stomach. I crawl back over to the door and stick my head out to retch. Molly, sweet Molly, who rarely spoke, but always gave kindness. Who taught me how to stitch a button and could calm Elizabeth with one touch when no one else could reach her. Molly is gone.

Molly is dead and Eric is a Cardinal guard. And the three of us are left out here in the emptiness of what used to be a home. This is the end of the things we used to consider good.

I pull my head back inside, but Elizabeth is still crying and it's more than I can take. I force myself back out the door. The cold wind is a welcome relief against my hot skin. In minutes I'm numb, which is so much better than feeling.

Outside, I sit in silence for hours and watch the sun make its steady descent toward the earth. No one wants to be out in the dark and cold except me. The sun is nothing more than a deep-purple haze on the horizon. Daniel pulls me back inside and lays me down on one of the beds. The only sound is the steady wind whipping between the buildings and the childlike whimpers of Elizabeth.

Twenty

Elizabeth walks with a purpose down the dirt path. Our feet crunch on the heavy layer of frost that coats everything. It shimmers in the early morning sunlight, casting the concrete buildings in glittery shades of red and orange. I might call it pretty if it wasn't the PIT. But it is.

We're farther north than I've been before, but considering our destination, I'm not surprised. No one would have thought to include the cemetery as a tour stop.

It's not really a cemetery. Even on the outside no one buries the dead anymore. Back home the memorial wall is set up right next to the Airbus station. Row upon row of orderly names are inscribed in the shiny black surface. I doubt the PIT has a memorial wall.

Behind another row of houses, the buildings stop and a frosty white field stretches out in front of us all the way to the fence. There isn't anything here. Maybe Elizabeth isn't thinking straight and brought us to the wrong place.

I follow her through the field and one by one small cairns of stones pop up around us. Nothing designates one small pile from the next other than the slight differences in shape and size of the rough stones. I understand. The people who lived here long before us chose this as the place to remember the dead the best they could.

Elizabeth is silent as she bends down to collect several small stones. I pick up a small, grey rock by my feet, but let it fall back through my fingers. She didn't put up a fight when I asked to come with her this morning, but this is still her journey. Elizabeth will want to hand-pick each of the rocks for Molly's memorial.

With arms full of round, white stones, she kneels down and piles them up, one by one. I feel silly standing there, watching her. Molly and I weren't close, but I need to do something to help honor her.

Crouching down between the piles of stones I pick up handfuls of fallen leaves and twigs that cover the ground. After several trips of dumping the frozen clutter several yards away, Elizabeth is almost finished with the pyramid of stones.

She picks up the last rock and brushes away any trace of remaining dirt before setting it in place on top of the small stack. I stare down at the pile. It doesn't come close to good enough for Molly.

But perhaps this is better than a name on a wall that some nameless Cardinal employee stamps on without caring about the person whose life is represented by the small, even letters. I think Molly would have liked this; something simple, yet beautiful, and made with our hands.

The tears fall down Elizabeth's cheeks and she wipes them away with the back of her hand, but she can't keep up with the steady flow. Drops fall faster and faster until she's sobbing, her damp hands clawing at the dirt.

Elizabeth's strong frame shakes with her cries and the raw emotion tears at me. I stay away, wrestling with my own emotions. I want to cry for Molly, too, but it feels selfish. Like my tears would intrude on Elizabeth's mourning.

She's just as weak as I am from our months in Quarantine so it doesn't take long for exhaustion to overcome her and silence her cries.

"I'm so sorry, Elizabeth." My foot taps out a nervous rhythm on the cold ground. "I know the two of you were close." My words sound empty in the odorless winter air, but they're all I have to offer her.

"Close?" Elizabeth rocks backs from her crouch and sits down on the newly cleared ground. "Molly and I weren't close. She was everything. The Cardinal didn't just take my best friend. He ended the love of my life."

My foot freezes mid tap.

"You didn't think I was in here for something stupid like hating the Cardinal, did you?" She gives me a half smile, but it doesn't last. "I always knew I'd end up here. The Cardinal would never let someone like me run loose in society, causing a ruckus by kissing girls."

She pats the ground next to her and I sit, still stunned by her revelation.

"That first year was…" She shivers, but I don't think it has anything to do with the cold. "I lost count of the times

I thought about just lying down in a bunkhouse until dehydration and starvation took me. Then I walked into the dining hall one day and found Molly. She gave me a reason to wake up each morning."

"I thought you and Daniel…"

She laughs, and this time it's genuine. "We found Daniel a few weeks later sitting at dinner talking about an old radio he found. He was smart and didn't make a face when I held Molly's hand. He rounded out our little group, but was never more than a replacement little brother."

"I guess that makes sense then. I always thought it was strange that you guys never kissed."

"Oh, wait until I tell Daniel you said that," Elizabeth says, slapping her leg and exhaling one big guffaw of laughter. "Why did you think we were together?"

"Eric told me."

Saying his name out loud brings the reason for our trip back to the present. If Eric hadn't betrayed us, Molly would still be alive.

"Yeah, well, turns out Eric is a much better liar than I ever gave him credit for."

It's peaceful out here, surrounded by little piles of rocks; physical reminders that even in the PIT there's still love. The harshness that usually lurks behind Elizabeth's words is diminished by the atmosphere surrounding the cemetery. This is probably my only chance to ask her the question that's been sitting in the back of my head since my first day in the PIT.

I keep my eyes focused on a blurry point in the distance. I won't be able to ask my question if I have to face her. "Why don't you like me?"

"I like you." Her response is too fast and we both know it for the lie it is. An uneasy silence settles around the mini memorials and we both huddle against the cold that goes deeper than the wintery breeze.

"I didn't want to be friends with you." Elizabeth's words sound like a reluctant confession. "I was so mad at Daniel for bringing you to our bunk that morning. The last thing we needed was a Goody Two-shoes running around. I thought for sure you'd fail the scavenger hunt."

I pull my arms tighter around me. I don't know if she's looking at me or not, but I don't have the guts to check. "If this is your way of telling me you don't hate me, you're not doing a very good job."

Elizabeth sighs and from the rustle of fabric I can tell she's turned toward me. "It's not that I didn't like you. I mean, I'm not gonna lie; you weren't my favorite person, but I didn't really have anything against you personally."

"Wow, stop," I tell her, my voice flat as I turn to meet her weary eyes. "I don't want all your praise to go to my head."

"I thought you were a liability," Elizabeth, says ignoring my sarcastic comments. "I knew I could trust Daniel and Molly. Eric, he's my brother, why wouldn't I trust him?" She presses her eyes closed for the length of a heartbeat. "But you were just some girl who thought too much and got herself thrown in the PIT. For all I knew, you still thought the sun shines out of the Cardinal's rear end. I was afraid you'd turn us in."

"Well, that worked out great, didn't it?"

"And I kick myself every night. Over and over, I run through those days leading up to our escape. I knew Eric was acting funny, but I thought it was nerves. I wrote it off as nothing, because I trusted him. Instead of picking up on the real reason behind his behavior, I watched you like a hawk."

"Why? What did I do to make you not trust me?"

"Nothing, and that was the problem." Elizabeth dips her head, her grief an actual weight bearing down on her. "You did everything we asked you to do. You never questioned the plan, never doubted it would work."

"Because *I* trusted *you*."

She lifts her eyes to meet my own. "Why?"

"What was my alternative?" I shrug and pull my knees tighter to my chest. "It was clear on day one I wouldn't survive in here alone. I could either trust you and go along with the plan or let the PIT eat me alive."

"Too bad trusting me didn't keep the PIT from chewing us all up." Her head droops to her knees, leaving her exposed, weak. Strong and confident Elizabeth, reduced to a ball of self-doubt and regret, and all because of him.

I jump up, my fists clenched against a sudden anger that boils up in me. "Don't you dare. Don't you even think about putting the blame for what happened on you."

"Becca, I—"

"No." My muscles are still weakened from months of atrophy inside Quarantine, but I have enough strength to push Elizabeth's shoulders until she's lying flat on her back against the cold ground.

She pushes herself off the ground and I brace myself, ready for her to fight back. Her jaw is locked in a grimace and she glares at me from two angry slits that hide her blazing blue eyes.

"The guilt is Eric's. He owns it all on his own and I won't let you go on thinking you share any part of it with him."

Her muscles relax by a fraction and she nods her head, a silent agreement to leave her guilt behind. Elizabeth kisses the tips of her fingers and leans over to touch them softly to the cold rocks marking a beautiful life lost forever. "Let's go."

The sun is higher in the sky on our walk back and the PIT stirs to life around us with people making their way to breakfast. I try not to think about Eric, but every word he ever said runs on a continuous loop through my head. How much of what he told me was a lie? All of it? Did he really love me or was that just another part of his deception?

Inside the dining hall, I follow Elizabeth through the line and we find Daniel among the crowded tables. His eyes follow every move Elizabeth makes, probably gauging her for another breakdown.

"Stop staring at me." She hits her bowl down on the table, but not hard enough to splash out any of her burnt oatmeal. "I'm fine now, I promise. Molly would want me to keep going. Now let's talk about something else."

I should keep my mouth shut, but the words tumble out before I can stop them. "Why would Eric ask me to marry him if he was going to turn us in?"

Daniel chokes on his lumpy breakfast. It takes several minutes and an entire cup of brackish water to bring his coughing under control. He rubs at his throat and raises a single eyebrow at me. "Way to ease into the conversation."

"Sorry, it's just something you said earlier." I turn on the bench to face Elizabeth. "What you said about Eric being a good liar."

"And now you want to know if he was lying about his feelings for you."

I nod. I can't explain why I care. It's actually a bit of a relief to not have him at my side every minute. I don't have to smile and pretend that his touch brings me comfort instead of confusion. And yet, no one has ever taken an interest in me like that before. What if the whole thing was an act?

"I think Eric loved you in the only way Eric knows how." Elizabeth's voice is resigned. This is a truth she's come to accept, but she doesn't like it. "He loved you for the Becca he thought you could be; the life he imagined he'd have with you. But you didn't love him."

Elizabeth and Daniel stare at me, waiting on the confession I thought I kept hidden from everyone. "No."

"I could tell the fake marriage was bothering you. Something more than just the rushed timeline." Elizabeth leans forward, letting her forehead rest in the palm of her hands. "I told Eric you seemed uneasy. Thought it might help you adjust better if your marriage felt more real. An engagement sounded like the perfect solution for both of you."

I can't blame her. She did what she thought was best. Eric made his choices and there's nothing any of us could have done to change who he is. The best thing for all of us is to forget what happened and move on. Whatever that looks like. "So now what?"

Daniel swings his legs over the bench and stands up stretching. "Now nothing, we keep going."

"You mean, we try again?" I ask, following him out into the cold morning air.

"No, not that." Daniel slashes his arms through the air with finality and keeps walking. "I mean we just live."

I rush to catch up with him. "But why? Why can't we try again?" I know it's not the same, but there has to be more than one way to get out of here.

Daniel turns and wraps his hands around my shrunken arms, his grip a little too tight. I grimace and he lets go, shoving his hands in his pockets. "They'll never even let us get close, Rebecca. By now, we're tagged and red-flagged in every file the Cardinal has. All of our supplies are gone and we're surely blacklisted from getting another job that might give us access to what we need."

I turn around to Elizabeth. Molly wouldn't want her to give up, but one shake of her head tells me she sides with Daniel. "He's right, Becca. I hate the idea of giving up, but what choice do we have? I'm not losing anyone else. I can't. Every day is precious and I won't waste any more living in a daydream of escape."

"But we can't stop." I reach for Daniel's arm, but he pulls back from me. "Please, if we just—"

"Stop it, Becca."

Daniel always calls me Rebecca. The sound of it rolls from his lips to tingle down my spine. My nickname, the one Eric used, doesn't roll. It spits from his mouth and knocks against my gut like a sucker-punch.

In his eyes, I can see it. All the driving force that pushed him to hack into the Cardinal's network and create new lives for us is gone. We aren't going anywhere.

Twenty-One

"Do you think Daniel can make something out of this?" I hold the broken broom handle up for Elizabeth to examine. "Maybe a hook or rod of some kind to hang our blankets to dry."

Elizabeth weighs it in her hands, inspecting the splintered end. "It's worth a shot. Might as well bring it back with us."

Daniel has used the past few months to channel his computer skills into those of a handyman. When I told him and Elizabeth about the way Constance and her husband set up their bunkhouse, they both poured themselves into the project. We all needed something to do.

"Might as well head back to the bunk. It'll be dinner soon and we wouldn't want to leave Daniel waiting." Elizabeth nudges me in the side with her elbow. I follow her without a word.

She's been making side comments and sending me winks for the past month every time Daniel is mentioned. It's not like I haven't noticed the way he looks at me. Now that I know he and Elizabeth were never together, I have to rethink every conversation and interaction we ever had.

But things are different now. We aren't leaving. This is our home. I don't know how to make a real relationship work inside the confines of the fence. I'm not sure I want to.

In the bunk, Daniel tinkers with a busted crate. He already built a small table and two very rough chairs. Not that we really need a table. It's not as if we'll be having any gourmet meals in here. He made the table for me, because I thought it would make the bunk feel more like a home. His willingness to work that much on something just to make me happy makes it even harder to tuck down my emotions when he flashes me a bright smile as we walk in.

I give him a quick smile, set our latest finds down on the table and head over to my bunk.

"Are you guys ready to eat? I need to step away from the woodwork before one of these crates ends up on the roof." Daniel stands and wipes his hands off on his pants.

"Oh, poor Daniel." Elizabeth wraps an arm around his shoulder, a look of mock sympathy on her face. "Is the big, bad crate giving you a hard time?"

"Ha, ha, laugh all you want. You won't think it's funny if I smash my finger with that blasted rock and can't make you any more furniture."

"Does that mean the rocking chair is out?" Elizabeth laughs and ducks away before Daniel can land the teasing punch on her arm.

It's good to see her laughing again. Those first few weeks had me wondering if we would ever get her back. She put on a brave face during the day, but her cries kept us all up more nights than not. It's been weeks since I've seen her cry, though sometimes I catch her staring off into nothing. That's when I know she's thinking about Molly and, like the rest of us, wishing she was still here.

Outside, the sky has turned overcast and grey. We take our usual path to the dining hall, but it doesn't look the same as it did on our walk to lunch. The closer we get to the courtyard, the cleaner things are. Piles of garbage that were a permanent part of the scenery are gone with nothing more than a damp spot of soil to mark their existence.

The main road running right down the middle of the PIT is completely clear of garbage. The normally rocky and pitted dirt path is smooth and even, as if someone has steamrolled the road.

"What's going on?" I can't believe what I'm seeing, but maybe this happens every year.

"I don't know, but I'm going to find out." Daniel keeps walking past the dining hall toward the Admin building. None of us have been anywhere near it since the night of our failed escape. Seeing him so close to those glass doors sends my heart rate racing. It's irrational, but I don't want us any closer to the Cardinal than we have to be.

Daniel keeps tight to the side of the dining hall and walks casually, as if he's headed to the dumpster. When he hits the edge of the building, he takes a few more steps toward a group of red-clad workers. Daniel bends down as if to tie his shoe. His head is down, but I know his ears are trained on the workers, taking in their every word.

The group breaks out into loud laughter and the workers walk off toward the Admin building. Daniel stands up and walks back to us, a look somewhere between confusion and amusement spread across his face.

"So, what's the story, secret-agent man?"

Daniel shakes his head at Elizabeth's question and motions toward the dining hall. Inside, we grab our bowls and let the din of the crowded room drown out our conversation.

"You remember last year's Acceptance ceremony?"

Elizabeth and I both shoot him a look of exasperation. As if we could forget the day her brother and I were Rejected from society.

"Okay, what I mean is, do you remember how they televised the ceremony? It was the first time people without a child going through Acceptance got to see the proceedings and it was a big hit."

"What does that have to do with cleaning up the garbage?" I'm just as confused as Elizabeth.

"Patience. Apparently, the Cardinal wants to make this year's ceremony bigger and better; really drive home the point about us criminals locked away nice and tight." Daniel leans across the table and Elizabeth and I bring our heads to meet his. "He plans to include live footage from the PIT as part of this year's broadcast."

"Great, we'll be like animals on display at the zoo," Elizabeth says.

"That's the general idea." Daniel sits back on his side of the table and all three of us take a minute to think about what this means.

"I don't get it." I flip my hands over on the table, my callused palms on display. "Before I got here, I couldn't care less what the PIT looked like. And if you'd have told me the roads were covered in garbage and the buildings falling apart, I would have said that's what criminals deserve. Why fix it up?"

I look to Daniel, but he can only shrug his shoulders.

* * *

A light rain taps out a steady rhythm on the roof, but the noise isn't keeping us from arguing. Ever since we got back from dinner, we've gone over every possible scenario for what the Cardinal is up to with his clean-up act. We've been at it long enough for the sun to set down below the line of buildings, but we don't have any real ideas.

"Maybe he's trying to get rid of anything that can be used as a weapon." Daniel sits on the edge of his bunk, his head cradled in his hands.

Elizabeth doesn't even try to hide the sarcasm in her response. "Yeah, because he really cares about us killing each other off."

"But he does care about his precious guards. Wouldn't want anyone we know getting hurt."

"Enough." My shout echoes off the walls. Daniel has the decency to look guilty for crossing the line. It's an unspoken rule to not talk about Eric. "It's not worth fighting over. Guessing what goes on inside the Cardinal's head is a waste of time."

"And what would you have us do? Sit around sewing doilies?"

"At least we wouldn't be sniping at each other."

"Not at all," Elizabeth says, rolling her eyes. "We'll be sharing a group hug when disaster strikes."

If I don't get out of the stuffy room, made even more crowded by Elizabeth's bad attitude, I'll say something I'll regret. We've finally come to a kind of friendly understanding between us and I don't want to jeopardize that with some stupid argument about what the Cardinal may or may not be up to.

It takes about three steps for the rain I'd forgotten about to completely soak my hair. Fat, warm drops seep into the coarse material of my dress, adding liquid weight to my frame.

I haven't thought of my mother in ages, but a vivid memory of her floods my brain. It had been raining for days. Much too long for a six-year-old to be cooped up inside. I snuck out while she was cooking lunch and splashed in puddles until I was soaked to the bone. My mother dragged me inside, lecturing all the way to the bathroom about the impropriety of little girls playing in the dirt.

She's not here now and I'm not a little girl anymore. I twirl once and jump. My feet slap into the shallow puddles cratering the ground.

"Rebecca, what are you doing out there?" Daniel stands at the door, his broad shoulders filling up the opening.

I lift my face to the sky. "Living," I shout back at him over the sound of heavy drops pinging against the dusty surfaces of the PIT.

"You want to think about living somewhere…drier?"

I laugh. Not a light chuckle or a polite laugh at a lame joke. Because that's what you do when someone tells a joke, even if it's not funny. I'm laughing because this is probably the most inappropriate time for laughter I can think of. I throw my head back and let the body-shaking hilarity bubble up from my belly, tickle my neck and burst into the night air.

"Rebecca?" Daniel walks out, ducking his head against the wet drops, and grabs my hands. "Are you okay?"

"I'm perfect." I tighten my grip on his hands and pull him around into a slow circle, my arms straight out in front of me, the bleakness of the PIT fading into a blur behind Daniel as we move faster and faster.

Daniel's laugh joins mine, adding a deep, booming bass line to the music of the rain. The dirt pathways are muddy slicks beneath my feet. I drop Daniel's hands, grab the skirt of my dress and pull it up till the hem brushes the top of my knees. My mother would have a fit. The thought of her standing in front of me, her hands punched onto her bony hips makes me laugh even louder. I jump into another puddle and yelp as cool drops of mud fly up to hit my legs.

"You've lost your mind." Daniel shouts at me and laughs as I twirl again, the short strands of my hair whipping out to smack against my cheeks.

"Maybe." I stand back and kick at a puddle, splashing mud onto Daniel's shirt.

Daniel's jaw drops open, his wet hands pulling at the front of his rain-soaked, mud-splattered shirt. "You shouldn't have done that." His eyes squint in the darkness, but he can't keep a straight face for long. A wide smile gives him away and he swings his leg back to pepper me with my own shower of mud.

I run away squealing, though the wet clothes and slippery roads keep me from going far or fast. I spin to move out of the path of his splatter, but my foot hits a slick spot and I fall down with a plop into the mud. The mud soaks into my dress instantly, but I don't care. I've never felt freer, even when I was.

Daniel squats down in front of me. His face is so close to mine I can see the drops of rain clinging to his eyelashes. For a split second, I let myself imagine what life could have been like if I had met Daniel outside the PIT. I would have fallen in love with him so easily. So different from how I felt with Eric, like our lives would have been a constant work in progress. With Daniel, I can imagine everything falling into place right from the start.

I blink and push the thoughts away. We aren't outside the PIT. We're here and not going anywhere, and I'm done living through a series of 'what if' scenarios. Daniel's smile turned more serious during my moment of weakness and his eyes are slightly glazed as if his mind was somewhere else, too.

"We better get inside before one of us gets sick."

Daniel holds out a hand to help me up. I smile back up at him, thankful for the friendship we have. Using my left arm as leverage I raise my right hand out to him. Instead of grabbing his outstretched hand I reach to his face and wipe my muddy fingers against the side of his cheek.

I sit in the mud and wait for his retaliation, but Daniel only takes my hand and pulls me back up. He shakes his head, water flying off his face and hair and hitches his thumb back at the bunkhouse. "I think Elizabeth is probably a little too clean and dry in there."

"She'll kill us. Both of us."

Daniel winks at me before bending over and digging both of his palms into the sloppy mud of the street. I may never be able to give him my heart the way I could if we weren't in here, but this, what we have right here, can be enough. I dip down and plant both hands into the mud next to his. I wink back at him before we head inside.

Twenty-Two

"Elizabeth, can you please sit still. You're driving me nuts with all that pacing." Daniel's the one who finally says something, but I've been thinking it for the past half hour.

Elizabeth and I would normally be out scavenging for chipped bowls or bits of wood for the bunkhouse, but we haven't been out in days. When the main road was cleared, everyone rushed out to gather what was left in the other alleys before it disappeared, too. We'd be lucky to find a moldy paper bag at this point.

"I'm sorry," she shouts back, not sounding sorry at all. "I pace when I'm thinking and in case you haven't noticed, I don't have anything else to do."

"I could teach you to sew." My offer is only halfhearted. Elizabeth and I know a sewing lesson from me would likely end in bloodshed—probably mine.

Elizabeth narrows her eyes at me.

"I don't know why you're letting this get you so worked up." I set down the dress I'm patching for the girl over in the clothing warehouse. I'm not practiced enough to talk and stitch at the same time. "We've been over this all week and we aren't any closer to coming up with an explanation for all the cleanup."

We walked the entire main road yesterday. The garbage was cleared all the way from the dining hall to the fence. The rocks are gone and the dirt has been smoothed and packed down. If I didn't know any better, I'd guess they're building a real road, but why in the world would they do that?

"I'm not going to be able to rest until we know what's going on." Elizabeth sticks her tongue out at both of us and starts another lap of the room.

"With the Acceptance ceremony coming up we should get some answers soon. We can be thankful for that, at least." I pick up my sewing needle, but set it right back down again. I can't get anything done with Elizabeth marching the room. "I'm going out for a little fresh air."

Daniel sets down the nail he's straightening. "Do you want some company?"

A lifetime ago I would have jumped at the chance for a pre-sunset walk with Daniel, but not now. He's still handsome and funny and smart and that's the problem. If I let myself open those feelings back up, there'll be no stopping them. After what happened to Elizabeth, I can't put myself in a position to be hurt that way. I'm not as strong as she is. I wouldn't survive.

"Maybe next time." I smile at him and his smile back says he knows I'll say no then, too.

"Don't be too long, then. It's almost time for dinner."

I nod and head out into the late-afternoon sun. I don't have a destination in mind, but my feet carry me toward the ocean. I'm able to use what used to be a wall to climb on the roof of a building. Too bad there's not an oil drum to climb on. They've all been cleared out. I'm not surprised.

I sit with my knees hugged against my chest, watching the water rush out toward the open sea only to be sucked back in and thrown against the beach. We tried so hard to fight against the waves, but were just as powerless as the salty water.

Maybe it was a bad idea to come out here. I can stare at the ocean all day, but it isn't going to change anything. No one leaves the PIT and it's just as well. Now that I know the real cost of our ideal society, I doubt I could live out there anymore.

I need to focus on my family here and keeping us safe. Nothing else matters. Not even figuring out what the Cardinal has in mind with his sudden interest in cleaning the main road. My focus needs to be on the people I care about.

Standing up, I hold my hands against the stinging wind. Nature's way of telling me I don't belong here anymore. Time to let someone else dream about freedom.

I turn and back down off the side of the roof, but something metal that shouldn't be there catches my eye. Scrambling back up, I hold my hand above my eyes as a visor to block the glare of the setting sun. On the main road, a line of evenly spaced metal poles, much taller than any of the buildings, sticks up out of the ground. What is going on out here?

I scoot off the roof and walk the short distance to the poles. Starting at the fence, about twenty poles are raised every few yards, puddles of still wet concrete circling each one. I study every visible inch of the closest pole, but there's nothing to indicate what it is.

"It's a fence post."

I spin around at the familiar voice and sure enough, Eric is standing there in his red uniform, a Noteboard in hand. He might have every answer in the world, but he's the last person I would believe. I bite my tongue and walk away.

"Becca, please, I need to talk to you." He's running behind me and it only takes a second for him to catch up to me. "It's important."

"I don't want to hear any of it."

"He's going to separate you."

It's like he knew the one thing that could get me to pay attention. "You have thirty seconds," I say, my arms crossed in front of me.

Eric takes a huge breath. "These are fence posts. I was sent out to inspect the concrete and make sure the poles are holding. They're building a fence to run right down the middle of the PIT. Women on one side, men on the other. They plan to finish it to correspond with the Acceptance ceremony."

I'm on him in a second, the collar of his red uniform gripped in my fists. "If you're lying to me, Eric, so help me, I'll end you."

"I swear," he says, his hands flying up in the air in surrender. "You've got a week, and then everything changes."

A sharp band of pain wraps around my chest, the pulsing squeezes making it hard to breathe. I push him back and wipe off my hands, disgusted from being that close to him again. "I have to go."

"Wait. I have something." Eric digs a fist down into the pocket of his pants and comes back out with something small and shiny. "A small shop by my apartment sells items confiscated from the PIT. You should have this back."

He takes a step toward me, but I hold out my hand to stop him. "That's close enough. Just toss it over."

Eric pulls back and tosses the item across the few feet separating us. I catch it with one hand. I know what's in my fist without looking. Resting in my palm is the delicate, woven knot of my grandmother's necklace.

I smile despite myself. After all the things I've lost in here, this was the last I ever thought I'd see again.

"I'm so sorry for what happened."

"No. You don't get to apologize. You don't get to feel better after turning us in, after getting Molly killed. "

"That wasn't supposed to happen. No one was going to get hurt."

"Is this supposed to make me feel better?" I hold the pendant up in my clenched fist. My mind fights against the dual instinct to hold the heirloom as close as I can and throw its tainted metal into the dirt. "Should I understand now why you betrayed your own family?" Why did it take me so long to see who he really is? I don't need him and I doubt I ever did. I'm stronger than anyone gave me credit for, including myself.

"Becca, I—"

"My name is Rebecca."

Eric opens his mouth, but snaps it shut. He nods his head as if he's meeting me for the first time. And he is. At least, he's meeting the new me. I turn and march away, but only get a few steps before Eric's cold voice has me turning back around.

"I suppose you think I should have kept my mouth shut," he says, hands splayed out to the side. "And we could be living unhappily together somewhere outside the PIT."

"How dare you?" My fists clench and I raise my tightened fingers to hit him, but Eric grabs my wrist before I can make contact. I pull away and he lets go without a fight. "Don't you dare pretend to know me or what makes me happy."

"What makes you happy will always be a mystery to me, but I have a pretty good idea that being married to me isn't it."

Heat creeps up my neck and I bet a piece of stale bread that a pink flush is spread across my face. "You don't...I might..."

"I've seen the way you look at Daniel. Staring at him when he explains something technical with the Noteboard like you can't soak up enough of him." Eric slides his hands into the pockets of his wrinkled uniform and looks at me for only a moment before turning his attention to a loose rock in the pathway. "With me, you were always kind and respectful. I like to think you even showed a bit of admiration for me. But not love. You couldn't give me your love when your heart already belonged to him."

He's right, though I'd never admit it. I can pretend that given enough time I might have come to love Eric, but I'd never truly love him. I love Daniel and constantly pushing him away isn't going to change that.

"I have to go." I turn away without saying good bye, but Eric isn't done yet.

"You'll tell them? Warn them what's happening?"

I turn around so he can see my face and know that every word I say is the truth. "What I do or don't do is none of your concern now. And neither are Elizabeth and Daniel. You gave up your family. I hope it was worth it."

I turn on my heels and run back to the bunkhouse as fast as I can, but without the landmarks of busted crates and piles of refuse all the streets look the same. The setting sun isn't making things any easier.

I dash down row after row until the buildings start to look familiar. Up ahead of me a tall, dark figure paces in front of a building and I keep running despite the stitch in my side. Daniel turns to the sound of my feet and I run into his arms.

"Rebecca, I was about to come looking for you. Where—"

"No time." I lean into his chest and swallow against my dry throat. "Inside."

Daniel doesn't argue with me, but pushes open the door and helps me inside to one of our creaky chairs.

"You're back. Becca, what happened?" Elizabeth stops pacing by the corner and kneels in front of me at the table. Daniel brings me one of our stolen dinner bowls filled with collected rainwater. I suck it down and lean my elbows on the table.

"Rebecca." Daniel sits down across from me and takes my hand. "What happened?"

"I know why they're clearing out the PIT. They had to make room."

"For what?"

"Out by the edge, they're putting up posts for a new fence."

"Why?" Elizabeth stands and leans both hands against the table. "They already fixed the broken spot where we tried to get out."

"No," I pound my fist against the table, desperate for them to understand. "This one isn't going around the PIT, it's going through it. After the ceremony, they're going to separate us. Men on one side, women on the other."

"How do you know?" Elizabeth asks, her voice leaking out, barely above a whisper.

I'm still holding my grandmother's necklace, but it feels like a hot coal in my hand. I pull back my arm and fling the silver knot into a darkened corner, the metal making a tinkling sound as it hits the wall and slides to the floor. "Eric told me."

Time freezes for a second as the impact of my words hits them. Elizabeth sinks to the floor in slow motion, her face locked, with wide eyes and open mouth. Daniel barely moves. His head, arms, legs are still as stone, but his fingers press deeper into my hand as if he can forge a link between us that can't be broken. I can't let them fall apart. I need them.

"We have to stop this from happening, so both of you snap out of it right now." Neither of them responds so I kick the table leg and pound my empty fist on the loose boards. Daniel at least looks up at me. Elizabeth makes an indefinable noise between a growl and a moan.

"I mean it. Get up." I kick the table again and this time they both respond. "Get up."

"What do you want us to do? Rage, storm, start a riot?" Elizabeth is back in the hole she fell into when Molly died, but we don't have time for that now.

"No, that's what they're expecting. They cleared the place out; we don't have anything to riot with but rocks and sticks. Besides, what's a couple thousand prisoners when you have the strength of the Cardinal? We need something that's bigger than just us."

Daniel's face holds a little bit of the old excitement he got whenever explaining something technical. "You have an idea."

I don't have a plan. What I have is anger, and right now that's good enough. "Acceptance ceremony is in a few days. They plan to broadcast a distorted picture of the PIT.

Show everyone how kind the Cardinal is. But what if we could show people what things are really like?" I look at Daniel because Elizabeth is still despondent on the floor. "What if they knew the truth about who gets put in here?"

Daniel lets go of my hand and walks a few paces away from the table before turning back to me. "You're talking about hacking into the live feed."

With his words, the plan takes shape in my head. "You can do it." I get up, and this time I'm the one grabbing his hand. "You're amazing with computers. I'll get one for you if I have to break into the Admin building every night and beat the doors down."

"You don't need to do that." Daniel bites his bottom lip and his eyes flash to the door.

"Yes, I do. I…we can't lose you."

He shakes his head. "That's not…" He looks over my shoulder to where Elizabeth is still sitting on the floor. "We can't do it."

"Don't say that." I sound desperate, miles away from the self-assured woman who put Eric in his place only a few minutes ago. I can't help it. "I can't risk losing you."

He pushes my hand away and takes a step back from me. The pain of his actions slices at my exposed emotions. His words shout at me across the few feet separating us. "They'll reject Patrice."

"Who's Patrice?"

"My sister."

Daniel told me a long time ago he had a sister back home, but in all this time he's never mentioned her again.

It's clear he hasn't forgotten about her. "She's up for Acceptance this year, isn't she?"

Daniel nods, the movement barely visible in the minimal moonlight shining through our window. "I won't destroy her chance to have a normal life."

I reach for his hand again, and this time he doesn't pull away. I need to say something, anything, that will convince him he can't give up, but anything I say will sound like I'm asking him to sacrifice his sister. "You can't be sure of what will happen." I hate myself for what I'm about to say, but it doesn't stop me. "She could be Rejected even if you do nothing."

Daniel throws my hand back at me. "Shut up. You don't know what you're talking about. You don't understand any of it."

"Then help me understand. You know more about the Machine than you're telling us." I force my arms to stay glued to my sides. I don't trust myself not to reach out to him again. "Please don't shut me out."

"No. It won't change anything." Daniel bends down to pick Elizabeth off the floor and guides her near-comatose body over to a creaky bed.

"You said my brain is what landed me in here. So let me use it. Tell me what you know."

"Don't you get it?" Daniel turns back to me, but refuses to meet my eyes. "What I know got me in here. I won't put you at more of a risk and I won't jeopardize Patrice's Acceptance."

Daniel tucks Elizabeth in. The resignation in his slumping shoulders is more than I'm willing to accept. "I'm stronger than you give me credit for and I'd be willing to bet Patrice is, too." His arms tense, but he stays silent. "I can't sit around here and watch you give up."

I'm out the door before Daniel can stop me. I have no idea where I'm going, only that I need to get away from the despair that hangs like a heavy layer of fog inside our bunkhouse. The streets are empty. Most people are probably at dinner now. It's not a good idea to skip meals around here, but I can't even think about eating. Not when my thin hold on normalcy is crumbling to pieces through my fingers.

I need to come up with a new plan, one that doesn't put Daniel's sister at risk, but I can't think. A sharp, cool breeze hits the front of my damp dress. How long have I been crying? Ever since we got out of Quarantine I've been pushing Daniel away, afraid of what could happen if I really opened my heart to him. But now that I'm staring at the real possibility of losing him forever, I realize I was only kidding myself.

I can turn down his offers for evening walks and sit on the opposite side of the dining hall table till the end of time, but none of that has prevented me from falling in love with him. Eric was right. I tried to keep my distance, but even he could see the way I felt.

"Hey there, what's a pretty girl like you doing crying all alone?"

The unfamiliar voice pulls me out of my stupor of self-pity. This is not an area of the PIT I'm familiar with. The streets are dotted with folks done with dinner and looking to fill the hours before total darkness claims the day. I've been gone much longer than I realized.

I turn around to retrace my steps back to the bunkhouse, but a coarse, grimy hand reaches out and grabs my arm. "Not so fast, pretty lady. I asked you a question."

The gangly man grabs my other arm and spins me against the outer wall of a nearby bunkhouse. His short, dark hair is matted on top of his head and I can smell a week's worth of filth on his skin when he leans in closer to me. He pushes one of his legs between mine and pins my shoulders to the wall with his skinny arms. I struggle against the pressure, but he's stronger than he looks under the layers of grease and grime.

"Something made the pretty lady sad. Bet I can give you something to cheer up your evening."

I scream out against the pressing darkness, but the people who dotted the streets just a minute ago have disappeared. The sun has all but set and I can barely see a couple feet to either side. I scream again, but the few people who might hear me don't care.

And why should they? When a girl in my own bunkhouse called out for help against the man assaulting her, I hid under my bunk.

"Please don't do this." My voice comes out as weak whimper between the sobs that wrack my chest. I kick out with one of my legs, but the effort puts me off-balance and my foul attacker only increases his pressure against me.

"Shut up now, if you know what's good for you." He presses his dirty nose against the side of my neck and inhales deeply, moving up past my ear. His pelvis pushes up against the front of my dress and another sob escapes from my throat when he lets out a low moan.

Pinned against the wall, I'm defenseless against him. He reaches an arm down and runs an unwelcome hand under my skirt and up my thigh, tugging at my thin underpants. I close my eyes. Please let it be over soon.

"Please." My words are little more than a whisper now. "For the sake of the Cardinal, please don't do this."

My attacker pulls back. He's going to let me go. Instead, he shifts his left forearm across my chest so he can raise his right hand up to strike me. "I thought I told you to shut—"

A crack echoes in the empty alley, and the rancid man who held me captive crumples into a heap at my feet. My legs won't support me and I slide down the wall, the crunching sound of a guard's baton beating against Molly's head running on a loop through my brain.

Strong arms lift me up into a cradle hold and practically run out of the alley. I should say something, anything, but I can't form words around the sickening crunch echoing in my skull.

The door to our bunkhouse opens, and the sight of familiar surroundings in the dim light of the moon finally re-engages my brain. "Daniel?"

"It's okay. We're home now. You're safe." He lays me on my bunk, but I'm not ready to let go of him yet. I cling to his neck the way a small child clings to her mother after a nightmare.

"You came for me."

Daniel guides my arms from around his neck but holds my hands against his chest until I stop shaking. "I'll always come for you."

"Daniel, I—"

"Tomorrow, okay?" He lifts my legs up to lay them on the bed and eases my head down onto the flat pillow. "We have a lot to talk about, but it can all wait until morning."

I grip his hand and pull it up to my cheek. His skin is rough but it feels like silk against my face. "Don't leave me."

Daniel reaches behind him with his free hand and pulls a makeshift chair over next to my bed. "I'm not going anywhere."

Twenty-Three

A soft tapping sound interrupts the sleep I thought would never come. The first hint of pink sunlight shines in through the window, painting the room in scarlet hues. Daniel is at the table, hunched over and moving his hands along the top. Elizabeth is still snoring softly in the bunk next to mine.

I lie still for a minute to watch him. He came for me when everyone else ignored me. I pull the blanket up tighter under my chin and push the ugly pictures out of my head. That's my savior sitting at the kitchen table and I'm going to keep him.

Daniel looks up from whatever he's working on and smiles at me. It's not his wide, dimple-revealing smile. This one is more timid, less sure. He gets up from the table and slides into the chair he left by my bed. "Hi."

I force my mouth muscles into a smile and push myself into a sitting position. I want to stay curled up under the thin cover, but there isn't time to waste in my fight to save our family. I still need to convince Daniel to help me.

"Rebecca, I'm so sorry about last night."

I grab his hand and squeeze as hard as I can. This beautiful man came for me in the middle of the night and saved me from...from what could have happened. Yet here he sits, apologizing to me. "I should be the one saying sorry. I'm sorry I ran out like that. I'm sorry I—"

Daniel lays his free hand over my lips, barely touching his skin to mine. I want so badly to nuzzle my head into that hand and let his warmth wash over me, clearing away every awful thing that's happened since I set my feet on PIT soil.

"I watched you walk out that door and the minute it closed behind you I realized how much I stand to lose when it comes to you. I can't let that happen."

I want him to help me. I need him more than ever, but I can't coerce him into it. If Eric's betrayal taught me anything, it's that going with the flow out of a sense of obligation will only lead to disappointment for everyone. "What about Patrice? I can't let you pick me over your sister."

Daniel smiles, and this time his dimples are back. "You are amazing, but I'm not picking you over my sister." He takes both my hands in his, covering my fingers with comfort and warmth. "I'm choosing everyone over my sister. It's time the truth was revealed."

I squeeze his hand. We're so close our knees are touching. Even that's not enough. I want to lean into him and never let go, but I have to focus. "Does that mean you're going to help me hack into the Acceptance ceremony?"

"I want to show you something." Daniel stands up, still holding my hands, and pulls me over to the table.

"What are you messing with over…?" A flat, grey tablet rests on the rough wooden surface. "How did you get that? The guards confiscated our bags. We went back and checked; they took everything."

"You better sit down." He reaches over to another chair and pulls off a sandy burlap bag to make room for me.

"Molly's bag." I grab it from him, tracing a finger along the faded red stamp of a potato on the front. "Where did you get this? Daniel, what's going on?"

"Sit down, please." I flop down into the seat and rest my elbows on the table. Daniel flashes me a sheepish smile. "You brought two Noteboards out of the Admin building, but I only needed one. I could have packed both of them in our escape bags, but…"

"But what?"

"I should have said something, but I thought I was imagining things. Seeing Eric for the way I wanted to see him. I didn't trust him, so I came up with my own backup plan. I took Molly's bag and buried the extra Noteboard in it out by the fence. If everything went as planned, I'd dig it up at the last minute and take it with us. If not, well, it would be there if I needed it."

Daniel stares at me, waiting for a response. His forehead crinkles above his nose. He's worried I'll be mad, but I can barely think about the Noteboard. "Was I the only one who didn't think something was wrong with Eric?"

Daniel looks over my shoulder to Elizabeth's sleeping form. "Her too?"

I nod. "I spent more time with him than anyone. Why didn't I notice what you guys saw?"

"It's not your fault. You believe the best in people." He reaches over and takes my hand in his, but I don't hold it back.

"You mean I'm weak. Naïve Rebecca believes every word she hears. Bought into the Cardinal's lies hook, line, and sinker."

"Trusting people isn't a weakness." He lets go of my hand and leans back in the chair, arms crossed. "The fault is mine for not saying something while I still had the chance to make a difference."

"It's not too late to make a difference." I push the Noteboard closer to him. "What do you think?"

"I think you're half crazy," He says leaning back toward the table and winking at me. "And half genius. It's going to be a mad rush to get it done in time, but you're right. We need to stop hiding in here. People out there need to know what's going on."

"I need to know what's going on." I sit up straight in the chair and clasp my hands in front of me on the table. "You know how the Machine works, don't you?"

Daniel slumps down into the chair and nods his head. He stares at the top of the table, refusing to meet my eyes. "The Machine does exactly what the Cardinal says it does. It detects chemical signals in the brain and compares them to the general population. Complex algorithms determine if you have a propensity for crime. Anyone above a preset threshold fails. It isn't perfect, but it works most of the time."

Nothing he's said so far is that different from the basic understanding that most people back home assume. There's got to be more to it. He looks up and there's a hardness behind his eyes I haven't seen since the first time he told me about the escape plan. "Every year after age sixteen at your annual physical, the reader records the same information as the Machine. A secret panel reviews the information and any changes are reported. If at any point, the data indicates the likelihood of criminal activity has exceeded the threshold, action is taken to remove the threat from society."

"I've never heard of someone older than sixteen being taken to the PIT."

Daniel shakes his head. This can't be good. "Taking additional people to the PIT would be admitting the Machine isn't perfect. The Cardinal's entire hold on power is based on the Machine's perfection. People who exceed the threshold after passing their Acceptance suffer from deadly accidents, or undiagnosed heart disease. They don't come here. They die."

"This is why they don't monitor the cameras in here anymore, isn't it? The Cardinal needed the manpower to monitor the annual screenings and...and..." I can't say it. Murder innocent citizens.

Daniel just nods his head. I don't have to say it.

My hands shake. I'm afraid to ask any more questions, but I need to know the truth. "What about people like us?"

"It's not enough to remove criminals. The Cardinal decided about a decade ago that other, less desirable, citizens should be eliminated. Anyone who doesn't fit into his idea of perfection. People like Elizabeth and Constance couldn't be allowed to pollute the population with their differences. But when you change the rules, people start to notice. People who might question the rules are a danger. Not to society, but to the Cardinal, and his power. People like me. Like you."

Tears roll down my cheeks unrestrained. I'm not surprised by what he's telling me, but it doesn't hurt any less.

"Everything we do is recorded. The books we read at the library, letters we write to family and friends, English class assignments, all of it. They watch who you're friends with to see if you socialize within the appropriate class circle."

Cheryl. Sweet Cheryl who I loved like a sister was a contributing factor to my Rejection. How many other innocent actions sent me here? Our English teacher assigned an essay last year about what we wanted in an ideal spouse. I added a paragraph about my fears of not finding a husband before I turned twenty-one. There was even a line about feeling bad for the girls who were forced into a Compulsory marriage. My teacher circled that paragraph, but didn't add any notes. I got an A and assumed he was making note of a well-written paragraph. What if he was making note of an abnormal fear that raised alarms on my file? "They knew before I ever set foot on that stage that I would be Rejected. Didn't they?"

Daniel nods and sinks his forehead into his hands. "It's all part of the show. The public Rejection reminds all the good citizens how much they need the Cardinal and his perfect Machine to keep them safe."

The effort to stay still is too much and I stand up to walk the length of the room. My anger builds with each pounding step. "Who knows about this?"

"All the council members. That's how I found out. I was searching my dad's office for a book I wanted to borrow. He had some files on his desk and curiosity got the better of me."

"They know and they do nothing to stop it." My voice is sharper than I want it to be. I slow my pace and take a few deep breaths to get control of my heart rate. "Why?"

"They shut their eyes and close their ears to the truth. Because even though they know it's wrong, deep down, they're glad the Cardinal is 'cleaning up' society. And they know that their continued power hinges on the Cardinal maintaining his."

I pass by Elizabeth, still asleep in her bed. I wish I could be her and undo the conversation I've just had. My head is about to explode and despite my empty stomach I might be sick. I stride to the other side of the room and rest my head against the cool concrete of the wall.

"Do you hate me now?"

Daniel's words pull me back to the table. I grab both of his hands in mine and force him to look at me. "Why in the world would I hate you?"

"I knew. I knew about all of this, and I was just as bad as the cabinet members." His hands pull at my arms, urging me to understand. "I kept my mouth shut and pretended like I didn't know. I never wanted to tell you because I'm ashamed. You have every right to hate me."

"No one would have believed you. Who would take the ludicrous statement of a kid who wasn't even a full citizen yet seriously? There was nothing you could do then."

"I'm going to make it right." Daniel stands up, tugging me up with him.

"We'll make it right, together."

Daniel wraps his arms around my waist and I fall into him. My arms stretch around his back and soak in his strength and warmth. My head fits perfectly in the slight valley of his chest. I pull closer and Daniel rests his chin on top of my head. The soft thumping of his heart strips away any defense I had left guarding my own. I could stand like this with him all day.

"If you guys are done with your love fest, do you think we can get some breakfast?" I step back out of Daniel's embrace. Elizabeth is sitting on the side of her bunk, one eyebrow raised and a slight smirk stretched across her lips. She stands and winks once at Daniel, whose face is the same shade as the dark-rose-tinted light streaming through the window. "Of course, I can always go on ahead if you guys need a minute."

Daniel grabs the Noteboard and shoves it under a pillow. He heads out the door without a word, Elizabeth and I right behind him.

* * *

The dining hall is full of people talking and laughing. The improvements have boosted everyone's spirits. All of them sit around joking and eating their burnt oatmeal like nothing has changed. They have no idea how bad things are about to get.

"So what do we need in order to make this happen?" I push my half-finished bowl of oats away. No matter how long we stay here, I'll never get used to burnt oatmeal.

"The Noteboard we've got, but I'll need some cables to splice into the feed. And we'll need a camera." Daniel counts the items off on his fingers. "Once they set up their video site, I have to re-route the signal to a transmitter that I can turn on when we're ready to cut into the broadcast. It's a lot to get done in just a few days."

"Gosh, you make it sound so easy." Elizabeth takes another big bite of oatmeal and glares across the table at us.

"We could use your help." I lean in to keep my voice from carrying to the other people at our table. "We need to find a location to use as a backdrop that doesn't have the new and improved PIT makeover."

"No, I won't have any part in this and I don't think you should, either."

"How can you say that? If we don't stop them, Daniel will be on his own." I can't lose him now that we have an actual chance to be together.

"Better stuck on the other side of some stupid fence than locked away for months in Quarantine again, or worse." She slams her bowl down and pushes it away even though it isn't empty yet. "How many times do you think they'll let us thumb our noses at the Cardinal before they decide to remove the problem permanently?"

"Don't you think Molly would—?"

Elizabeth pounds her fist on the table and several people look over at us. "Leave Molly out of this."

"I just think—"

"Then stop thinking. You can leave me out of your plans." Elizabeth doesn't wait for another argument. She swings her legs over the bench and races out of the dining hall.

Daniel is as still as stone next to me. Is he going to follow her out and forget about the plan? I can't do this without him. I wait for him to get up, but he stays on the bench, eyes staring at the door Elizabeth disappeared through.

"Do you think we need to be worried about her giving us up?"

Daniel shakes his head. "No, she'd never betray us like that, but she's definitely not going to help. We should probably not talk about it around her too much."

"Right. Are you ready?" Daniel hasn't eaten much more of his breakfast than I have.

"Not really, but we don't have the time to wait for me to get there." He holds out his hand. "Let's go."

Twenty-Four

A huge rock in my stomach weighs down each step as we get closer to the southern edge of the PIT. If Eric told the other Cardinal guards about the old security building full of computer castoffs, our chances of finding everything we need are slim. Even before the recent cleanup, electronic equipment was a rare find in the cluttered alleys. Now, it's a near impossibility.

The outside of the security building looks the same as it did the last time we were here, but it's the inside that counts. Daniel and I both pause outside the door. If the building is cleared out, it's likely we'll never find what we need and our plan is ruined.

Daniel looks at me and I nod. I close my eyes when he pushes the door open so I can hold on to an extra few seconds of hope. "Sweet Cardinal."

I open my eyes and my legs collapse beneath me. Inside the room, every table, shelf and workbench is empty.

Completely cleared of the countless pieces of machinery that were essential to my happiness. We have nothing.

"No." I pound my fists against the hard-packed dirt floor of the building, ignoring the throbbing pain traveling from my bruised hands up my arms. "No, no, no!" Hot, angry tears prickle against my cheek. I use the dusty sleeve of my dress to wipe them away. The PIT doesn't get any more of my tears.

"Rebecca, I—"

"No." I stand up and push his hand away. The empty building isn't his fault, but I'm angry and Eric isn't here for me to yell at him. "Unless you have another buried burlap treasure, we're…we're screwed."

"Rebecca Jane Collins."

My hands shoot up to cover my mouth and I'm absolutely mortified. Never in my life have I used such foul language. My mother always said gutter language was for Rejects. A panicked giggle bubbles up from inside and slips between my fingers before I can stop it. What would she say to me now? "I'm sorry, I just… Wait a minute. How do you know my middle name? I never tell anyone."

"Oh, well…" Little lines form between Daniel's eyebrows and a light blush creeps up to redden the beautiful brown skin of his cheeks. I want to touch his face to see if it's warm. "I might have peeked when I was setting up your OneCard profile."

I hold out my hand palm up and curl my fingers. "Fair's fair. You have to tell me yours."

"I don't have one."

"Who doesn't have a middle name?" My hands migrate to my hips, and I squint my eyes in my very best 'you better not be lying' look.

"Honestly." Daniel holds his hands up as if I accused him of stealing. "It's a tradition in my family that the men don't have middle names."

"Then I guess you'll just have to tell me something else about yourself. Something I don't know about you."

Daniel's eyes flash wide for a second before a resolved calm steadies his face. He wipes his hands on the side of his pants before taking a step closer to me. "I have a secret." Another step closer. "One I've wanted to tell you for a while." Another step brings him within inches of me.

The small room was already a bit stuffy with the warmer spring air, but it's suddenly a hot box. My arms tingle from the remembered contact of the hug we shared this morning. I want to close the gap between us, but my feet are bolted to the floor and I'm afraid the slightest movement will collapse the tenuous hold I have on my ability to stand.

Daniel's hand reaches up and tucks a yellow curl behind my ear. "I think you're beautiful."

I open my mouth to say thank you, because that's what I'm supposed to say when someone gives me a compliment. Daniel slides his hand over and blocks my lips with a raised finger. "And not just because you have the kindest green eyes and a disarming smile that you share with anyone and everyone. You're stunningly beautiful because you never lose your ability to trust even after you've been cheated, and when something bad happens you worry about how it impacts everyone else first, and you did everything we asked you to, even though it made you unhappy."

Daniel dips his hand down under my chin and pulls it up until I'm staring right into the depths of his coal-dark eyes. I blink away the tears pooling in the bottom of my eyes. I don't want to miss a second of the way he's looking at me.

"We never asked what you wanted and I'm sorry about that. It was wrong to assume so much and I promise to never do that again. Which is why I need to ask you a question." His thumb strokes the side of my chin and I lean my head into his hand. "Would it be alright if I kiss you?"

I nod my head, because 'yes' doesn't feel potent enough for how much I want him to kiss me right now. Daniel fills the remaining distance between us, wraps his free arm around my waist, and bends his head down to match his lips with mine.

I kiss him back, not because I'm supposed to or because I don't want to hurt his feelings. I kiss him because I want to. Because I've wanted to for longer than I ever admitted to myself.

Daniel pulls me tighter until our bodies line up like the final piece of a puzzle sliding into place. My arms wrap around his neck and I let go of the stress from the past twenty-four hours. His lips are warm and soft against mine.

This is nothing like the only other kiss I have to compare it to.

My first kiss on the roof. His mouth was hard against mine, demanding more than I could give him. Daniel's kiss is tentative, inviting. Kissing Daniel is like coming home, and his arm wrapped around my waist is the most natural thing on earth.

His hand traces the line of my jaw from the bottom of my ear to the tip of my chin. His mouth pulls away from mine and I whimper a protest. His lips trace the same line as his finger and my protest turns to a moan I've never made before. A shiver runs across my shoulder blades despite the overwhelming warmth of the room.

Daniel's mouth moves from my chin down to the side of my neck and I tilt my head to invite him to more of my skin. His fingers move up and down my spine, stoking the fire growing in the pit of my belly.

Warm lips find mine again and this time I'm the one demanding more, pushing my lips into his, pushing to take in more of him. His tongue dips out to slide along my bottom lip and I open my mouth to him. Daniel's body hardens against mine and he spins me around until my back is pressed up against the cool concrete wall. My body hums like a live wire. He wants me as much as I want him. As much as I need him.

This is what was missing all those months, what I tried to pretend I had with Eric. I can almost laugh at how ridiculous it was. A chaste kiss on the cheek and a hug that lingered just longer than my father would have approved of. We were children playing a game of love.

But now I know it can't be faked. You can't light a candle and pretend it's a furnace. This is what I'm fighting to protect. I won't let the Cardinal have this.

Daniel pulls back slightly and kisses one eyelid, then the other before leaving the lightest of kisses on my lips. We lean against the wall for a minute, our foreheads pressed together, while we bring our breathing back down to normal speeds. His warm hands on the side of my face have a calming effect.

"You have no idea how long I've wanted to do that." Daniel's face is still so close to mine that the heat of his words tickles my nose.

I laugh at the absurdity of the situation. "Probably about as long as I've been pretending I didn't want you to."

Daniel pulls back to match his dark-brown eyes with mine, and then we're both laughing. Because it's easier to laugh than cry. Because all this time we wasted not being together and we might only have days left before the Cardinal separates us for good, or worse.

Daniel takes my hand and pulls me outside into the blinding noon sun. "I need to show you something."

We walk in silence along the edge of the fence. It's strange how I can experience two completely opposite emotions at the same time. Part of my heart sings with Daniel's hand around mine, his thumb rubbing soft circles along the top of my skin. But my happiness isn't complete. We don't have any of the equipment Daniel needs to hack the Acceptance feed and with the old security room empty I have no idea if we'll ever find it.

A few rows away from the security building Daniel stops outside of one of the countless rundown shacks that make up the edge of the PIT. It looks the same as any of the others except for a dingy scrap of fabric tied around the frame of a busted window. Inside, the stench of rot is suffocating. It doesn't take long to see why. The back corner is stacked to the ceiling with moldy mattresses.

I choke back a gag and use my fingers to pinch off my nose. My voice comes out weak and nasally. "What are we doing in here?"

"Why don't you wait outside? This will only take a minute."

I step back out and watch Daniel from the safety of the broken window. Using the neck of his shirt as a defense against the odor, he goes to work pulling mattresses off the pile. When the right side of the mound is moved away, he reaches back into the corner and pulls out a huge box.

"What is that?"

Daniel doesn't stop to show me. He runs to the empty building next door and calls over his shoulder, "Not out in the open."

I catch up to him just as he pulls a huge cable out of the box and sets it on the ground next to where he's crouched over the mystery box. "Did you just pull another burlap bag trick?"

Daniel pats the floor next to him and continues to pull out random items, spreading them out around him. "The day we left, you went for a walk with Eric." He pauses to inspect a small switch, but I keep my mouth shut. This is a story I want to hear.

"I was so mad, at both of you."

"What? Why?"

Daniel sets the switch down on a growing pile next to him and stops to look at me. "I guess that's not fair. Maybe

I was just mad at the situation. Mad that you were going to marry Eric, even though I could tell you didn't want to, despite what you said. And furious that Eric would get to marry you, even though it was clear he didn't see you for the amazing woman you are."

I grab Daniel's hand and wish I could go back in time and erase so many things. All that time I spent trying not to think about him, pretending it didn't hurt to see him with Elizabeth. To know he felt the same way, hid the same pain. Such a waste.

"I needed to get away and I knew no one would bother me out in the security building. I wasn't planning on anything, but once I got inside, I realized it wouldn't hurt to shore up my back-up plan. The Noteboard was already buried out at the fence, but having some spare equipment would be handy as well."

"So do you have the equipment we need?"

Daniel goes back to sorting through the box, laying everything into one of two piles. "I have no idea. There wasn't time to be picky so I grabbed a box and loaded it up with anything that didn't look broken. The stinkhouse was a bit of good luck. Unlikely anyone would bother combing through there for loot."

I reach into the box and pull out a bulky rectangle with a cracked digital display on one side. All the wires and gizmos are a mystery to me, but this was my idea and I feel like I should help. "So what exactly are we looking for?"

Daniel pauses in his search, but before he can give me a description of what we need, he snatches the object out of my hand and kisses me hard on the mouth. "This is what we're looking for."

My head is a little woozy from his unexpected kiss, but I gather my thoughts enough to form words. "What is it?"

"This is a transmitter. We'll use it to broadcast our own signal over the one being used by the ceremony." Daniel stands up and brushes off the back of his pants before offering me a hand up.

"What about a camera?"

"I'll get the camera tonight." Daniel stuffs the transmitter into his full pockets and takes my hand to head back home.

"But where are you going to get one?"

"I have my choice, seeing as how there are two right outside the Admin building."

I stop walking and his hand tugs against my arm. "No, no way. It's too dangerous. There are guards all over the PIT right now. We can't risk it."

Daniel turns around and brings both my hands up to his lips. "I have to. We need a camera."

"I just got you. I can't lose you now."

"And that's why I have to get the camera. We have to do this, Rebecca. You were right. Getting the truth out is our only chance at stopping the Cardinal in his tracks."

"Then I'll help you."

"No," he says pulling my hands down and lowering his face till it's even with mine. "It's enough to put me at risk. We don't need both of us in danger."

"Going alone is asking for trouble. I can help keep a lookout. Make sure no one catches you off guard."

"Rebecca—"

"I'm going, it's final. This was my idea and I'm making an executive decision. Let's go get Elizabeth for lunch and then get back to the bunkhouse. We need to make a plan if we're going out tonight."

Daniel crosses his arms and gives me his dimple smile. "Just out of curiosity, when did you decide to become Miss Take Charge?"

"When the Cardinal decided to mess with my family." I cross my arms to match his pose. "Is that a problem?"

Daniel throws his hands up, palms out. "Nope, no problem here." I catch the smallest of smirks on his face as he turns around.

I loop my arm through his and we walk back to our home.

Twenty-Five

"I think our best bet is to go right before dawn. The moon will be at its lowest. It makes it harder to remove the camera, but it also gives us the most cover." Daniel draws another line in the dirt next to our bunkhouse to mark the final road leading to the courtyard and then the Admin building.

"Fine," I smudge out a little 'x' on the diagram with my toe. "But I'm not waiting all the way over by the wash house. I won't be able to give you any real warning time and besides, it stinks."

"Any closer and your warning will have to be run."

"Not if I get up on the dining hall roof. I'll be able to see everything going on in the courtyard and several alleys over. I can give you plenty of notice to take cover and the guards are never going to check the rooftops so I'm perfectly safe." I take the stick and mark an 'x' on the square he's drawn to indicate the dining hall. "I'm here, you're right next door at the Admin building, and we're both home before the sun rises."

"And if something goes wrong?"

"Then I promise to stay on the roof until it's safe to come down and then run like a good girl back to the bunkhouse."

Daniel takes the stick back and uses his foot to wipe away our drawing. "This isn't a game, Rebecca."

"I know." I step across the smeared picture and wrap my arms around his waist. My forehead pushes against his chest. "But it's easier if I don't think about how risky this is. If it's just a quick trip to the Admin building, I can pretend there's no risk of losing you."

Daniel links his hands behind my back. "Fair enough."

"I'm going to dinner." Elizabeth steps around the corner of the house. "If you guys can bear the separation, you can come with me."

Her mood hasn't improved any throughout the day. Daniel and I tried to explain what our plan is, but she won't even stay in the bunkhouse if we're talking about it. I had hoped when we came back with the transmitter she might change her mind, but that backfired when we told her about tonight's mission to steal the camera.

The dining hall is packed and everyone is still in high spirits about the general improvements. Faces through the crowd are smiling and laughing as if the Cardinal announced a holiday, complete with cake.

"Is it just me," Daniel says, sliding onto the bench, a bowl of greasy rice in hand, "or does everyone seem a little too excited about some cleaned up garbage?"

"I was thinking the same thing." I poke a finger into the rice and prepare myself for the first awful bite.

"You two stay here for a minute. I'm going to do a little investigation." Daniel stands back up, a casual smile on his face as he walks over to a group of boisterous men a few tables away. One of them must be telling a joke, because on cue the whole table breaks out into gales of laughter, Daniel included.

He sits down and joins in the conversation, his face never betraying the true intention of his social visit. Daniel leans in to say something and everyone else instantly turns to more smiles and exaggerated arm movements. A wide smile breaks out on Daniel's face, but the little lines above his nose give away the real concern hidden behind his jovial expression.

Daniel stands and shakes hands with one of the men, before walking a bit too quickly back to where Elizabeth and I wait. He sits down and the easy smile he wore just moments ago is gone without a trace.

"The new fence posts have finally caught everyone's attention."

"Then why does everyone look so happy?" I give up on the bowl of rice. "I expected rioting in the street or at least an angry mob."

Daniel pushes the bowl back at me. "You need to eat." He takes a bite from his own bowl to prove the point. "They don't know the poles are for a fence. The workers told them the Cardinal ordered construction of new buildings throughout the PIT."

My bowl is halfway to my mouth, but I set it back down at Daniel's words. "You're kidding. So they think what? The Cardinal decided we deserve new bunkhouses?"

Daniel pinches the bridge of his nose with his thumb and index finger. "That's exactly what they think. The men I spoke to were all bragging about the workers letting them help hold the poles while they poured the cement."

"So what?" Elizabeth says, wiping her mouth with the back of her hand. "So they spend the next few days on cloud nine until the fence goes up. They'll be mad and then they'll move on like the rest of us." She stands up and marches away from the table.

"I'll see you back at the bunk." I stand up and push through the crowded room to follow her.

Outside, a steady stream of people are making their way to dinner, but I finally spot her at the edge of the courtyard. "Elizabeth, wait for me." If she hears me, I can't tell. I run to catch up with her. "Wait a minute; I want to talk to you."

Elizabeth whips around, her hands on her hips. "What do you want?"

Her glare stops me a few feet away. "I thought we moved past the place where you hate me?"

"We did, until you convinced Daniel to go along with this ridiculous plan." She turns to walk away again, but I hook her by the elbow and force her to stay and talk to me.

"This is our only chance of staying together."

"All you're doing is increasing your chances of ending up in Quarantine again." She jerks her arm back out of my hand. "I'm warning you. If Daniel gets caught tonight, it'd be best for you to not even bother coming back to the bunk. We'll be done."

I stand in the middle of the empty alley and watch her sink into the crowd. So much for not feeling the pressure of tonight's mission.

* * *

Our heavy footsteps are the only sound interrupting the still night. There are only a few hours until sunrise, so we have to move fast. Daniel leads me around the edge of the courtyard, darting from shadow to shadow until we reach the back of the dining hall.

"Don't you want to go over the hand signals one more time?" Daniel weaves his fingers together to create a foothold.

"Stop stalling and help me up." I put one foot into his hands and use the boost to reach the top of the dumpster. From there I have to jump up to catch the ledge of the roof. A year ago, I wouldn't have had the strength to pull myself up, but months in the PIT have changed me in more ways than one.

Daniels stands on the ground ready to catch me if I slip. I grab the ledge and, in a very unladylike move, swing my legs up onto the roof.

Crouching down to keep a low profile, I crawl to all four corners and make sure no one is around. Rushing to the back, I lean over the edge and give Daniel a quick thumbs-up. He grins back at me, his dark face almost disappearing in the night.

I follow his movements to the front of the Admin building. Using one of our chairs from the bunkhouse, he climbs up toward the inactive camera and works to loosen the first screw. Satisfied that he's alright for the moment, I make my first round.

My knees are raw after only a few yards, but I can't risk standing up and giving away my position. At the front of the building I scan the courtyard and darkened alleys beyond for any sign of movement. Nothing stirs so I head back along the southern side of the building to check on Daniel's progress.

He's moving faster than I thought he would. The camera is already hanging at an odd angle from the missing screws. He has to be at least halfway done.

It's tempting to sit and watch him work, but I need to stay alert if I want to keep him safe tonight. I start another circuit along the northern wall toward front of the building again. I bet the view of the sunrise is amazing from up here, but Daniel and I need to be long gone well before that happens. Still no movement in the courtyard. I keep moving, ignoring the pain in my knees.

A scuffing noise on the ground stops me mid-crawl. It could be just Daniel finishing up with the camera, but I need to be sure. I flatten my belly to the roof and scoot until my face is right at the edge of the building. My eyes scan every inch of ground in front of me, searching for a movement to match the noise.

The courtyard is empty and quiet. I must have imagined the sound. I scoot back from the edge, but stop when the ripple of a shadow catches my eye. Then another, and from an alley, two red-uniformed workers walk into the courtyard.

In a fraction of a second I'm up, half running, half crouching back toward the rear of the building where Daniel is still working to remove the camera. I press my lips together the way Daniel showed me and blow out a hard puff of air. The squeaking noise is just loud enough to get his attention.

I roll my fingers around each other, point toward the courtyard and hold up two fingers. Thank the stars Daniel forced me to learn a few quick hand signals after dinner tonight.

Daniel nods, but doesn't stop working. I puff out another breath of air, but he doesn't even look at me this time. Just nods and moves his hands to take off another screw.

Scraping off most of the skin on my knees, I speed crawl back to the front of the building. The workers are halfway across the courtyard now and clearly headed for the Admin building. Judging by their pace, Daniel has just over a minute to get out of there.

I race back to the building, cramps shooting up my side, to check on Daniel's progress. The camera is down and he's using the sharpened edge of a clamp he found to clip the wires. I let out two quick squeaks of air. This is supposed to be our 'you're out of time so get out of there' signal but Daniel keeps working.

The men's voices carry up to my spot on the roof. Daniel's shoulders tense. He hears them, too. I can't whistle again without the men hearing me, but Daniel doesn't need me to tell him he has to get out of there.

"Two more days and we can get back to our regular routine."

"I can't wait. This fence is a bear to put up and the night shift is not helping my digestive system."

"What are you talking about?"

"My wife's dinners aren't that great fresh. Reheated, they're plain awful."

The men laugh and the sound is way too close to be comfortable. Any second they'll come around the corner of the dining hall and see Daniel.

"Hey man, hold up a minute?"

Daniel finally has the camera disconnected from the wall, but he's too late. He freezes on the chair, clutching the stolen equipment to his chest. I stare at his face and try to memorize every line, knowing this might be the last time I ever see him.

"My shoe's untied. Wait for me."

I exhale a silent breath. Daniel's been given a last-second reprieve, but only if he can move it. He jumps down off the chair, picks it up with one hand, and dashes across the empty space between the Admin building and the dining hall. Moving quickly and silently, he throws the chair up onto the dumpster and shoves the camera down between two black bags.

"Let's get out of here."

There isn't time to get him up on the roof. He smiles up at me, winks, and wriggles down into the garbage, pulling bags of rotten potato peels over his head.

"I hear the day shift is in charge of the actual divide." I watch as the pair of men walk over to the Admin building door. One of them looks around and I'm panicked that he heard Daniel getting into the dumpster. Instead of moving toward our building to investigate, he reaches into the pocket of his uniform and pulls out a pack of contraband cigarettes.

The two of them sit down on the dusty ground and light the ends of the tobacco for a post-shift smoke.

"Yeah, I'm glad I won't be here for that. I heard they're gonna corral all the pit-stains into the courtyard and make them watch the entire Acceptance ceremony. And while they're all standing there, trying to catch glimpses of freedom, the day shift will finish off the fence." He takes a long drag from the grey stick and exhales slowly, letting the smoke curl up into little puffs in the sky. "When the show's over, they'll separate everyone out."

His partner nods his head like this is a perfect plan and exhales his own, less showy, puff of smoke. He can't be more than a year or two past Assignment. "Here's what I don't get, man. Why bother with all that?"

The older man spits into the dirt by his feet and grins at him. "You weren't here last summer or you wouldn't be asking a question like that. Some of these pieces of garbage got it into their heads they were too good for the PIT. Made an escape attempt out by the eastern fence. They would have made it if Dunstan hadn't turned them in."

The younger man whistles and lets out a string of curse words that would make even Elizabeth blush.

"Exactly. Word is the Cardinal felt the PIT had gone soft. He switched out all the guards and sent down orders to build the fence. That'll teach 'em to test the generosity of the Cardinal. It's not punishment enough, if you ask me." He digs the stubby end of his cigarette into the dirt and tucks what's left into his pocket.

"Let's go. I need to get a shower and wash this PIT filth off." The two men stand and swipe their cards to get in the building. The lingering smell of tobacco is the only evidence they were there.

I count to one hundred and dangle my legs over the side of the roof, landing with a dull thud on the lid of a dumpster. Daniel pushes up on the bags over him and climbs out to help me down over the edge.

Neither of us says a word as he hands me the camera and reaches in to grab our chair. The sun will be up any minute. We hustle back across the courtyard and through the maze of neat and tidy alleys until we reach the bunkhouse. Daniel's hand pauses on the door and he looks back at me. "Not a word to Elizabeth."

I nod my head. We won't be telling Elizabeth that everything changes in two days because of us.

Twenty-Six

Only two days left. How in the world are we going to make this work? I focused so much of my effort yesterday on the logistics of hacking into the feed that I didn't give any thought to what we'll actually say once we do it.

I've been running through speeches in my head all day, pacing up and down the room while Daniel works on connecting the camera to the transmitter. Everything I come up with sounds ridiculous.

Who's going to believe Daniel and me, standing in front of the camera, swearing we aren't criminals after we hack into the Acceptance ceremony feed? It's crazy. I'm crazy and I'm going to get us killed.

"Rebecca, your pacing is driving me nuts."

"I know. I'm sorry." I pull out a chair and join Daniel at the table. "I can't come up with a viable scenario in which the two of us convince the entire population of the

Territories that the Cardinal is lying to them about who gets sent here."

Daniel sets down his tools and takes both of my hands in his. "This is why the Cardinal sent you here. Because you're smart and you know what to say to make people believe you. You are going to figure this out."

"Maybe if I had another month or a week. I'll never get it by tomorrow."

"Okay, that's it. Too much time cooped up in the bunkhouse." He pulls me up and marches me over to the door, practically shoving me out into the sunlight. "Go for a walk and clear your head." Daniel bends down and gives me a quick kiss. "Just don't go too far." He ducks back inside and pulls the door closed in my face.

"Great. A walk. Because the PIT is so inspiring." I mutter the words under my breath, but Daniel can't hear me anyway.

I set off down the alley, not really caring which direction I walk in. Every street looks the same and none of them hold the answers to how I'm supposed to change things.

Lots of people are out today enjoying the warm sunshine before summer takes over and it's hot enough to roast a chicken outside. I don't really want to be around others right now, so I duck down a smaller alley and head into a deeper part of the PIT I don't normally come to.

I don't think I've been back this way since Eric and I were searching our grid for escape supplies. That was a lifetime ago, but nothing has changed. A small spot of yellow from an early weed separates one bunkhouse from another.

Dandelions! Two people might not say much, but four people begin to tell a story. I spin around in a circle to orient myself. I think her bunk is a few alleys over. I dash down the clear paths and hope she's home. If I can convince Constance and Thomas to work with us, we might actually stand a chance.

There's only one bunkhouse on the street with curtains hanging in the window. I rush to the door and knock hard three times.

Please be home. Constance opens the door and I flash the biggest smile I can. "Rebecca, I thought we'd seen the last of you. Come in."

Inside her house, not much has changed. The same rectangle door-table still dominates the room, though she's managed to get ahold of enough fabric to make a new blanket for their bed.

"Sit, sit. I've heard rumors about your little adventure last summer, but no one seems to have any real details. But here you are after I heard you were dead from a crotchety old gossip two roads over."

Last summer's disaster is the last topic I want to talk about, but I need Constance to trust me. "Well, I'm not dead. I spent a bunch of months in Quarantine when the guards caught us trying to escape."

"Hmm…so that part is true, then. Though I did hear that one of the girls in your group didn't make it." I don't think Constance is trying to be mean. Death is a regular part of the PIT, but Molly's death is still painful.

"Molly, she was my friend. She died trying to protect us so we could try to get out."

"I'm sorry." Constance reaches across the table and lays one of her hands on top of mine. "Really, I mean that. No one should have to watch a friend die."

I nod my head. It's now or never. "I'm hoping Molly didn't die in vain."

Constance leans back, away from the table. "You aren't going to try to escape again, are you? The PIT is crawling with guards these days."

"No, leaving isn't an option. But there's still a way to get out."

"What are you talking about?"

I have to trust her. She might go straight to a guard the minute I walk out the door, but I refuse to believe it. Not everyone lives like Eric, getting ahead by backstabbing the people who trust him. "We want to tell people what's really going on in here, who the Cardinal sends to the PIT. Tomorrow, during the Acceptance ceremony, we're going to hack into the feed and tell people the truth." I grab for her hand and squeeze it too tight. "I want you and Thomas to join me. Tell the Territories your story."

Constance jerks her hand away from me. "Are you crazy?" She stands and walks in a slow circle next to the table. "Even if you could do it, who would believe you?"

"No one would believe me, but the more of us willing to stand up and tell the truth the more plausible our story."

"Why would I do this?" She stops pacing and sets both hands down on the table. "Why would *you* do this? You realize the minute they see what's happening the guards are going to track you down. You'll be lucky if they send you to Quarantine. All of this because your friend died?"

"No, all of this to keep from losing what little I have left." I push up from the table and meet her gaze. "Those posts aren't going up so the Cardinal can build us new bunkhouses. Tomorrow morning, while we're all standing around watching the ceremony, they're going to put up a fence running down the middle of the PIT. They're going to separate us, women on one side, men on the other."

Constance stares at me, her eyes blinking in rapid-fire succession while the rest of her body sits frozen at the table.

"Thomas," she whispers and runs to the door, flinging it open and running out into the street. Her hands claw at her head while she swings her face from side to side, looking for the husband she's about to lose.

Without a word, she marches back into the house, slams the door behind her and walks over to the bed. She pulls the corners of the blanket free from where she's tucked them in. I follow her around the room while she collects random objects and piles them up in the middle of the blanket.

I grab her arm when she picks up the cracked bowl from their makeshift washroom and sets it on the blanket with the rest of their worldly possessions. "What are you doing?"

"What does it look like I'm doing? I have to get everything packed. As soon as Thomas gets back we have to get out of here, out to the edge where no one ever goes. We can hide there for a few days until everything is set."

"You can't do that. Don't you think they'll notice one of you living on the wrong side of the fence? You'll have to leave the bunk for food eventually."

"We'll have to make it work," she says, tying up two corners of the blanket. "One of us will have to sneak food. We'll make do with half portions."

"Constance—"

"Enough." Her shout echoes around the tiny room. "I can't lose him. I won't." Constance grabs my hand, walks me to the door and pushes me out. "Thank you for telling me about the fence. You secret is safe with me, but I can't help you."

Constance slams the door shut and I'm left standing alone outside the home of the one person capable of making this work.

Twenty-Seven

I throw open the door of our bunkhouse. It bangs against the wall and sends dust from the ceiling floating down to coat everything in the room. I don't care. My emotions cycled between despair and anger the whole walk back from Constance's house and settled on anger when I reached the door.

"Hey, what gives?" Elizabeth stands in the middle of the room shaking dirt out of her dark, spiky hair.

"Where's Daniel?"

"He went out to the courtyard to look at the setup for tomorrow's broadcast." Her finger points off in some vague direction and the sour expression on her face shows exactly how she still feels about our now-doomed plan. "Now, you want to tell me what's got you all riled up?"

I storm across the room until I'm right in front of her, lifted on to my toes so I can look her in the eyes. "Riled up? I'll tell you all about it, Elizabeth Dunstan."

"Don't call me that. That's not who I am anymore."

"No? What should I call you?" My index finger points into her chest with each word, pushing her into a fight I'm itching to have. "Coward? Quitter?"

Elizabeth's lips transform into a thin line and her eyebrows pull down into a sharp 'V'. I wanted a fight and now I have one. "You little…" She raises one fist, but shakes it back down. "After everything I've done, all the risks I took for you."

"But when it counts the most you sit in here and pretend everything's fine." I grab her hands and pull them up to my chest. "They're going to take Daniel away from us tomorrow. Don't you care?"

"Of course, I care," she says, pulling out of my grip and walking toward our one window. "I may not love Daniel the same way you do, but that doesn't mean the idea of losing him doesn't hurt me. He's my brother more than Eric ever was."

"You're right, I do love him and so do you. So why won't you fight to keep him?" I need something to throw, but we really don't have anything. I grab a pillow off the bunk next to me and hurl it at her head.

Elizabeth grabs the pillow out of the air and swings it into my chest. "I'm fighting to keep him alive, you stupid" — pillow shot to my right side—"idiotic"—pillow shot to my left side—"little girl!" Pillow slam on top of my head. She lets the pillow fall to the floor and drops down onto a bed. "I can't lose anyone else."

"And what about Daniel? Don't you care that he's going to be all alone over there? Do you think that makes him safe?"

"No, I just—"

"He's going to be in danger every day with no one to watch his back." The fight is drained out of me, and I sink down onto the bed next to her. "I can almost understand why Constance doesn't want to help me, but you have a stake—"

"What does Constance have to do with this?"

"I went to talk to her. I thought if she knew what was going to happen she might be willing to help. If she and Thomas would tell their stories, that would make four of us. It's not a lot, but it might be enough."

"She said no?"

I shake my head. "She thinks they can hide out and stay together."

"It won't work. The guards will find them."

"Of course they will. But she doesn't get that." I kneel down in front of Elizabeth, ready to play the last card I have. My voice is barely more than a whisper. "She's never seen how far the guards are willing to go."

"Don't go there."

"Why not? Do you think you're the only one who cared about Molly? Do you think her sacrifice didn't touch all of us?"

Elizabeth stands up, pushing past me, but I'm not ready to give up yet. "It was dark that night, but not so dark I didn't see what she did. That guard was going to club you. Molly ran out from our hiding spot on a broken leg and blocked you."

"She shouldn't have done that." Her voice is gravelly, but her back is to me so I can't see her face.

"Maybe not, but she did." I walk up behind her, my hand raised, but I stop myself from resting it on her shoulder. "She stood up so the rest of us could escape. She had to know the odds of getting out were against us with all those guards, but that didn't stop her from giving everything she could to give us a chance."

"I can't."

I've never heard Elizabeth admit defeat to anything and I'm not about to let her start now. "You can't, or you won't?"

Elizabeth turns to face me, a hardness behind her eyes. "I have to go."

"Elizabeth, wait." My words don't slow her down. She's out the door before I can even try to stop her.

This is what I get for trying to take control of my world for once, everything falling apart around me. I sit down at the table and wait. There's nothing left for me to do. I still don't know what I'm going to say tomorrow, but I don't think it matters anymore. I don't know how I ever expected this to work. And now I've wasted my last few days with Daniel and alienated the one person that could have helped me after the fence goes up.

The door squeaks open and startles me out of my sulk. Daniel is back from checking out the broadcast setup.

"Good, you're here." He lifts up the mattress from one of the bunks and takes out the Noteboard and video camera. "I want to run these out to the stinky-mattress building during dinner. Most people will be in the dining hall and the workers should be on break so it should be clear."

"I don't think we should go."

"Do you think it will be safer at night?" Daniel sets the equipment on the table and sits down with me. "I'm worried that with everything going down tomorrow, they might have extra guards out tonight to protect the broadcast area from vandalism."

"No, I don't think tonight is a better plan. I don't think anyone should be asking my opinion and we're both crazy for thinking this will work." I get up from the table and walk to a bed so I don't have to look him in the eye. "I don't think we should go at all."

"Hey," he says, following me to the bed. "Want to tell me what crushed your soul?"

"Elizabeth hates me and stormed out of here, because all I have is some half-thought-out plan that will probably end up as a great big disaster and just might get us killed. Not to mention Constance thinks the whole thing is crazy without even the slimmest chance of success and I'm beginning to agree with her." I tell him about Constance's plan to hide out until after the fence goes up. I grab his hands, hoping to absorb some of his strength. "Maybe that's what we should do, too."

Daniel squeezes my hand and brushes a curl out of my face. "Is that really what you think we should do?"

"I wish you would stop asking my opinion. Haven't I made it clear that I make horrible decisions on my own? Honestly, do you really think this is going to work, because nothing else I've done has? I told Eric how I really felt and it made him turn us in to the guards. Then I come up with this crazy plan that's going to get us both killed."

"I don't see it that way. You told Eric the truth. He made a bad decision all by himself. And that's what your plan is all about; telling the truth. Maybe it will work, maybe it won't, but we're doing something. Instead of sitting around and letting the Cardinal lie to everyone, you're going to fight back. Some people will react like Eric and make bad decisions, but some people will hear you and start looking for their own truth."

"But we both know what will happen when the guards track our signal and shut us down."

Daniel takes my face in his hands. "We both know what might happen, but that's a risk I'm willing to take. I'm not going to hide like I've done something wrong."

"I don't want to lose you."

"You can't lose something that's a part of you." Daniel tilts my face up and leans in until his lips are pressed to mine, taking my mind off all the uncertainties that tomorrow will bring.

Daniel leans back and ends the kiss too soon. As much as I'd love nothing more than to spend every minute we have left together sitting here soaking him in, we still have work to do.

Daniel grabs the camera and sticks it in his pocket before handing me the Noteboard. "I want to keep these separate just in case. You'll need to keep that out of sight."

"I don't have pockets. Where am I supposed to put it?"

The smirk on his face tells me exactly where it needs to go. "I'm afraid down your dress is the only option."

"Of course." Nothing says high class like smuggling a Noteboard in your bodice. I turn my back to him. "I need you to undo a few buttons so I can get it down the front."

It's my turn to smirk as Daniel fumbles with the buttons at the back of my dress. The tips of his fingers brush down my spine sending tingles along my arms. My face is on fire, but at least he can't see it. I shove the computer down to rest against my stomach and wait for him to redo my buttons.

Daniel finishes the last button, brushes his hands along my shoulders and places a single kiss on the back of my neck. My legs are having a hard time holding me up. I hate the PIT for letting me finally find love only to rip it away again. We have to make this work.

Daniel takes my hand and we walk out the door.

He's right about this being the perfect time. Everyone is making their way to the dining hall and no one notices the two of us walking in the other direction. A few blocks from our bunk, the cleaned up version of the PIT fades away to reveal rundown buildings where the garbage has crept back in. It's just a short walk to our new headquarters.

Overly loud laughter stops our silent walk only a few streets away from the stinky bunk. None of the prisoners have a reason to laugh that hard. It can only be guards or workers. Their boisterous voices get louder but there isn't anywhere for us to hide. We don't need a bunch of guards wondering what we're doing out here instead of eating dinner.

Daniel shoves me up against the side of a mostly collapsed building and presses his body up against mine. His head bends sharply and he whispers, "Kiss me."

I don't hesitate to lift my face to his, but this isn't like our other kisses. We press our lips together but neither of us can relax or enjoy the moment. If we get caught with this equipment the plan is ended before it even gets started.

The voices get louder and I grip the front of Daniel's shirt like a drowning woman clinging to a life preserver. They come up along the side of us, their eyes burning holes into the side of my head. Daniel's hands cut into my waist and his shoulders press farther into me as if he's trying to hide me completely.

I want to yell at them, tell them to keep moving, but I bite back the words and chant *go away* over and over in my head.

A harsh voice barks, much too close for comfort. "Enjoy it while you can, trash." They laugh, it must be half-a-dozen different voices, but no one moves to stop us. Their cackles fade with their pounding footsteps off to terrorize someone else. Daniel and I hold our pose until we're certain we're alone.

Daniel straightens up, but I pull him back to me. We need to keep moving, but I need a moment for him to really hold me because in his arms I can pretend everything is fine and our lives aren't in danger. He wraps his arms around me and rests his chin on the top of my head until I stop shaking.

"Almost there, okay?"

I nod and relax my hold on him. He takes my hand again and we walk the last few blocks to the deserted building where we'll make our last stand. Inside Daniel helps me with my dress again and we hide the camera and Noteboard behind the stack of mattresses. It's the best we can do to keep them safe until tomorrow.

In the dining hall, most people are already done with dinner. The masses head back to their bunks or wherever else people go in the PIT to stay out of or get into trouble. I'm jealous of their ignorance. Without any idea what's coming, tonight will be just like any other night.

I've checked every table, but Elizabeth isn't here. Daniel catches me looking around for her. "I'm sure she already ate. It's late."

"Yeah," I say after swallowing a mouthful of weak broth. "I guess she's already back at the bunkhouse."

Elizabeth isn't back at the bunk. Daniel makes a quick check of the surrounding blocks before it gets too dark, but she isn't anywhere nearby.

"She was really mad at me, but I never thought she wouldn't come back." I sit up from where my head is buried in my arms on the table top. "You don't think something happened to her?"

"No. Not again." I can't tell if he's telling me nothing happened or pleading that it didn't. Daniel opens the door and looks out one more time in the growing darkness.

I walk up behind him, adding my eyes to the search, but there's nothing to see. Going out to find her would be useless. She could be anywhere. "Wherever she is, I hope she knows what she's doing."

“Me, too.” Daniel joins me at the table and we sit silently, holding hands across the rough wood surface. There’s really only one thing to talk about and it’s the last thing I want to discuss on what could be our final night together.

The sun kisses the horizon and the darkened room is bathed in shades of red that make everything look sinister. It falls below the surface and the light in the room fades until I can’t even see Daniel’s face a few feet away.

“Tomorrow’s a big day,” he says, his chair scraping against the floor as he stands up. “We should get some sleep.” Still holding my hand, Daniel guides me toward him for a goodnight kiss.

Pressed up against him, his lips greedy for mine, I try not to think about how few kisses we might have left. Instead I wrap my arms around his neck and hold on tight. His hands pull against the small of my back, drawing me in even closer.

This is what I need. A lifetime of these moments. Of standing in the dark in our fake kitchen and pretending like right outside our door is a normal world where people don’t get sent to the PIT for knowing the wrong things or questioning the actions of our leaders. Inside this world our time would be measured in decades, not hours, and tomorrow wouldn’t feel like the end of everything.

But we can’t live in that world, not yet, and maybe not ever. Daniel pulls away and I grudgingly let go. We stumble to opposite sides of the room and the squeak of bedsprings is the only sound.

I close my eyes, but sleep is out of the question. I can't relax. I can hardly breathe. A weight like a boulder crushes my chest. This hurt is almost enough to wish I'd stuck to the original plan and tucked away the feelings I had for Daniel. Almost. Now that I've known that kind of love, I don't know that I would give it up. Even if it meant never knowing this kind of pain.

I want to be strong for him, but that's not who I am, no matter how Daniel sees me. The day I was Rejected, I thought that was the worst pain a person could feel. Then Quarantine numbed me from feeling anything and I thought that numbness and lack of feeling was the worst hurt imaginable. But I was wrong. It's not the pain of experience, but the death of a chance for experience that hurts the most.

I bite back the tears for as long as I can, but the tightness builds until I can't hold them in any longer. I suck in a huge breath and a single wet sob escapes in the exhale before I can pull it together. Daniel is on my side of the room in an instant.

Without a word, he crawls into the tiny bed next to me, his chest a warm security against my back. He wraps his arms around mine, our hands finding each other in the dark and tangling in a desperate mesh of fingers.

I could hold on to a small piece of hope that somehow this will all work out, but I'm afraid of what that might cost me. Deep down we both know that we'll either end up dead or separated forever in Quarantine. I push those thoughts away. We still have this one night left to comfort each other before the real pain begins.

I could kick myself for all those months wasted, too unsure of myself to own my true feelings for Daniel. We could have had that time together to solidify these emotions destined to burn hot and quick. Does he even know how much I love him?

I picture Candace and Thomas lying in a deserted, crumbling bunk out near the edge. They're lucky they've had so many years out here together. No matter what the Cardinal does tomorrow, he could never undo their years of marriage. What if the Cardinal couldn't take that from me either?

"Daniel?"

"What, my love?" I can't see him, but his voice is warm against my ear. The darkness makes the words easier to say.

"Will you marry me?"

The silence is a cacophony of noise in my ears. Long, slow minutes pass waiting for him to answer me.

"I, Daniel Whedon, take you, Rebecca Collins, to be my wedded wife, to have and to hold from this day forward, till death do we part."

My chest swells with his words. This moment is as far from a white dress and fancy wedding as you can get. Nothing at all like what I pictured in my head before my Rejection, when I still had the luxury of day dreams. It's perfect. If we die tomorrow or by some stroke of luck live to be one hundred, I will never doubt Daniel's love for me.

I squeeze his hand and roll to my side. His face must be only inches from mine and I lean in to press my lips to his.

"Hold on," he says, pulling back from my kiss. "I didn't hear 'kiss the bride.' Now it's your turn."

I press my free hand to my chest and try to still my surging heartbeat enough to match Daniel's vows. "I, Rebecca Collins, take you, Daniel Whedon, to be my wedded husband, to have and to hold from this day forward." I suck in a deep breath, unable to recognize an end of my love for him. "Not even death shall part us."

With my last words, Daniel's lips find mine in the darkness and we share our first married kiss. I focus on my joy and try not to think about how few kisses I'll share with my new husband.

Sunlight streams through the windows after too few hours. I squeeze my eyes tight and pretend I don't hear the stirring of people outside, heading to breakfast. Daniel must have the same idea. Behind me, he pulls his arms tighter and nuzzles his head down into my shoulder.

After a few more minutes of blocking out the world, we both know our moment of peace is up. We have to get to breakfast, sneak back to the building where we stashed our equipment and get everything set up in time for our big television debut.

Elizabeth still hasn't come back. I hope that wherever she is, she's safe, but I don't have enough space in my head to worry about her today.

There isn't anything for us to do in the bunkhouse except put on our shoes, but we both linger over our laces, taking the extra moment to be here. It's a dreary box with a leaky roof, a dirty window, and wobbly fake furniture, but it's been my home for the past year.

I take a minute to make all the beds and push the chairs up around the table. Maybe when we're gone, someone else will find this bunk and make it their home. It makes me happy to think of a group of women or men coming here after a day of working in the kitchens or picking up trash to sit around the table and share a story or a quick joke. This house deserves to hear laughter again.

The PIT has a holiday-like atmosphere today. I understand, there aren't a lot of entertainment options available to us, but I don't get the draw of watching the Acceptance ceremony. Maybe everyone is excited about the idea of seeing who'll be joining our ranks before they actually get here. Or maybe they're hopeful they'll see friends or family in the crowd. Whatever the reason, people are smiling and laughing and the ceremony is the topic of conversation at every table in the dining hall.

Elizabeth isn't at breakfast. I have to assume she knows what she's doing, but I'm sad she's not here. We may not be as close as I would have liked, but I still wish I could tell her good-bye. If she were here, I'd thank her for letting me be a part of her family, for accepting me even when she didn't want to, and for sharing in the few moments of happiness I've had in the past year.

Daniel's eyes stay glued to the door. He must be hoping to get another chance to see her, too.

We sit in the dining hall as long as we can, but time isn't something we have a lot of today. Daniel sets down his bowl and spreads a forced smile on his face. "Are you ready?"

I nod and hold out my hand to him.

"Attention prisoners." Up at the front of the room a guard in a pristine red suit stands up on top of a table. "All prisoners are to report to the courtyard for a mandatory viewing of today's Acceptance ceremony. No exceptions. All prisoners should finish eating and make their way to the courtyard immediately."

Daniel gives my hand a quick squeeze and leans in so his words aren't overheard by anyone nearby. His warm breath tickles my neck and I lean in to get closer to him. "I'll head out first and act like I'm going to the bath house. Wait here a few minutes and then make your way to the fence." He brushes his lips against my ear and leaves a light kiss on the side of my neck. "I'll see you out there." With one last squeeze of my hand, Daniel strides out of the room.

I should be nervous, or scared, or even sad. Instead, it's hard to say I feel anything at all. Daniel and I said our good-byes last night in the best way we knew how. Other than Elizabeth, I don't have anyone else I want to see before the end. And I know this will be the end.

It actually brings me a bit of peace to accept the truth of the situation. I'll get on camera with Daniel and we'll fight back in the only way we can. When the guards come for us, and they will come, we won't go quietly. We'll fight and they'll fight back and that will be the end for both of us. But we'll be together. I won't let the PIT separate us.

Outside, the courtyard is packed with everyone jostling to get a good view of the huge screen that's been erected to show the ceremony. Other than meals there isn't another time that everyone is all together, and even then people tend to congregate in shifts so they can have a place to sit while they choke down the burnt rice. The size of the crowd is overwhelming. I have to shove my way through to the far side by the bath house.

I find my way to the edge of the mass of bodies and walk as quickly as possible without drawing attention to myself. I need to blend in if I have any hope of getting out of here undetected. The bath house is only a few feet away and I'm home free, but a pair of rough hands grab me by the upper arms and spin me around.

"Are you too stupid to understand what mandatory means?" The red-uniformed guard jabs his hand into my back and pushes me toward the boisterous voices of the congregated prisoners. "Get back to the courtyard. Now."

"I just need to go to the bath house." My voice is a panicked whine in my head, but I can't help it. I need to get out of here. I need to get to Daniel. "I'll hurry. I promise."

"Hold it." A sneer slides across his mouth. What does he care if a prisoner is in discomfort?

"What's going on?" Eric's familiar voice joins in the argument and I don't know if I should be thankful or concerned.

"Caught this one trying to sneak off to the bath house."

"And?" Eric doesn't look at me. I have no idea if he even realizes I'm the subject of the conversation.

"Our orders were clear. Everyone stays in the courtyard. You want to explain to the boss why one of them wasn't there?"

"You want to explain why the Cardinal's broadcast of the PIT includes a woman standing in a dress covered in piss?"

"I…well…"

"Right." Eric grabs my upper arm in the same harsh manner the other guard did and pushes me ahead of him. "I'll take her." He shoves the back of my shoulder without another word and we march off toward the bath house.

What am I supposed to do now? We reach the bath house without Eric saying a word to me. I reach out an arm to push open the door. Eric grabs my arm before my hand makes contact and drags me wordlessly to the side of the building. In the shadows of the cramped walls, we're hidden from the prying eyes of the packed courtyard.

There isn't any reason to trust Eric, but I don't have a choice. There isn't time for me to sit around and make up excuses for why I have to leave. "Eric, I can't stay here. Please let me go."

"I'm not stopping you." Marching in front of him, I didn't get a chance to really see him, but now I do. Eric's uniform is wrinkled. I might think he slept in it, except the dark circles under his eyes are evidence he isn't getting much sleep these days. "I don't know what you're up to, but I hope it's worth it. Now get out of here."

He stands there, head down, hands in his pockets. He's putting himself at risk letting me go. When my face flashes on the screen, the guard he shamed into letting me go will know Eric was responsible for letting me get away. "Thank you."

His head jerks up. The hopeful pleading of his eyes is pathetic. The confident Eric who kissed me on the roof of an abandoned bunkhouse is gone. "If I could go back and do it all over again, I'd do everything different."

"I know." I know he's sorry. I know he wishes things could be different. I know he wants my forgiveness. What I don't know is if I can give it to him.

Eric lets his chin drop back down to his chest and turns around toward the courtyard, kicking a loose pebble from the path. "Tell my sister…" He stops, his head turning to stare off into the PIT. "Never mind. Nothing I say is any good to her now."

I count one, two, three of his steps before the words come tumbling out. "I forgive you." Eric stops but doesn't turn around. "I hope you don't get in trouble for this."

A harsh laugh shakes his shoulders. "What are they going to do? Send me back to the PIT?"

"They might."

"Maybe that wouldn't be so bad." Pain pours out of his red-rimmed eyes. "The Cardinal may have let me out of the PIT, but I'll never really get my freedom back."

I wish there was more I could say, but we've both used up all our words. All that's left for me is to suck up huge breaths of air to keep the tears at bay while Eric walks back to the life he wishes wasn't his. I turn and race toward the end of the life I'm dying to save.

Twenty-Nine

Pain stitches up my side, but I don't have time to slow down. The humongous speakers in the courtyard blare the sounds of the ceremony and I can hear them all the way out here by the fence. The band is in high spirits, but that means the Cardinal's speech isn't far behind. We're running out of time.

My feet pound so hard against the ground I almost miss the sound of the approaching guards. They must be making a sweep of the PIT, making sure all the good little prisoners are tucked away in the courtyard so they can put up the fence without a riot breaking out. I slide into a doorless bunkhouse and hold my breath, waiting for them to pass by.

I catch my first break of the day and they don't bother to check inside any of the buildings. I pause, leaning against the concrete wall, to make sure they're far enough away. By now, Daniel's probably wondering what happened to me.

I have one foot out the door when the band stops and the Cardinal's booming voice pumps through the air. I have to keep moving, but I keep one ear out for other guards and one tuned in to the Cardinal's words.

"…everything to make the Permanent Isolation Territory a place where those who can't live among us can make a life for themselves. As you can see, they have everything they could need."

I imagine the Cardinal at his podium while shots of a decluttered PIT flash behind him.

"Yet, despite these efforts, there are those inside the PIT who don't appreciate the second chance at life they've been given. Just this past summer, a small, ineffective group of dangerous criminals attempted to break out of the PIT."

A gasp of shock echoes back through the microphone and plays out of our speakers. This is clearly the first the crowd at the ceremony has heard of our little ineffective escape. "There is no reason to be alarmed. Rest assured, I will never allow those who would undermine our society to escape. But let this serve as a reminder that there are dangerous people out there. The people we send to the PIT cannot be rehabilitated or trained, regardless of the benefits provided to them."

The Cardinal is laying it on thick this year. Are there people out there with doubts about the system? A sliver of hope opens up in my head. If some of the citizens are questioning the Cardinal, maybe they'll believe us. It might be too late for me and Daniel, but there's a chance we can stop the Machine from Rejecting more people who don't belong in here.

I turn the corner and run smack into Daniel. He gathers me into his arms and squeezes tight enough to cut off the scream I was about to let loose. "You're alright," he breathes into my hair. "I was so worried."

"I'm fine. Eric helped me."

Daniel raises his eyebrows, but I ignore his silent question and pull him back into another hug. Even with a hundred lifetimes, I could never stop wanting his arms around me. I convinced myself last night I was at peace with our good-bye. I was lying to myself.

The tears come out in loud bursts from the middle of my chest. Deep sobs that shake my torso and force me to my knees. Daniel kneels as well and I cling to him with all the strength left in me. I'm not ready to give this up.

"Shh…it's okay. I'm right here." Daniel holds me close, smoothing the tangled curls on the back of my head. We don't have time for a breakdown, but he lets me have my moment. When the sobs slow down, he pulls back, one hand on my shoulder and the other cradling the side of my face. "You don't have to do this. You can turn around and run to the courtyard and pretend you don't know anything about this."

"But you're staying?" My hands are like a vise on his wrist.

"I don't intend to live without you."

There's nothing left for me to do but stand up and walk into the building. I won't leave him out here to die alone. I can't sacrifice a single minute of the life we have together, no matter what that time will cost me. That is a choice I can still make.

Daniel was right. It really is all about maintaining control. The Cardinal and I have that much in common. Of course, the Cardinal wants control of an entire nation, while I'm just looking for a little control over my own life. But I know better now. I can't control my life. I didn't control it before the PIT and I certainly don't control it in here. All I can control is how I react to what life hands me. Today, I fight.

We head into the building, but we can still hear the Cardinal's voice blaring over the courtyard speakers. This close to the fence his words are blended with the sounds of hammers and metal scraping as the workers rush to get the fence up while everyone is distracted. The clang of bolts being driven into the posts is like the ticks of a time bomb counting down the minutes of this life we have together. It does nothing to help ease the queasiness in my stomach.

Daniel pulls the camera and transmitter out of their hiding spot and plugs them into the Noteboard. "I just need to finish programming in the signal they're broadcasting in Cardinal City."

"How do you know what signal they're using?" I watch him type away into the machine, even though I don't know how any of it works.

"That's what I was doing yesterday. They set up the display after lunch and the receiver was already booted up." Daniel hits a few more buttons before unplugging the Noteboard from the camera. "Okay, we're ready."

He hands me the camera and grabs a few boxes he managed to salvage from the remaining trash that decorates the edge of the PIT. Outside, the sun is higher in the sky.

Daniel sets up the boxes a few feet from the side of the building to create a makeshift camera stand. "Stand against the wall and I'll get the camera focused."

Daniel positions the camera moving the lens back and forth. The Cardinal isn't speaking anymore, but a dreary music is pumping from the speakers. I wonder if he's showing more shots of the PIT. The Cardinal described this place like a criminal paradise. If he had shown the same footage last year would I have been appalled at the conditions or outraged at our 'amenities'?

"Rebecca?" Daniel pulls my focus back to the task at hand. "We're ready."

I nod, but freeze at the sound of footsteps walking in our direction. From the volume, it has to be several people and they're moving quickly. Daniel's wide eyes meet mine. He grabs the camera in one hand and my wrist in the other, before running back into the building.

I slam the door closed behind us and Daniel shoves the camera under the mattresses. Standing against the back wall I hold my breath and listen for the sounds of whoever is walking nearby.

Back at the courtyard, the music stops playing and the Cardinal's voice breaks back in over the sound of amplified applause. Whatever they showed the crowd in Cardinal City, they loved it.

Footsteps shuffle by the door. Whoever is out there isn't talking like the other workers we've run across the past few days. Did the other guards notice that Eric didn't return with the prisoner from the bath house? Are they looking for me? Keeping my eye on the door, I reach for

Daniel's hand as the footsteps stop right outside the building.

The hiss of a whisper is barely detectable over the Cardinal's boisterous words. Daniel gives my hand a squeeze while we wait for the inevitable.

The door creaks open, but the backlight of glaring sun makes it impossible to see who's come to take us down.

"So are you guys still going to crash the Cardinal's party or did I drag all these people out here for nothing?"

My eyes adjust to the light and reveal Elizabeth standing in the doorway. I'm so happy that I get to see her and that she's not a Cardinal guard that I rush over and tackle her with a hug, almost knocking both of us to the ground.

"Whoa, I love you, too, but you're making it hard to breathe." Elizabeth pries my arms from around her neck and looks over my shoulder.

"I didn't think I'd get to see you again." Daniel is right behind me, a slow smile revealing his dimples for the first time in ages.

"And let the two of you have all the fun? Never." Daniel wraps her up in his arms and Elizabeth hugs him back.

"Wait, what do you mean all these people?" I move past her out the door, but stop before I get two feet in the sunshine. At least a dozen men and woman are standing outside the building biting their lips, running hands through their dirty hair and fussing with their threadbare clothes. In the front of the ragtag group are Constance and Thomas.

"I heard what you said," Elizabeth says behind me. "About making a sacrifice, even when the odds are small."

"But how?"

"I've been here a lot longer than you, girly. I managed to meet a few people before I started hanging out with the wrong crowd." Elizabeth moves to stand with her group and winks at me and Daniel. "Once I convinced Constance, everyone else was easy. We've got all kinds of Rejects, from your mentally slow to physically challenged. All the people I know who shouldn't be here."

I want to meet them all, hear their stories, but there isn't time. I finally know what I'm going to say and the timing is critical.

"Daniel, get the camera. Everyone else, come line up over here against the wall."

I stop to listen to the Cardinal's words. Based on last year's speech we have just over a minute.

"Quickly, now." I grab Daniel's arm as he runs by with the camera. "When I point to you, I need you to cut in immediately. Can you do that?"

"Never doubt my technology skills." He sets the camera down and we take time we don't have for one last kiss. It's brief and bittersweet and doesn't even come close to the kiss we really deserve. But then, that's kinda the point. This is what none of us deserve. "I love you."

"More than you can ever know." I let him go and turn back to the others, swallowing the tears I can't afford. "I'm going to say a few words and then it will be your turn. We won't have long before they find us and shut down the feed so we don't have time for speeches. Just give your name, your Territory and the real reason why you're here. This is what people need to know."

The Cardinal's voice rises and I know we're out of time. This is the end of his speech. Now or never. Something small and cold hits the front of my chest. I dip my chin and the beautiful simplicity of my grandmother's pendant strung on a dirty shoestring rests against my breastbone.

Elizabeth's voice whispers in my ear from where she stands behind me. "So you never forget. This is why you're here."

I spin around and she's motioning with her arms to all of us standing there. I understand what she means. This was what the Cardinal feared when he sent me here. Afraid I'd turn my voice against him. I can almost be grateful.

If everything had gone the way I expected at my Acceptance ceremony last year, I would be outside right now, living the boring life planned out for me and never know what true love is like. Life might be safer on the other side of the fence, but that doesn't equal better anymore.

"I'm sorry for—"

I stop Elizabeth's words with the palm of my hand. "How many times do I have to tell you that none of this is your fault? The guilt for this one belongs to the Cardinal and it's time for everyone else to know it, too."

I turn back to Daniel and take a second to meet his eyes. I try to say enough words for the next fifty years in that one gaze. I'm glad we don't have time for a long good-bye. I could never make him understand how much he means to me. I nod my head and wait for the small green light on the front to blink on.

Looking right into the camera I smile as wide as I can. I smile for Daniel and Elizabeth for believing in me, for Constance for showing me what real love looks like. I smile for Molly and all those who came before her who'll never smile again. Even Eric. I smile for all of them. And then I stop smiling.

"You know us. We're your children, your classmates, your brothers and sisters. We aren't criminals. Each of us is here because we're different. We're here because the Machine doesn't decide who's worthy of freedom, the Cardinal does. We're here, and any one of you could be next."

Elizabeth squeezes my hand and Daniel smiles at me from behind the camera. They give me the last bit of courage I need to keep going. "Ladies and Gentlemen of the Territories, before you stands the future."

Thank you so much for traveling with me on Rebecca's journey. From the first word, her story always felt like one that demanded to be told. While I always knew how her story would end, Rebecca (and the others) surprised me with how they would get there. I really don't feel like their author, but only the person lucky enough to share their adventure with others.

It's my hope that you've loved this book as much as I loved writing it. If you did, or even if you didn't, I'd love to hear from you. You can write to me at SarahNegovetich@Gmail.com.

And finally, if you feel so inclined, I am always grateful for readers who share their opinions with others. If you loved this book, please tell a friend. You can also leave a review on Amazon, B&N, Goodreads, or anywhere books are discussed online. Our fellow book lovers are a constant guide to helping us find out next favorite novel.

Thank you again for being a part of Rebecca's story.

Before you stands the future!
Sarah

This book has been a labor of love that never would have been born without the help of so many. Thank you to my wonderful partners in crime at SAW. Not only would this book have a completely different (and kinda stinky) first chapter without your help, I never would have had the courage to share Rebecca's story with the world. Write on, writers! To my wonderful online friends and beta readers, Rachel, Sarah, & Beth, thank you for chewing me up and cheering me on at the same time. A big thumbs up to my editors, Brent, Zoe, and Tanya. You guys were a dream-team to work with and I know I'm a better writer thanks to you. To my agent, Marisa, thank you for believing in this story, even when everyone else said Dystopian is dead. And finally to my amazing little family, Nick, Sophia and Isabella, thank you doesn't feel like enough. Your support gave me the time and space I needed to bring this story to life and your love gave me the motivation to be the best writer I can be. Love you, mean it!

About the Author

Sarah Negovetich knows you don't know how to pronounce her name and she's okay with that.

Her first love is Young Adult novels, because at seventeen the world is your oyster. Only oysters are slimy and more than a little salty; it's accurate if not exactly motivational. We should come up with a better cliché.

Sarah divides her time between writing YA books that her husband won't read and working with amazing authors as an agent at Corvisiero Literary Agency. Her life's goal is to be only a mildly embarrassing mom when her kids hit their teens.

You can learn more about Sarah and her books at **www.SarahNegovetich.com** or follow her antics on Twitter @SarahNego.